"It's not fair to ask you to put your business, your whole life, on hold while you baby-sit me. I'm not your responsibility." Not anymore.

"Yes, you are." Ray took the two steps that separated them and placed his hands on Grace's face, forcing her to look up at him. "You came to me," he said softly. "When you were scared, when you didn't know where else to go, you came to me. Do you think I can turn my back on you now? Pretend nothing has changed?"

"Nothing *has* changed," she said weakly, trying, so hard, to mean what she said.

"Gracie Madigan," he whispered, his mouth moving toward hers. "Everything has changed, and you damn well know it."

Dear Reader,

You've loved Beverly Barton's miniseries THE PROTECTORS since it started, so I know you'll be thrilled to find another installment leading off this month. *Navajo's Woman* features a to-swoon-for Native American hero, a heroine capable of standing up to this tough cop— and enough steam to heat your house. Enjoy!

A YEAR OF LOVING DANGEROUSLY continues with bestselling author Linda Turner's *The Enemy's Daughter.* This story of subterfuge and irresistible passion—not to mention heart-stopping suspense—is set in the Australian outback, and I know you'll want to go along for the ride. Ruth Langan completes her trilogy with *Seducing Celeste,* the last of THE SULLIVAN SISTERS. Don't miss this emotional read. Then check out Karen Templeton's *Runaway Bridesmaid,* a reunion romance with a heroine who's got quite a secret. Elane Osborn's *Which Twin?* offers a new twist on the popular twins plotline, while Linda Winstead Jones rounds out the month with *Madigan's Wife,* a wonderful tale of an ex-couple who truly belong together.

As always, we've got six exciting romances to tempt you—and we'll be back next month with six more. Enjoy!

Leslie J. Wainger

Leslie J. Wainger
Executive Senior Editor

Please address questions and book requests to:
Silhouette Reader Service
U.S.: 3010 Walden Ave., P.O. Box 1325, Buffalo, NY 14269
Canadian: P.O. Box 609, Fort Erie, Ont. L2A 5X3

Madigan's Wife
LINDA WINSTEAD JONES

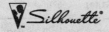

INTIMATE MOMENTS™
Published by Silhouette Books
America's Publisher of Contemporary Romance

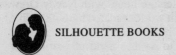 SILHOUETTE BOOKS

ISBN 0-373-27138-7

MADIGAN'S WIFE

Copyright © 2001 by Linda Winstead Jones

All rights reserved. Except for use in any review, the reproduction
or utilization of this work in whole or in part in any form by any
electronic, mechanical or other means, now known or hereafter
invented, including xerography, photocopying and recording, or in
any information storage or retrieval system, is forbidden without
the written permission of the editorial office, Silhouette Books,
300 East 42nd Street, New York, NY 10017 U.S.A.

All characters in this book have no existence outside the imagination of
the author and have no relation whatsoever to anyone bearing the same
name or names. They are not even distantly inspired by any individual
known or unknown to the author, and all incidents are pure invention.

This edition published by arrangement with Harlequin Books S.A.

® and TM are trademarks of Harlequin Books S.A., used under license.
Trademarks indicated with ® are registered in the United States Patent
and Trademark Office, the Canadian Trade Marks Office and in other
countries.

Visit Silhouette at www.eHarlequin.com

Printed in U.S.A.

Books by Linda Winstead Jones

Silhouette Intimate Moments

Bridger's Last Stand #924
Every Little Thing #1007
Madigan's Wife #1068

LINDA WINSTEAD JONES

has loved brooks of all kinds for as long as she can remember, spending her leisure hours with Nancy Drew and Miss Marple, or lost in worlds created by writers like Margaret Mitchell and Robert Heinlein. After years as an avid reader she decided to try her hand at writing her own story. Since 1994 she's been publishing historical and fantasy romance, winning the Colorado Romance Writers' Award of Excellence for her 1996 time-travel story, *Desperado's Gold*. With the publication of *Bridger's Last Stand,* her first book for Silhouette Intimate Moments, Linda stepped into the exciting arena of contemporary romance.

At home in Alabama, she divides her time between her husband, three sons, two dogs, reading whatever she can get her hands on and writing romance.

For my brother Tom,
who introduced me to Lyle Lovett's music
and even graciously loaned me a few CDs. Thanks.
Now might be a good time to tell you—
you're not getting them back.

Chapter 1

The effect of a Ray Madigan grin could be devastating on the unprepared female. Grace popped a potato chip into her mouth as she watched him smile at the waitress and ask for a refill of his coffee and a piece of lemon icebox pie. Darn it, he should be older, slower, less attractive than she remembered. How else was she supposed to get him out of her system once and for all?

Not a speck of gray marred the honey-toned softness of his light brown hair. She knew plenty of almost-thirty-four-year-old men who had a liberal dusting of white around the edges, or the beginnings of male-pattern baldness. Not Ray. Just a little bit too long, a mixture of wavy dark blond and golden brown strands curled at his neck and over his ears.

He apparently hadn't gained a pound in the past six years, either. In fact, he might've lost a couple. Tall and lean with wide shoulders tailor-made for resting a head upon, he looked just as she remembered; too good-looking for his own good and tempting as hell, darn his hide.

These days, Ray always wore the same uniform: a T-shirt, a plaid or checkered button-up shirt over that tee, blue jeans and well-worn leather work boots. He wore the loose shirt, she knew, to conceal the gun he tucked in the waistband at his spine.

No, nothing had changed. Ray played the good ol' boy flawlessly, when it suited him. To the casual observer he looked like a hundred other rednecks interested in nothing more than a good time, a faithful truck and a six-pack of beer. They didn't always see the spark of intelligence in his eyes, the way he watched everything and listened to every word. Grace saw, though. She always had.

His eyes had always done her in.

As the waitress walked away Ray planted his eyes on Grace once again. She did her best to appear calm and uninterested. Unaffected. Casual to the point of aloof.

"So," he said, stirring a single pack of sugar into his coffee. "How's Dr. Doolittle treating you these days?"

"Dr. Dearborne," she corrected without rancor. "And I have to admit," she said with real admiration, "you were right. I went to his office the morning after we had lunch last time, and told him I expected to be treated like a professional. I told him I'd have to start looking for another job if he didn't stop making improper suggestions when we found ourselves alone. He hasn't made a pass at me since."

"He doesn't want to lose his office manager," Ray said, his smile gone. "Folks aren't exactly lining up, panting to go to work for smarmy dentists."

"Dr. Dearborne isn't smarmy," she said without enthusiasm. "He's just…challenged in the personality department."

"He's a creep," Ray muttered as the waitress placed the lemon icebox pie before him. "Trish went to him with a toothache a few months back, and he actually made a pass at her while he had his hand in her mouth. The bastard called her every day for two weeks."

"Trish. She was your second wife, right?" Grace asked, as if she didn't know perfectly well who Trish was. Wife number two, blond, a party girl. She and Ray had met in a bar, gotten totally wasted and decided they were perfectly suited for one another. The marriage had lasted all of three months. Well, officially the marriage had lasted for three months. Word was they hadn't lived together a full two weeks.

Ray nodded. "I called Patty and she fixed Trish up with her dentist." The look he gave her was censuring. "I can't believe you're working for that jerk."

Patty was wife number three, a nurse who'd tended Ray in the emergency room more than once. A more level-headed woman than the flighty Trish, she'd made her marriage to Ray last almost eight months. They'd parted amicably, or so she heard.

Grace thought it damned unnatural that the three of them, Ray and Trish and Patty, were friends. Of course, it was kinda unnatural that she and Ray were sitting here, together, right now.

Unnatural for most, maybe, but not for Ray. She'd rarely seen him angry; he took everything in stride. Sadly, she suspected he didn't care enough about anything or anyone to get truly angry. People came and went, in and out of his life, and he carried on as if nothing had changed.

She tried to steer the conversation away from her boss and Ray's ex-wives. He never seemed satisfied with the explanation that she worked for Dr. Dearborne because the pay was good and the benefits were better, and talking about Trish and Patty always made her teeth ache.

"How can you eat like that and not get fat?" she said, pointing accusingly at his huge piece of pie.

"I inherited my father's metabolism," he said with a grin.

"One day that metabolism of yours is gonna give out," she said, wondering if it was true. Last time she'd seen Ray's father he'd been fifty-nine years old, fit as a fiddle, and wolfing down a meal fit for three teenage boys. That had been nearly nine years ago. Ray and his father were not close, and didn't visit one another often. Of course, on the few times she'd seen them together there hadn't been any animosity, either. They acted like old acquaintances who got together now and again because they felt like they should, not because they wanted to see one another. "You should come running with me sometime."

He made a face as he dug into the pie. "Run? On purpose? I don't think so. Besides," he cocked one eyebrow at her. "You run at the crack of dawn." He shook his fork at her and deepened his lazy, honeyed Southern drawl. "It ain't natural."

With his pie finished and the last of his coffee drained, Ray settled his eyes on her in a way that told her he was about to say something she wouldn't like. She saw the man behind the charmer, the intensity flashing in the friendly blue eyes he locked to hers. Her stomach flipped uneasily. *This* look hadn't changed in years.

"You remember Stan Wilkins?" he asked.

"Sure. He moved south a few years back, didn't he?"

Ray nodded, a slow, deliberate motion. "Yep. He's in Mobile. He called me a couple of days ago."

Grace wanted to believe it had been a purely social call,

but the fluttering in her stomach suggested otherwise. "Great," she said indifferently. "How's Mary?"

"Fine," Ray said with a small smile. "Their oldest is in high school, can you believe it?"

Had it been so long? Deep down, she shivered. Yes, it had been. One day melted into another, and then another, and then another, and the next thing you know years have passed. Days you can't get back are gone. "Hard to imagine."

Ray leaned forward, forearms on the table, eyes clear and guileless. He looked like a man who could do no wrong, who knew what he wanted and would do anything to get it, the rest of the world be damned. Darn his hide, she knew this look, too. No good ever came of it. He hesitated, drummed his fingers on the tabletop, and in an instant Grace knew what was coming.

"Stan's heading up the narcotics unit in Mobile, and he's looking for someone to come in and work undercover. When he heard what had happened up here…"

"You're not considering it," she said softly. Her face paled—she could feel it, as if her skin turned suddenly cold. "Tell me you're not even *thinking* about…"

Unrepentant, Ray said casually, "I told him I'd call in a few days and let him know."

Taking a deep breath, Grace reminded herself that she shouldn't be angry. She should be able to take anything and everything Ray Madigan did in stride. Unfortunately, that was easier said than done.

"You've been off the Huntsville force for a year," she snapped, trying to keep her voice low. "Your P.I. business is going well, you told me so yourself. And you haven't been shot once!" Her heart leapt into her throat, but she worked hard not to show it. "Dammit, Ray, you know what happens when you get involved in something like this.''

He didn't look surprised by her response. ''I told Stan I'd think about it.''

All of a sudden she remembered, too clearly, why she'd left him in the first place. The worry, the horror, the feeling that at any moment someone would knock on the door and reach deep inside and yank her heart out again were too much for her to bear.

She started to slide from the booth, but Ray's quick hand on her wrist stopped her. His fingers manacled her, long, strong fingers tight and warm against her pale wrist. She stared at his hand on her arm for a long moment, marveled, for a heartbeat, at the size and power and undeniable masculinity of that hand.

She'd been so careful not to touch him, so cautious on the occasions they'd met for coffee or lunch, like any two civilized human beings might be. They didn't hug hello, they didn't kiss goodbye, they didn't even shake hands. And now here she sat motionless while he held her in place, his hand firm and heated on her wrist. The sensation brought back so many memories…good and bad.

He peeled his fingers away from her skin, slowly, as if he'd just realized what he'd done. ''Sorry.''

She settled back in her seat, still rattled but no longer furious. ''You were shot three times while you were working narcotics, Ray. Three damn times!'' Her heart clenched as she remembered that third, most horrifying time. ''What on earth would make you want to walk into that again?''

He didn't have an answer for her, but he wasn't ready to give in, either. She saw the determination in his eyes, the flicker of restlessness. He hadn't yet told her why he'd quit his job with the Huntsville Police Department, but she knew there had to be more to it than a simple early retirement or the need for a change. He'd loved his job too much, he'd devoted too much of himself to it. He'd given up too much for the job; including her.

Grace hadn't looked up many old friends since her return to Huntsville, but she had called Nell Rose and Sandy. Cops' wives, both of them. They were more than happy to catch up, have lunch, go shopping and gossip about Trish and Patty, but when Grace had asked why Ray left the force she got the runaround. Nell Rose said she had no idea and then decided she wanted dessert after all, launching into a glowing rave about chocolate. On another afternoon, Sandy's soft answer was, "same ol' same ol'," just before she reached for a pair of suddenly exciting half-price black heels.

"I told him I'd think about it, that's all," Ray said softly. "I haven't made any promises."

No, Ray Madigan didn't make promises.

The waitress came back and dropped two tickets on the table. Separate checks, always.

Grace dug in her purse for a ten-dollar bill, more than enough for her barbecue plate and a generous tip.

"At least listen to me," Ray said softly. "I know you don't like what I do…"

"I don't care what you do, not anymore," she said coolly, hoping her fury didn't show. She tried so hard not to care. "If you want to go to Mobile and get yourself killed, go right ahead." She slid quickly from the booth and tried to walk past him.

"Dammit, Gracie, sit down." Ray reached out and grabbed her wrist *again,* effectively restraining her as she tried to make her escape.

"Let me go." Her voice didn't rise above a whisper. Something unwanted welled up inside her and made her long to sit beside him, lay her head on his shoulder and beg him not to go to Mobile. She'd fought these feelings for a long time, and she fought them now.

"Just sit back down," he insisted softly, refusing to release his grip as he assaulted her with his most cajoling, most seductive voice.

"No."

"Gracie..."

"No," she said, just a little bit louder.

The waitress walked by to pick up Grace's check and the ten-dollar bill. Maybe she sensed the tension, maybe she was concerned about the other customers who stared over their own coffee and pie. To defuse the situation she smiled, winked and said, "Why don't you just marry the poor guy and put him out of his misery?"

Grace gave the young girl a wide, unconcerned, very calm grin. "Been there, done that, got the T-shirt."

The waitress's eyes widened in surprise. Ray lifted a lazy hand. "Tamara sweetheart, this is Grace. Mrs. Ray Madigan number one."

He leaned back in the booth and watched Grace walk away, and the smile he'd worn all through lunch faded. Her thick dark hair, longer than she used to wear it, bounced around her squared shoulders. She didn't toss a glance back as she walked away; he didn't expect her to. Gracie Madigan didn't look back, ever.

In her silly moss green suit and sensible low-heeled shoes she looked joyless. Annoyed. And too damn good. His gaze lingered on her legs, well revealed beneath an almost too-short green skirt. She'd always had great legs, he mused as she disappeared from sight.

Well, he'd known she wouldn't like the idea of him going back into narcotics, though he hadn't expected her to lose her temper. After all, they weren't married anymore, hadn't been for six years now. As of two months ago, they'd been divorced as long as they'd been married.

He knew too well what Grace thought about his chosen profession. She hated it. After all, that was the reason she gave for leaving him. Yeah, she was real good at walking away when the going got tough.

"So that's number one," Tamara said as she began to efficiently clear the table, balancing plates and glasses on a small round tray. She flashed him a wicked smile; too wicked for one so young.

"Yep," he said.

"She's pretty," Tamara said, careful to keep her tone conversational. Just a trace of curiosity crept into her soft voice to give away her interest.

"Yep." Pretty and sexy, the kind of unforgettable pretty and sexy that got under a man's skin and stayed there. Having Grace back in his life in such a platonic way was torture; a torture he wasn't about to give up. A friendly lunch every two weeks or so was better than nothing, so he purposely refrained from talking about the past. He kept the conversation light and friendly and safe, so she wouldn't run off again.

Until today.

Hellfire, this was getting complicated. The best thing he could do for himself would be to hurry back to the office, call Stan, and agree to be in Mobile on Monday.

He paid for his lunch and walked back to the office, trying to enjoy the sun on his face and the gentle breeze that wafted past. Spring in Alabama was always a reminder of why he stayed here, why he'd made Huntsville his home. Up north they were still fighting snow and ice in some places, but down south the girls had started sunbathing and the kids ran around in shorts and T-shirts after school. Dogwoods bloomed, birds flitted and chirped, summer was just around the corner.

And Mobile was just a hop, skip and a jump from Gulf Shores, the Redneck Riviera.

There wasn't anything on his calendar that couldn't be farmed out to another P.I.; an insurance fraud case he was about to close up and a couple of divorce cases—the least favorite and most profitable part of his business.

But beach or no beach, he wasn't leaving just yet. Gracie was the one who did the running away, not him.

The modest offices of Madigan Investigations were situated on the ground floor of an old redbrick building in the heart of downtown Huntsville. The furniture was cheap, the sign painted on the glass door discreet and tasteful. He got a lot of his business from the lawyer on the second floor.

"You had two phone calls," Doris said the minute he opened that door. She waved two pink slips of paper before her and then dropped them on the desk. "One about business, one from that second ex-wife of yours. She's getting married again, and she wants you to give her away." Doris showed her disapproval with a wrinkling of her nose and a pursing of lips. "Can I go to lunch now? I swear, every time you have lunch with that *first* ex-wife of yours I end up half starved before I get out of here."

In Doris he'd found the perfect secretary. Built square and solid, she was old enough to be his mother, sassy one minute and mothering the next, more than competent where her secretarial duties were concerned, and—most important—he'd not been tempted even one time to ask her to marry him.

"Take the rest of the afternoon," he said, well aware that his lunches with Grace usually ran long. "I can answer the phone for a couple of hours."

Doris smiled as she walked by, stopping just long enough to reach up and give him a maternal pat on the cheek. "You're a good boy, Ray."

Rather than go into his own inner office, he sat at Doris's desk to read his messages. One of his most persistent clients had called; a man who was certain his wife was cheating on him, even though Ray hadn't been able to discover that the woman did anything more illicit than floor it through the occasional yellow light. When he read the other message he smiled.

He'd have to call Trish, wish her luck and decline her request. He hadn't met her fiancé, but even the most saintly man would have to balk at having his bride walk down the aisle on the arm of her ex-husband.

Oddly enough, he wouldn't actually mind giving Trish away. She was a sweet girl and he wanted to see her start a new, wonderful life. She deserved it. And if Patty ever married that doctor she'd been seeing for the past year, he'd be there with bells on, he'd toast the bride and groom and wish them a long and happy life together.

If Grace ever decided to get married again…his smile faded. Hellfire, no matter how nonchalant he tried to be about Gracie, he couldn't quite pull it off. No matter how hard he tried—and dammit he gave it his best shot—he still thought of her as his wife.

To take his mind off of a subject he'd rather not ponder, he recalled a more pleasant memory; the look on Dr. Doolittle's face when the dentist had opened the door to his fine home two weeks ago and found Ray standing there. The way the creep had paled when Ray had very calmly threatened to rip out his spleen if he ever harassed Grace again, and then threatened to do the same if he ever felt the need to share the details of their conversation.

Hell, a man could live without a spleen, Ray thought as

he positioned his locked hands behind his head and leaned
back in Doris's chair.

Since the house she rented was situated near downtown
Huntsville, Grace had the pleasure of taking her morning
jog down quiet streets lined with old houses and even older
trees. A small neighborhood park was especially beautiful
in the spring, with the flowering dogwoods and pear trees
in bloom growing gracefully around a small pond.

On occasion she'd see another runner, but most mornings she had the sidewalk and the park path to herself. It
was worth getting up while the sky was still dark, leaving
the house before the sun actually peeked over the horizon.
She loved jogging in the gray light, watching the day come
alive.

Ray lived close by, a fact she'd been well aware of when
she chose her house. He rented an apartment over a garage,
just a few streets north. She'd told herself, more than once,
that knowing Ray was near had nothing to do with her
decision. Living in Madison or South Huntsville would
require driving every day in rush hour traffic on the Park-
way or I-565. The house she rented, a rather small old
house that had been recently remodeled, was convenient.
And she liked the neighborhood. In order to convince herself of this truth, she never ran down Ray's street. In fact,
she made it a point to run in the opposite direction.

This morning she couldn't completely clear her mind,
as she usually did when she ran. She kept thinking about
Ray, wondering if moving back to Huntsville had been
such a good idea, after all. It had seemed so when she'd
made the decision. The offer from Dr. Dearborne had been
a good one, and besides, she needed to get over Ray, to
put what they'd had in the past and move on. As long as
she continued to make him more than he was, in her mind,

that would never happen. A good dose of reality would remind her of the reasons she'd left him in the first place, and then she'd be able to get on with her life. Maybe with Ray finally in the past where he belonged, she'd be able to think about getting married again, having children, being happy.

So far it wasn't working. Until yesterday, when he'd mentioned the job offer in Mobile, she'd been in serious danger of falling in love with him all over again. He could be charming, when it suited him, and there were times she forgot the problems that had driven her away and remembered the nights he'd come home to her.

The nights he'd come home after a hard day to forget all that had happened outside their house. Those times when he went undercover for weeks at a time, but sneaked into the house and the bedroom and the bed in the middle of the night on occasion. Just to hold her, he said. Because he couldn't bear to be without her.

Some nights she still woke from a dream feeling the dip of the mattress as if Ray were climbing into the bed to lie beside her. For an instant, a heart-stopping, impossibly bright instant, she thought he'd come to her; that the years had rolled away and he had come to whisper in her ear, take her in his arms, and love her.

Some mornings she'd actually lie in bed and close her eyes and pretend she could hear Ray singing in the shower. Lyle Lovett songs, always. Off-key, but just a little. He hadn't sung in the shower every morning, but usually, after a long, wonderful night when they'd gotten little sleep, she'd come awake to hear him singing. She knew his favorite Lyle Lovett songs by heart. "She's No Lady." "If I Had a Boat." "Here I Am." As she ran, an unwanted smile briefly crossed her face.

This was getting dangerous. She had to erase these

thoughts and remember the bad days; like the first time
Luther had come to the door to tell her Ray had been shot.

Even running and working up a sweat, she went cold at
the memory. Luther had assured her, that night, that Ray
would be all right, that the wound wasn't serious. She
hadn't believed him, not for a second. She'd thrown a coat
on over her nightgown, stepped into a pair of tennis shoes,
and as Luther drove her to the hospital she wondered how
she'd ever survive without Ray.

She couldn't, and she knew it. Ray was too much a part
of who she was, and without him she was nothing. *Nothing*. Riding in Luther's silent car she'd tried to imagine
her life without Ray in it. Long before they reached the
hospital she'd felt hollow and achy, like someone had
reached inside and ripped out her heart. When she'd sniffled and wiped away a few relentless tears, Luther had tried
to assure her that Ray was all right. She hadn't believed
him, not until she walked into the hospital room and saw
Ray sitting up, his shoulder bandaged, a couple of buddies
laughing at some joke she'd missed.

He'd been pale, she remembered, and his hands trembled a little; something no one else seemed to notice.
When he'd seen her he'd smiled. *Smiled!* Suddenly her
untied shoes and her nightgown peeking out from the
knee-length coat seemed ridiculous, her tears seemed silly.
But even though Ray was fine, the emptiness didn't quite
go away. She had a new and very real fear to deal with,
now: losing Ray to a job he loved.

She rounded the corner, her mind a million miles away.
The squealing of tires brought her to the present.

A car jerked to a stop at the curb as a man rolled from
the open passenger door, over the grass, onto the sidewalk.
She jogged in that direction to see if she could be of any
help.

The man who'd fallen tried to get up but couldn't. Even from here she could see that he shook, and she heard what could be crying. He was apparently badly hurt. Someone else, a rather large man in a baseball cap and a wrinkled tan trench coat, stepped from the driver's side of the car. His attention was on the man on the sidewalk as he ran around the idling car.

Grace was still a good distance away, in the shadows of the trees that lined and shaded the sidewalk. The man on the sidewalk lifted his head as the driver approached and reached down to help him up. Some friend he was, Grace thought as she drew closer. The poor man who'd fallen from the car was jerked to his feet, and the driver wrapped an arm around his neck in a way that had to hurt, and then reached up to lay his hand on the side of the injured man's head. He quickly executed a powerful wrench, twisting the head unnaturally.

She heard the crack, and the bone-crushing sound brought her to a halt. The man who'd fallen from the car…no, she realized with a chill, he hadn't fallen, he'd *jumped*…went limp and silent. The big man had broken his neck.

Grace stood on the sidewalk, no more than eighty feet away and frozen to the spot. She couldn't believe what she'd just seen, and her mind searched rapidly for an alternate explanation she couldn't find.

The big man in the tan coat lifted his head and saw her. For a split second their eyes held; she held her breath as she met the murderous gaze of a cold-blooded killer. He dropped his victim, and the dead man crumpled to the sidewalk.

Grace turned and ran. She didn't jog, not this time, she ran as fast as she could away from the murder she'd witnessed. Her feet barely touched the ground; her heart pounded fast and hard. It wasn't long before she heard footsteps behind her, heavy footsteps that gained on her too quickly.

The killer wore hard-soled shoes. His steps clipped heavy and loud against the sidewalk. She hoped the shoes would be a disadvantage, but that hope died quickly. He continued to draw closer.

Her right hand settled over the canister at her waist. Bless Ray for insisting that if she was going to jog alone she carry this spray. For dogs, he'd said, but she knew Ray too well, she knew how he thought. He saw danger everywhere, and this time he was right.

If she waited much longer it would be too late. If the man in the trench coat caught her from behind he could very well snap her neck just as he had that poor man who lay on the sidewalk. If she turned too soon, he'd have time to prepare. She waited—a few more steps, let him come a little closer—and then she plucked the pepper spray from her waistband and turned to face her pursuer.

The move surprised the killer, she could tell by the way he suddenly slowed his step, and by the startled widening of his eyes. No time to think about those pale eyes, she thought as she raised the canister and sprayed directly into his face.

The murderer came to a halt with a howl, covering his face with two beefy, strong hands. While he had his hands over his eyes, Grace kicked him between the legs, as hard as she could. He screamed again, louder, and hunched down to shield the newly attacked area with both hands. Taking a deep breath, she lifted her knee and snapped her foot out to kick him once more, in the face this time. The big man went down hard.

She turned and ran, picking up speed with every step. Her heart pounded furiously as she listened for movement behind her. If he got up after taking those two kicks, the best she had to offer, she was lost. She was dead.

Chapter 2

Ray rolled over in bed and glanced at the alarm clock. Who the hell was ringing his doorbell at this time of the morning? It was barely light outside. He mumbled a curse as he swung slowly out of bed, grabbed his Colt from the bedside table and made his way to the door, flicking off the safety with his thumb as he yawned. Whoever was out there didn't let up on the buzzer.

He cursed again as he threw open the door, but stopped as soon as he saw Grace standing there, trembling, sweating and much too pale. He took her arm and pulled her into the room, and she fell into him.

Still half-asleep, he intuitively cradled Grace protectively. She lay almost limp against his chest, a surprising and somewhat disturbing place for her to be. For a second, maybe two, he closed his eyes and just held her. Didn't he dream about this? The way she felt lying against him, soft and shapely, strong and still yielding. The way she smelled, so sweet and warm.

He had to force himself fully awake, he had to remind himself that something was terribly wrong. Grace breathed much too laboriously, as if every time she inhaled it hurt. Her entire body shook, from head to toe. Much of her dark hair had fallen out of its ponytail; sweat dampened tendrils fell across her face and shoulders.

Forcing himself to clear his mind and face reality, he kicked the door shut. "Okay," he said calmly, "tell me what happened."

She took a deep breath and tried to talk, but couldn't. Not just yet. Her lips trembled; she still wasn't breathing right.

"Take your time," he said, struggling to remain calm, tightening his arm around her. There was nothing else he could do; he practically had to hold her up. If he let go she'd probably fall to the floor. He held her tight with one arm, placing his hand against her spine. His other hand, the one with the Colt in it, hung at his side. He clicked the safety into the on position.

He could feel and hear Grace's breathing return to near normal. She took one deep breath and then another, inhaling slowly, exhaling warmly against his chest. The trembling subsided, but her heart continued to beat against his chest; too hard and fast.

Grace was fragile, feminine and delicate, but she'd never been helpless. It wasn't like her to fall apart. She was falling apart now, right here, with her head buried against his chest as if she were trying to hide from the world. Still, he found the time to note, again, that she smelled like heaven, that she was soft and sweet and alive. And here.

Suddenly he wished he'd taken the time to step into a pair of jeans, maybe a shirt as he made his way to the door. All he'd grabbed as he left his bed to the jarring ring of the doorbell was his pistol. Standing here practically naked, wearing nothing more than a pair of boxer shorts while he held a woman he'd tried his best for the past six years to forget, was almost more than he could stand. For a moment his mind flitted to impossible notions; about kissing her to calm her nerves, about holding her close long after whatever had scared her into his arms was gone.

And then he noticed the canister of pepper spray in her hand.

"Gracie," he whispered hoarsely. "What happened?"

She lifted her head, stared warily at him, and stepped back; as if she'd just realized where she rested. "I saw a man murdered," she said, her voice so soft he could barely make out the words. "The killer, he just…snapped this poor man's neck like it was nothing." She swallowed hard and lifted her hands to look at them, as if she couldn't understand how anyone could have so much strength, or could use their hands in such a way. "He chased me, when he realized that I'd seen what happened. I thought he was going to catch me, so I used the pepper spray, and then I kicked him. Twice."

"Good girl," he whispered.

"And then I ran."

Here, she didn't say. She didn't run home, didn't run to the nearest phone to call the police. She ran *here.*

"First things first," he said, gently taking her arm and leading her to the couch. She apparently didn't need to hang on to him anymore, but he wasn't sure she was ready to stand on her own, either. Not just yet. As she sat, tense and shaky still, on the edge of the couch, he grabbed the phone and dialed Luther's home number.

"Did he follow you?"

She shook her head frantically. "No. I didn't look back

for a long time, but when I did…he wasn't there. Not the man or the car.''

He nodded. ''That's good. Now, where was the murder?'' Luther still hadn't picked up the phone.

''The corner of Magnolia and Lincoln on the park side,'' she said. ''He just snapped the guy's neck and let him fall to the sidewalk.'' Once again, she numbly stared down at her own hands.

Luther finally answered with a low growl.

''Meet me at the corner of Magnolia and Lincoln,'' Ray said curtly.

Luther mumbled into the phone. ''When?''

''Now.''

He hung up while Luther complained, profanely, into the phone.

''Luther's been in the homicide unit for almost two years now,'' he said, watching as Grace relaxed until she looked nearly catatonic. He almost preferred the fear. Right now she looked like she could feel nothing, like what she'd seen had numbed her.

But then she turned clear, intelligent eyes to him. Her brown eyes were so dark, so warm, there were moments he wanted to fall into them. He'd always loved her eyes; he'd never told her so.

Sometimes the years melted away. When he said something funny at lunch and she laughed, when they argued about her working for Dr. Doolittle, when she smiled in a certain way or looked at him…the way she looked at him right now. It was, for a moment, as if she'd never left him, as if nothing had changed.

She took a deep breath. ''Thank you.''

He shrugged his shoulders as he turned his back on her. Who was he kidding? *Everything* had changed. ''For what? Look, I gotta get dressed. It won't take Luther more than fifteen minutes to get downtown, and he'll be pissed if we aren't waiting for him.''

"Sure," she said, and then she sank into the soft cushions of the couch.

"Right here," Grace said, pointing down to a perfectly innocent-looking section of the sidewalk. "A man jumped out of a moving car…at least I guess he jumped. I didn't see that part. When I first saw him I thought maybe he'd fallen out of the car.''

She noted the skeptical glance Luther cut in Ray's direction. No longer frightened out of her wits, she was offended by his obvious disbelief.

"What kind of car was it?" Luther asked, holding the tip of a pencil to his small notebook.

"Dark," she said, "and kind of big.''

Luther glanced up at her and wrote down nothing. "Dark and big. A van or a SUV?''

She shook her head. "No, it was a car.''

Okay, it was a poor description, she admitted silently, but she'd never been good with cars. Darn it, she'd been surprised and terrified. Noting the make and model of the car idling at the curb hadn't been her major concern at the time.

The weary homicide detective apparently decided it would be a waste of time to write "big dark car" in his notebook, so he snapped it shut and looked around with sharp, narrowed eyes. Light traffic whirred past on the street, and a few early morning walkers claimed the sidewalk. All was apparently perfectly normal here. In bright sunshine, it seemed impossible that a murder had recently taken place in this very spot.

Luther reached into the pocket of his dark suit jacket and pulled out a piece of hard candy, slipped off the cellophane wrapper and popped the sweet into his mouth. "I'm trying to quit smoking," he explained as he placed the wrapper back into his pocket. "It's hell. Pure hell, I tell you."

He looked like hell, to be honest. Tired and haggard and worn out, he showed the years Ray did not. They were the same age, within three months, but today Luther appeared to be several years older. He'd always been the more serious of the two, the cop who took everything to heart, who wanted to right every wrong. Maybe he'd finally figured out that he wasn't going to change the world after all. Life's disappointment showed on his face.

Ray hung back while she answered Luther's questions, but he stayed close enough for her to feel he was with her, that he supported her. Silly notion. She hadn't leaned on Ray, hadn't *depended* on him, for years. The lessons weren't always easy, and some days they were damned hard, but she had learned to depend only on herself.

"Tell me what the man looked like, the one who was driving the car," Luther asked as he sucked on his candy.

She did have a better description of the killer than of the car. When she'd turned to attack him with the pepper spray she'd gotten a pretty good look. "He was a big guy, maybe six-two or -three, with kind of a Neanderthal face. Lots of forehead, square jaw." This Luther deemed noteworthy. "He looked strong," she added. "Like maybe he works out."

"Hair?" Luther asked, raising his eyes from the notebook.

"Under a baseball cap, and since I didn't see much I'd guess it's pretty short. Brown," she added. "Not as dark as yours, not as light as Ray's."

She described what he'd been wearing, his broad face, his pale eyes—those eyes she remembered well, though at the moment she couldn't be sure if they were blue or green. Luther wrote everything down, but she could see he was supremely unimpressed.

Inside, she was still unsettled by the experience. Her heart beat too fast, her palms were sweaty and her mouth was dry. The memory of what she'd seen remained solidly in her mind, too vivid. Too real. If it wasn't for Ray she'd be a basket case right now, she knew it.

So much for her newfound independence.

The three of them walked down the sidewalk to the place where she'd sprayed and kicked the murderer. Again, there was no sign of violence; no blood, no dropped clue. Nothing. Everything appeared to be normal, as if nothing unusual had *ever* happened here.

Luther closed his notebook again and shoved it into the pocket of his dark suit jacket. He dressed more traditionally these days, thanks to his job in homicide she supposed. Black suit, white shirt, gray tie. His hair was shorter, too, cut in a quite conservative style. She didn't remember Luther being so conventional. He'd always been as wild as Ray, just in a different way.

"Maybe the man isn't dead," he offered tiredly and with a brief spark of optimism. And more than a spark of condescension. "Maybe you saw two men fighting and you panicked and thought..."

"No," Grace interrupted, annoyed that she had to try so hard to convince Luther of what she'd seen. Dammit, she'd heard the crack, she'd seen the murdered man crumple like a rag doll. "He's dead."

Luther grumbled and turned to walk back toward the curb, where his car and Ray's were parked; one nondescript gray sedan parked before another, vehicles that were forgettable, invisible, anonymous. Cars that would remain unnoticed on the street. Neither of them wanted to be noticed when they worked.

"There's not much to go on, but I'll keep an eye out for missing persons and see what comes up," Luther said casually. "Would you recognize the victim if you saw a picture?"

"I don't know," she said honestly. "It happened fast, and I wasn't very close. He had dark curly hair, that's all I can be sure of."

The homicide detective sighed: a long suffering, weary, "why do I bother?" sigh.

How could she convince him of what she'd seen? Grace tried not to give in to frustration. Luther would know the truth soon enough, when the body showed up. Then he'd listen to her. She took some comfort from the fact that Ray stood supportively beside her. *He* believed her.

Deep down she knew she shouldn't find comfort in the fact that Ray remained with her, reassuring and strong and constant. They weren't married anymore, and she didn't lean on him the way she used to. She didn't lean on *anyone*. Ray Madigan was no longer a part of her life.

And yet, after this morning's harrowing experience she did feel much better when she turned her eyes and thoughts to Ray. The world stopped spinning, and it was almost like the old days, when he was a part of her and she couldn't imagine life without him.

Luther shook his head and bit down on the last morsel of his hard candy with a loud crunch. "So, how do you like being back in Huntsville?"

"Fine," she said, puzzled that he wasn't more concerned about the murder.

"Are you going to stick around this time?" he asked as he threw open his car door.

She heard censure in the question, undisguised, open

hostility. Of course he was hostile; he was Ray's friend, had been his partner for years. Ray had forgiven her for leaving, but apparently Luther never had.

"For a while, I guess," she said uneasily. "You'll call me when the body's found?"

Luther gave her a quick, joyless grin as he slipped into the driver's seat. "If anything turns up, I'll give you a call."

If?

Her heart fell as she watched Luther drive away. "He doesn't believe me," she said softly.

"I know," Ray answered. He didn't sound at all concerned.

She looked at Ray, really *looked* at him. He was dressed in soft, cool blues, yet the morning sun made him appear golden and warm. The light shone favorably on slightly waving pale brown hair and tanned skin. His stance was casual, easygoing, but for the hint of tension in his hands and the set of his neck.

He squinted slightly against the bright sunlight, deepening the new wrinkles around his eyes, and her heart leapt. All her work, her dogged determination to put Ray behind her, had been for nothing. A waste of time. Because right now she was overcome with the certainty that she could hide in the shelter of his arms and he would protect her from anything, from everything. She had the urge to go to him right now, to press her face against that chest and breathe deep, to hold on...just for a while longer. Heaven help her, what she felt for him was so much more than a need to hide.

He'd touched her. She'd touched him. Old desires she'd thought long gone flitted to the surface to tease and taunt her. He looked so deliciously inviting she was tempted to fall into his arms again and stay there. She didn't, of course. Reluctantly wanting Ray was one thing. Relying on him to fill the void in her life would simply be asking for trouble she didn't need.

Ray never gave away much with his facial expressions, and this moment was no different. There was no emotion on his handsome face, no annoyance or concern or affection. He was cool and calm, almost indifferent. In spite of it all, she was glad he stood beside her. Where would she have run if not to Ray?

"You believe me, don't you?" she asked as he headed for the curb.

Before he reached the car he spun around to face her. "Of course I do." He said the words as if *not* believing was unthinkable.

She nodded her head as she joined him. He opened the passenger-side door and she dropped into the seat. "Thank you," she said as he closed the door. She had to learn to put her mixed feelings for Ray aside and accept their present circumstances. He was a friend, the best friend she'd ever had. Anything else was impossible.

She trusted Ray with her life, but she did *not* trust him with her heart. Not anymore.

He shut the door without responding to her thanks, and for a moment Grace gazed out over the park. It was too early, still, for mothers to be out with their children, as they would be later, so the place was almost deserted. Still she felt a chill, as if someone were watching.

She wrote the warning chill off to nerves as Ray cranked the engine and pulled away from the park.

Cops. He could smell them a mile away, and those two, with the woman, they were definitely cops.

Standing behind a wide-trunked tree and watching the second of the two gray cars pull away from the curb, Fred-

die laid a hand over his cheek where the woman had
kicked him. For a little thing she packed quite a punch.
Quite a surprising punch. His jaw still hurt like hell, but
fortunately nothing was broken.

He lowered his hands and thrust them impatiently into
the pockets of his trench coat, silently cursing the woman.
She'd surprised him, caught him off guard. And she didn't
fight fair. If he wasn't in public he'd cradle his battered
privates, as well.

He should kill the woman simply for hurting him, but
he never, *never* killed anyone in a fit of anger. This was
business, and he was a professional. Besides, killing the
witness now would only give credence to her claims. He
couldn't have that.

At the present time he wasn't particularly worried. There
was no evidence that a crime had been committed. That
one cop, the one who had arrived alone, obviously didn't
believe her. Freddie gave in to a crooked smile. The body
that currently rested in the trunk of his car wouldn't be
found for weeks, maybe even months. The death would be
made to look like an accident, as the client had requested,
so odds were no one would even make a connection to the
woman's wild story and the tragic accident that took the
life of one of Huntsville's most respected businessmen.

He walked away from the tree and towards his parked
car, limping just a little in deference to his throbbing, ach-
ing privates. Just to be safe, he'd dump the old Thunder-
bird coupe. Dammit, he hated to do that. It had been a
good car. But, he thought without rancor, it was just a car.
It could be replaced.

This afternoon he'd be paid the second half of his hefty
fee. He should get out of town immediately, but he didn't
like to leave loose ends. Maybe he'd keep an eye on the
woman for a while. Just to be safe.

Chapter 3

Ray wasn't surprised to see Luther come strolling into his private office unannounced. Doris had always been a little afraid of the irascible Detective Luther Malone; she let him have the run of the place. She was usually such a stickler for making clients and visitors wait, guarding his domain from her post in the outer office like a friendly but potentially dangerous guard dog.

"So," Luther said, propping himself on the edge of a messy desk. "What's up with Grace?"

"I took her home to shower and change clothes, and then I drove her to work," Ray said, closing the file before him. "She's still shook up, but figured working would be better than sitting around thinking about what happened."

Luther raised his eyebrows and shot Ray a look of sheer disbelief as he reached into his pocket for a piece of hard candy. Peppermint. "You didn't buy that story, did you?"

He'd known from the start, as Grace had, that Luther was skeptical about her account; they'd worked together too long not to be able to read each other's reactions to any given situation, not that Luther was exactly subtle these days. "Why would she make it up?" he asked calmly.

"I was hoping you could tell me."

Until recently, they'd had an unspoken agreement not to speak about Grace. She was a forbidden subject. Right now Ray saw more than skepticism in Luther's eyes; he saw a detective's unquenchable curiosity. Luther had a ton of questions that had nothing to do with murder.

Ray leaned back in his chair, not quite ready to satisfy that curiosity. "I'm telling you, she was spooked when she showed up at my place."

"Really?" Luther said dryly. "That's another thing that bothers me. She ran all the way to your apartment, instead of stopping at one of the *many* houses she had to pass to get there."

"Instinct," Ray said slowly. "She was scared so she went looking for someone familiar."

"You guys are divorced and have been for years," Luther grumbled. "Why would she go to you, of all people, when there's trouble?"

Ray flashed a wide smile. "You know all my ex-wives still adore me and depend on me to take care of them. Gracie's no different."

His smile didn't falter as Luther shot him a biting glance that said, too clearly, that Grace *was* different. Luther knew too much.

"I have no body," Luther said in a low voice. "No blood, no sign of a struggle, not a single corroborating witness, even though this supposedly happened right out in the open. I'm looking for a big dark car, and a big guy with medium brown hair under a baseball cap, a trench coat and hard-soled shoes, and evil pale eyes. Blue or green, take your pick.''

''And a temporary limp,'' Ray added lightly.

Luther delved in his coat pocket for another piece of candy. Strawberry, this time. He played with it instead of placing it in his mouth, rolling it in his palm and between his fingers. ''She might as well have given him a hook and sent me chasing after the one-armed man. Why can't I get something easy like the Taggert case? A body, a murder weapon, blood, fingerprints, enough evidence to convict the guy twice...but no, that jerk Daniels has the easy cases fall into his lap, and I get a hysterical woman's fairy tale.''

Ray wasn't yet ready to admit that Grace might be lying. He couldn't forget the vulnerable expression on her face as she'd looked at him and said, *You believe me, don't you?*

''Maybe it happened the way she said, and maybe she saw something and just overreacted,'' he reasoned. ''I don't think she'd make this up.''

''You don't?''

He knew she'd been terrified when he opened the door to his apartment, when she'd fallen inside and into his arms. She'd have to be terrified to forget her unspoken rule and actually *touch* him.

''I don't,'' he finally said.

Luther shook his head. ''Well, think about it. Has anything happened lately that might upset her? Something that might send her off the deep end.''

''We had lunch yesterday.''

''That'll do it,'' Luther cracked.

Ray's smile faded. ''I told her about the Mobile job offer.'' He didn't like the niggling seed of doubt that settled uneasily in his brain.

Luther stood and lifted both arms wide. His dark suit

jacket gaped to reveal his shoulder holster and the snub-nosed six-shooter in it. "That's it. Don't you see? She figures if you stick around here to protect her from some big, strong killer in a trench coat and a mysterious dark car you'll forget about the undercover job."

The theory made too much sense. He might not like the idea, but he couldn't immediately dismiss it, either.

"She always hated the undercover work," Luther added needlessly. "Divorced or not, I think she'd do anything to keep you from going into that again."

He remembered the look on her face yesterday, when he'd told her about the job offer. Terror, anger, revulsion. She hadn't even tried to disguise her true feelings. Would she lie to keep him from taking that job? Did she know he wouldn't leave town if he thought she was in danger?

Of course she did. Like it or not, she knew him better than anyone else ever had.

"Well hell," he drawled, as if this new wrinkle didn't make a bit of difference. "If a body shows up with a broken neck, or if you get a missing persons report on a man that matches her vague description of the victim, then what?"

"Then we reevaluate," Luther said as he made his way toward the door. "Frankly, I don't think anything's gonna turn up. I think Grace pulled a nasty trick out of her hat to make sure you stay right here in Huntsville for as long as she wants you here."

"And if she didn't?" Ray asked as Luther opened the door.

"Then we could all be in a heap of real trouble," Luther said, and then he closed the door softly.

The numbers on the computer screen added up perfectly, as usual. Things had been a mess three months ago when she'd taken this job, but the accounts were beginning to look good. Everything on the screen before her made perfect sense. Losing herself in the menial task had almost made her forget this morning's horror.

Grace heard a soft noise, a shuffle and a sigh behind her, and she glanced over her shoulder to see Ray standing in the doorway, leaning against the doorjamb with a smile on his handsome face and his arms folded across his chest. He looked like he didn't have a care in the world. She had never been more glad to see anyone in her life.

She didn't want to depend on Ray, to *need* him the way she once had, but again her heart gave a little leap at the sight of him. Why did he have this effect on her? Her heart melted; she felt a rush of warmth and tenderness in her body. She'd never been able to completely get Ray Madigan out of her heart, no matter how hard she tried. And she did try.

"Almost finished," she said. "Come on in and have a seat." She gestured to the single unoccupied chair in the room, a rather uncomfortable, hard chair against one wall.

She returned her eyes to the computer screen, even though she'd finished with this particular task. Ray's presence unnerved her, and she needed a moment to gather her wits. She moved the mouse and clicked the icon to save her changes, again.

Running to Ray this morning hadn't been a mistake, or so she'd told herself again and again during this long day. Falling into his arms, *that* had been a mistake. A big one. She liked being there too much, even though she knew they had no future together. He would never forgive her for leaving him, and she couldn't live with the knowledge that there would always be an enticing, dangerous job waiting for him around the next corner. An enticing, dangerous job he loved more than he'd ever loved her.

She swiveled in her chair to face him.

"How are you feeling?" he asked. She had the strange notion that something new lurked beneath the surface; a wariness in his voice and in his blue eyes.

"Fine, I guess. Did Luther find anything?"

Ray shook his head. "No."

She didn't think there was any way the killer could find her, but she worried just the same. What if, somehow, he knew where she lived? What if she walked into her house tonight and found him waiting for her? She shivered as she recalled the way he'd so easily snapped a man's neck. She'd surprised him and gotten away once. She didn't think she'd have the opportunity again.

"You're really worried about this, aren't you?" Ray asked softly. He stared at her obstinately, as if trying to read her thoughts. If anyone could...

"Yeah," she admitted.

Ray looked comfortable in his uncomfortable chair, at ease in a cramped office he'd never set foot in before. But then, he always looked at ease. He fit in, wherever he happened to be.

"Grace," a gratingly familiar voice called from the hallway just before stepping through the doorway into her office. "Did you finish..." Dr. Dearborne suddenly stopped speaking, as he saw Ray sitting against the wall. He even took a half step back. "What are *you* doing here?" A hint of revulsion touched his voice, and he paled. Just a little.

"Hi, Doc," Ray said with a wide smile.

"You two know each other?" Grace asked, more than a little confused.

"We've met," Ray said casually.

Their meeting had probably had something to do with Trish's unpleasant encounter with the dentist, Grace reasoned. Ray could be downright old-fashioned about some things; like honor and the way a lady should be treated. It was the Southern gentleman in him, she supposed. Still, he sometimes went too far.

Dr. Dearborne put his less than steady eyes on her. "Never mind, Ms. Madigan. What I wanted to speak to you about can wait until tomorrow. Or Monday." He gave her a sad, weak smile as he backed out of the office. "Nothing important."

Grace hadn't been working for Dr. Dearborne all that long, but she recognized fear when she saw it. The poor, personality-challenged dentist was so anxious to get out of the room he tripped over his own feet. After a quick recovery, he disappeared down the hallway.

"What on earth did you do..." she began.

Ray stood, quick and graceful. "How about I buy you dinner?" he interrupted.

Just as well. She didn't need to hear how he'd so gallantly defended ex-wife number two from the man he insisted on calling Dr. Doolittle.

But dinner sounded too much like a date. "I don't feel like going out," she said as she reached into the bottom drawer of her desk for her purse. But oh, she didn't want to be alone. Not yet. "I can cook you dinner."

He made a face, screwed up his nose and squinted his eyes until she could no longer see the vibrant blue. "What have I done to deserve this?"

She smiled as she stood. "I'm a much better cook than I used to be. Give me a break. I was just nineteen when we got married. At the time all I could do in the kitchen was make macaroni and cheese out of a box and open a can of soup."

She wished she could take the statement back, or at least reword it. Suddenly she remembered the times they'd made love in the kitchen. On the table, against the counter, on the floor. Ray would come home and find her trying her best to hone her abysmal domestic skills, and with a touch and a whispered word or two the recipe was forgotten. He'd lift her up or lower her down and she dismissed everything else. Everything. How many pots had she burned? How many leathery roasts had they laughingly tossed in the garbage? It was no wonder she hadn't learned to cook until after the divorce.

Her face felt warm. Once the memories came they were hard to shake. She tried to put the heated recollections in perspective. So, they'd had great sex. She'd learned the hard way that you can't build a lasting relationship on lust. Eventually you need stability, commitment, compromise. Ray didn't know the meaning of the word *compromise*.

"And if it was the kind that said 'add water' we were in trouble," he said.

"What?"

"The soup," he clarified.

If he knew what she was thinking about he didn't show it. But then, Ray was a master at concealing his feelings. No wonder working undercover came so easily to him. He could become whomever and whatever he wanted; he revealed only what he wanted to reveal.

"Steaks," she said, headed for the door with her purse clutched in her hands. "Salad and baked potatoes. We'll have to run by the grocery store, though." She glanced over her shoulder to see that Ray followed; close but not too close.

"No problem," he said, as he ushered her out the door and to his car.

Ray hadn't expected he'd ever find himself sitting on the couch in Grace's new house. Sure, they saw one another now and then, but she always managed to keep her distance, to keep things casual. In order for her to actually invite him here, she had to be either really scared, or else desperate to keep him from going to Mobile.

He wondered, as he watched her work at the bar that separated the long, narrow kitchen from the living room, just how far she'd go to keep him around.

He had no illusions about Grace. She'd loved him once, and she still cared for him; at least a little. She cared for him enough to worry on occasion, and she trusted him enough to come to him when there was trouble. Enough of a spark remained between them to provide the occasional uncomfortable moment, like in her office just a short while back.

But she didn't care enough to stay. Sometimes he had to remind himself of that fact.

In a flash he knew Luther's suppositions about the murder story being concocted just to keep him in town were bull. Grace hadn't made anything up. She didn't care enough to stay; she sure as hell didn't care enough to fight.

Annoyed at himself for studying Grace so intently, he turned his attention to the room. This house was old, but had been recently remodeled. Instead of a small parlor and eat-in kitchen, there was now one main room that consisted of a living area with a sofa, chairs, television and small stereo; the open kitchen and the bar that separated it from the living room; and a smaller space for a round oak dining room table with four chairs. The layout was simple and practical.

He saw Grace in this room, in the comfortable caramel-colored furniture, in the fat pillows scattered about the seating area. He saw her in the thriving plants and the lace curtains and the knickknacks on the single bookshelf. Snow globes. She loved snow globes. He recognized a couple of them as gifts he'd given her, years ago. A big snow globe with a white carousel horse, given to Grace for her twentieth birthday; a smaller one with a little boy and a little girl leaning forward for an innocent kiss, presented on their fourth anniversary.

She chopped vegetables for a salad while the potatoes baked, keeping her eyes on the knife and the cutting board and the vegetables. A strand of hair fell over her cheek, a long, dark strand that looked so soft and tempting his fingers itched.

What would she do if he walked into the kitchen, put his hands on her face, and kissed her long and hard? If he pulled that body up against his and quit pretending he didn't want her? He had a feeling that before this crisis was over, they were going to find out.

When they'd come in from their trip to the grocery store, she'd declared microwave potatoes "not the same," so they waited for the real thing: big fat potatoes baking in the oven. The steaks were marinating, a gas grill awaited on the patio out back, and the ice cream he'd sneaked into the grocery cart sat in the freezer. And if Grace chopped those vegetables much more they would be baby food, not salad.

"Gracie," he said softly. "Come in here and sit down. I'm not so old that I can't chew my own food."

Her hands stilled, and she looked down at the vegetables on the cutting board as if she hadn't realized what she'd been doing to them. Very carefully, she laid her knife aside. "I guess I'm still a little distracted by what happened this morning," she said as she wiped her hands on a dish towel and tossed it aside.

She stepped out of the kitchen and headed straight for the chair adjacent to the couch. Ray had no illusions that she might actually sit on the couch next to him. That would be too close, much too dangerous. Did she think he didn't notice the way she reacted when he touched her? The way her eyes went wide and her lips parted and her heart raced?

But no matter how Grace reacted, she continued to manufacture a false barrier between them. She hadn't even taken the time to change out of her work clothes, as if to slip into something more comfortable would send the wrong signal. She wore a straight, knee-length brown skirt and a tan blouse, very businesslike, very professional. On coming home she'd taken off the matching jacket and hung it in the closet, but she still wore panty hose and low-heeled shoes. She hadn't even let her hair down. Just that one stubborn strand touched her face, one misbehaving lock of dark hair that had fallen from her oh-so-sensible hairstyle.

A nervous Grace didn't settle back into the overstuffed chair, but reached for the remote control that sat on the coffee table and turned on the television. "Maybe there will be something about the murder," she said as she re-turned the remote to the table.

The news was on, and investigative reporter Sam Morgan's face filled the screen. Ray's instinctive reaction was to snag the remote for himself and turn the television off. "There won't be. Luther will contact us if anything comes up."

"Still," she said, snatching the remote off the coffee table and switching the TV on again. "You never know."

And, of course, if the television stayed on she wouldn't have to talk to him. She could keep her eyes and her attention on Morgan and pretend nothing was going on, here. This time after Ray turned the television off, he placed the remote on the couch beside him. It would be safe there.

"Do you want to talk about what happened this morning?'' he asked, managing to make Grace even more skittish.

She placed luscious big brown eyes on him while she twiddled her thumbs in her lap. Her knees were clamped together, her spine straight; she looked like she'd just finished a class on how to sit like a little lady. She looked like a scared little girl.

''Not really. I've told you everything already. Talking about it isn't going to make me feel any better.''

''Are you sure?''

Grace gazed longingly at the remote control. ''I'm sure,'' she said softly. Poor girl, she was about to jump out of her lovely skin. ''You know, I'd better check those potatoes,'' she said, practically jumping to her feet.

Without thinking, Ray reached out and snagged her wrist. With a gentle tug, she fell back and into his lap, landing there soft and wonderfully, arousingly heavy. She didn't stay there long, but slid off his lap to sit beside him. As she landed on the remote, the television came back on. At least Morgan wasn't on camera anymore.

''The potatoes won't be ready for at least another half hour, and you know it,'' he said, refusing to release her wrist when she tugged gently.

''But I really should…'' she began weakly.

''What are you afraid of?''

He hovered over Grace, and she lifted her face to him. She didn't tug against his grip again, or try to slide any farther away. He reached out and tucked that strand of hair behind her ear, his fingers brushing lightly against her face and grazing her ear as he accomplished the task.

''I'm not afraid of anything,'' she whispered, but the fear in her eyes told him she lied.

''Not even the man who chased you this morning?''

Her eyes widened. "*Him?* Of course I'm afraid of him. I'm not stupid."

Her short slide across his lap had caused her skirt to ride up, just a little, and when he glanced down he caught a glimpse of shapely, silk encased thigh. He placed his hand there. Grace trembled.

No matter how hard he tried he couldn't forget how it had been with them. He touched her and she was his. She laid her head against his chest and he forgot everything. When they came together there was power, and heat, and lightning. Like a spring storm, they lit up the sky and rocked the world.

He lowered his mouth to hers and kissed her, soft, tender, tentative. He felt the tremble of her lips, the gentle sigh of acceptance that touched his mouth. His mouth lay over hers, fixed for a long moment. God, she tasted good. Warm and soft, sweet and real and hungry. There was something akin to relief in the kiss, like he'd had an itch in the middle of his back for six years and someone had finally scratched it. The unexpected comfort of the kiss terrified him, but he didn't move away.

Feeling bold, fearlessly greedy, he moved his lips against hers, ever so slightly. Grace answered with a soft, gentle draw of her own. A tender sucking, a deep and arousing reception. Everything inside him tightened and heated, as if a bolt of lightning coursed through his body.

His hand, resting on her leg, inched higher until his fingers brushed her inner thigh. The flesh he stroked was giving, soft and warm, enticing and irresistible. This was familiar territory, even though it had been years, six long years, since he'd touched Grace this way. She trembled, but didn't take her mouth from his.

Ray Madigan was not a complete fool. He didn't love Grace anymore; how could he? She'd left him, she'd hurt him in a way no one else ever had or ever would. She'd taken a world he'd thought was safe and happy and blown it apart. No, he didn't love her, but he did *want* her. Yes, dammit, he did want her.

If the response of her mouth against his was any indication, she wanted him, too. She moved her lips against his and inhaled as if gently sucking the life out of him, as if she wanted to taste deeply but was afraid. Soft and hesitant and almost innocent, she brushed her lips against his.

He leaned over her, pressing her back into the soft cushions of the couch, and deepened the kiss. When he slipped his tongue into her mouth she gasped, and her hands went to his face, his head. She touched his cheeks and speared her fingers through his hair, and she answered the kiss, for an all-too-brief moment.

And then she pushed his head back, forced his mouth from hers. "I can't," she whispered. Unshed tears made her dark eyes sparkle, the flush on her face made her look nineteen again.

"Why not?"

She shook her head. "I can't sleep with you, Ray. I can't."

"I wasn't exactly thinking about sleeping, sweetheart," he said huskily as he moved closer. Her thighs fell slightly apart; she had to feel his arousal pressing against the inside of her thigh. He could so easily take her, here and now. He needed it; she needed it.

"You know what I mean."

Ah, she was serious. "What's wrong? Have you gone back to your ten date rule?" he asked lightly, as if it didn't make any difference one way or another if they finished what they'd started. As if he didn't want to ask her, here and now when there was no escape for either of them, why she'd left him.

He'd never understood the way she'd left. A damn note on the refrigerator, like a grocery list. *Milk. Eggs. Good-bye.*

He would never ask. The question would sound too much like pleading, and he would *not* grovel in front of Grace. Not now, not ever. He wanted her as much as he ever had, right now he hurt for her, but by God he did not need her.

"Don't you think a ten date rule is a little excessive in this day and age?" he asked casually, holding his body against hers. He felt and savored every breath she took, the tension in the length of her bewitching body.

He remembered how she'd explained it to him, the first time he'd tried to make love to her. Still a virgin, she'd concluded that she wouldn't know a man well enough to sleep with him until they'd had at least ten dates. Never a patient man, he'd asked her to marry him that night, on their third date. She'd said yes and they'd been married three days later. He'd been so sure that what they had was real and deep and lasting, that Grace was the one person who would always be there. He'd been young and stupid.

"And if that's it, do I have to start all over?" he smiled as he delivered the joke. "Can't I at least get credit for the dates we had before we were married? How about all those lunches at Pop's?" Suddenly he knew why she'd never allowed him to buy her lunch. "Is that why we *always* go dutch these days?" he teased.

"Be serious," she said, as she tried to gently push him away.

He wasn't going anywhere. Not yet. He pressed his body to hers, hovered above her so close he could feel her intense warmth and the beat of her heart, the slight tremble of her legs. Already she was inside him, as if he'd inhaled her, as if she seeped beneath his skin when he held her tight.

"Tell me, Gracie, when was the last time you had a tenth date?"

She pursed her lips, a sure sign she wasn't going to answer. He raked his body against hers, moving slowly, and kissed the side of her neck. When he did let her go, he wanted to make damn sure she left with the same torturous longing he felt growing inside him. He allowed his lips to linger, tasting her, feeling her heartbeat beneath his lips and his tongue before he released her.

As soon as he let her go she scrambled off the couch. "I imagine," she said, almost steadily, "that a ten date rule *does* seem excessive to you." She tried to hide her anxiety, but she couldn't disguise the faint quiver in her voice. "You probably wish willing women would just show up at your door naked."

"Bearing food," he added lightly.

She turned to stare at him. Her face was flushed, her lips damp and slightly swollen, well kissed and, like it or not, craving more. And such pained incredulity lurked in her luscious eyes. What had she expected, that he'd give her some romantic song and dance about wanting her and no one else? He didn't wear his heart on his sleeve; he didn't lie or make promises he wasn't prepared to keep.

"Preferably pizza," he added. "After all, it's good hot *and* cold."

His smile faded as she spun away to return to the task of mutilating the vegetables. Damnation, he wished he was already in Mobile. No good could come of this, no good at all.

If Grace actually thought they were going to get through this without ending up in bed together, she was crazier than she was making him.

Chapter 4

Freddie hated to run, and blamed the woman for this unpleasant morning jog. It was early and as cool as the day would be, and still he'd already worked up a sweat.

As he ran he glanced down side streets, watched the park trails, eyed the other runners. Betting, all the while, that the woman who'd witnessed the hit had been running a regular route. She must live in the area.

His hair was now blond and much too short, cut close to the scalp. He wore brown contact lenses, in case he should come face-to-face with the witness. The pale gray-green eyes, his mother's eyes his grandfather had always told him, were too distinctive. It was his one curse. A touch of expertly applied makeup covered the small bruise on his jaw, completing the facial transformation.

He no longer wore the conservative clothes he favored, and his trench coat had been packed away, for the time being. For this part of the job he would take on another look. The sleeves of the T-shirt he wore on this warm morning had been ripped out to display his muscular biceps and a tattoo that read Martha. The bicycle shorts he wore were too tight and too bright a shade of red. From a distance he looked like a punk. Up close he probably appeared to be a middle-aged man going through some kind of midlife crisis, trying to look younger than he was. To keep up the front, and because she was pretty, he grinned and winked at a shapely redhead who ran past, going in the opposite direction.

She looked away, ignoring him with her nose in the air. Bitch. Freddie spun around to glare at her bobbing red ponytail. For a moment he ran backwards, his eyes on the woman's back.

His irritation at her rebuff didn't last long, and he soon turned about and resumed his recon. He had collected the second half of payment for the job yesterday afternoon, as planned, and the body was planted at the foot of a small mountain at the south end of town. The victim's car, the one he'd been driving when Freddie had stopped him, was well concealed. He'd pushed it over a cliff on a deserted, curving stretch of road, so it would appear that the victim had driven over, missing the sharp turn and plummeting down the embankment. The car had rolled down noisily, through and past and over saplings and thick bushes, landing brilliantly behind a thick copse of trees. If the body wasn't found for a while, it would be impossible to tell that the driver's neck hadn't been broken in a tragic car accident.

The cops would never even suspect foul play, as long as no one looked too close, as long as no one listened to that damn woman who'd seen him yesterday.

A man in sweats jogged past, smiling and nodding, offering a friendly "good morning." Freddie returned the smile and muttered his own greeting. There were no other runners on the street, no nosy dark-haired woman who could ruin everything for him *and* for his client.

Once things calmed down a bit and the cops dismissed her claim as fantasy or fabrication, she might have to meet with a tragic accident of her own. Just as a precaution.

But first he had to find her.

Sensing a presence, Grace spun away from her computer and saw Ray lounging in the doorway of her office, that smug you-can't-fool-me grin in place.

"What are you doing here?" she asked, trying to stay calm. Last night's near disaster on her couch lingered with her, still. She'd been so close to giving in, to forgetting why she couldn't love Ray anymore.

"I thought I'd come by and check on you, maybe buy you lunch."

"I'm not very hungry," she said in a small voice.

His grin faded. "Come on, Gracie. You gotta eat."

The truth of the matter was, she felt secure here in her office. She'd felt safe last night, too, with Ray sleeping on her couch while she hid under the covers and remembered what he tasted like, what he felt like. She'd lain in bed and relived the moment his mouth had finally touched hers, the weight of his body, the warmth of his arms and his hands.

It didn't make a lot of sense that Ray's presence had made her feel safe from danger. A sleeping man in another room didn't provide much protection, but knowing he was there, a few steps away, comforted her...and kept her awake at the same time.

"I'll buy," she said, reaching into the bottom drawer of her file cabinet for her purse.

"What's the matter?" he asked softly, taking her arm as she reached the doorway. "Afraid I'll start counting?"

"Ray..." She balked, just a little.

"Never mind," he said, leading her down the hallway, past rooms occupied and unoccupied. "Forget I said anything about counting. This is not a date, it's business."

"Business?"

The waiting room was crazier than usual. A harried mother and her triplet toddlers were here to see Dr. Dearborne for their first checkup. A crew from a local television station was covering the human interest story.

Shea Sinclair was one of the few friends Grace had made since returning to Huntsville. She was a friend of Nell Rose's, and the three of them had had a girls' night out a couple of times. A movie, a sandwich and a daiquiri, a little girl talk and then home well before midnight.

Grace stopped to say hello. "Looks like you have your hands full."

Shea, professionally crisp in her bright blue suit and flawlessly applied makeup, turned her back on the mother of the triplets, crossed her eyes and stuck out her tongue. So much for her professional image.

"Yeah," she said softly. "This is hard news. My dream come true."

"Gotta start somewhere," Grace said with a wide smile.

Shea shook her head. "They have me doing the weekend weather now, can you believe it?" she said in a lowered voice. "I'm not a meteorologist, I have no experience, and they want me to stand there and read about fronts and airflow systems like I know what I'm talking about."

"Sorry," Grace said with a sympathetic tilt of her head. She turned to Ray, noted the sour expression on his face, and introduced him anyway. "Shea, this is a friend of mine, Ray. Ray, this is Shea Sinclair." She didn't say Ray Madigan, not wanting to answer questions about the shared last name right now. And curious Shea would definitely have questions.

She waited for Ray to turn on the charm. He didn't.

"Nice to meet you. Grace, we need to go." He took her arm and headed for the door.

Once they were outside, he picked up their conversation as if it had never been interrupted. "Strictly business. We can talk about the murder you witnessed, if you feel up to it." Ray led her into the sunshine and to his car, opening the passenger door for her.

"Why were you so rude to Shea?" she asked as she sat down.

He didn't deny it as he leaned forward, placing his face close to hers. "I hate reporters," he drawled softly. "All of them."

"Well, that's not fair..." He slammed the door on her protest.

When Ray sat behind the wheel and they headed out of the parking lot, Grace turned to study his profile. Already his rare moment of displeasure had faded. You'd think he didn't have a care in the world.

"Have you talked to Luther today?" she asked.

He glanced at her quickly, then returned his eyes to the road. "Yeah. They still haven't found anything."

"Have they looked?" she snapped.

"Where are they supposed to start?" he answered without malice.

She settled back into her seat and accepted the fact that Luther didn't believe her, that they didn't have enough clues to even begin an investigation.

"I could always go to Shea and see if she can get it on the news. If I go public, the police will have to do something."

"No."

"Why not? Because you hate reporters? And when did you develop such an aversion…"

"If the man you saw is still in Huntsville," he interrupted, "why provide him with your name and another good look at your face?"

Grace slid lower in her seat. "I never thought of it that way."

"Don't worry," Ray said in a soothing voice. "Eventually a body's bound to turn up, or else someone will file a missing persons report on a man who matches your description of the victim, and then Luther will have something to go on."

Eventually wasn't very comforting. "Well, if we don't have anything, what kind of business are we supposed to discuss over lunch?"

He turned into a bumpy parking lot, pulled into a space, and brought his car to a stop. Grace looked through the windshield to see The Hamburger Shack, affectionately called The Shack by those who dared to brave their big burgers and greasy fries. The building hadn't changed, except perhaps to become more weathered over the years. The concrete block building had been painted yellow years ago, and the door was a bright red. Wooden picnic tables sat randomly on a cracked brick patio.

"Lunch first, business later," Ray said, opening his door and crossing to open hers. "Grab us a table and I'll get the food."

She started to reach into her purse, but Ray stopped her. "If I count it as a business expense it's not a date, so hang on to your money, all right?" He sounded annoyed, like he was seconds from losing his temper. And Ray never lost his temper.

"All right."

She sat at a picnic table in the sun, her back to the

parking lot where she could see the door Ray entered. Two other tables were occupied, but they were on the opposite side of the patio. Here she and Ray would be relatively alone. She wasn't sure if that was a good idea or not.

When school was out you couldn't find a parking space at The Shack, much less a table. How many meals had she and Ray eaten here? Too many to count. She wondered if he'd brought her here on purpose, to remind her of better days, or if he just had a hankering for a really good burger. You could never tell with Ray.

She slipped off her plum jacket and placed it on the bench beside her, and rolled up the sleeves of her white blouse. It was a warm day. Besides, with the jacket on the bench beside her Ray would be forced to sit across the table, not right next to her like he used to. After last night she knew she was going to have to be careful. Very, very careful.

She lifted her face to the sun, momentarily taking it in, allowing herself to relax. It was a beautiful day, even with all that had happened. How did Ray know that a simple lunch in the sun would make her feel this way? Free and light, unafraid.

Ray wasn't long getting their food. He backed through the red door, a tray laden with two baskets and two tall paper cups in his hands. "I hope I remembered right," he said as he placed the tray on the table. "Medium well, no onions, fries extra crispy, strawberry shake."

She glanced into the basket he placed before her. "I don't remember the burgers being this big. And there are enough fries here to feed a small family. I can't possibly eat all this."

He looked down at the jacket on the seat beside her, and without comment sat on the opposite side of the table. "Sure you can," he said.

She did her best, but there was no way she could eat everything Ray had brought her. Besides, she didn't eat like a nineteen-year-old anymore! Ray did, though. He didn't leave a speck of food in his basket.

When she pushed a half-full basket away Ray lifted his eyebrows and grinned. "That's pathetic," he said lightly. "I remember a time when you wouldn't leave so much as a crumb of one of Arthur's burgers untouched. His feelings are going to be hurt when he sees this."

"Arthur's still here?" The owner of The Shack had been elderly when they'd first come here, twelve years ago.

"Some things never change," he said in a low voice, and she remembered last night, the way she'd been tempted by a kiss. Did he intend to remind her?

"Can we talk about the murder now?" Grace asked, trying to turn the discussion around. She'd rather relive that terrible morning than sit here mooning over her persistent and troublesome attraction for her ex-husband.

Ray's smile faded, and he placed his forearms on the table and leaned toward her. "Gracie, are you absolutely sure what you saw was a murder?"

Not him, too! "No," she snapped. "I made it up. That's how I get my kicks these days."

She started to rise, but Ray reached out and grabbed her wrist, holding her in place.

"Sit down."

She did. "Just forget it," she said lowly, shaking off his grip. "If you don't believe me..."

"It's not that I don't believe you," he said in a soothing voice. "But we have to consider the possibility that what you saw was...shall we say, less fatal than you think. Maybe it was a fight that got out of hand, but no one's dead. Maybe the guy you saw jump or fall out of the car was hurt, but not murdered."

"And the man who chased me?"

"Maybe he wanted to explain what had happened, so you wouldn't panic."

"He didn't look like he wanted to explain anything, Ray," Grace said. "He looked…he looked…" Deadly. Downright mean.

"I know."

She'd been an idiot to think he believed her!

"Would you stop speaking to me like I'm a child?" She looked him square in the eye across the table. "I know what I saw."

He gave up. Leaned back and relaxed. "Okay. I just had to be sure you didn't have any doubts."

"None," she said tersely.

Ray's gaze flitted past her to the parking lot, and he groaned softly.

Grace looked over her shoulder to watch a middle-aged man in an ill-fitting suit headed toward them from the parking lot, his eyes unerringly on Ray. The badge and gun on his belt identified him as a cop.

"Madigan," the man said as he reached the table. "How the hell are you?"

Even though Ray worked up a smile, Grace could tell he didn't like this particular cop much. "Daniels. I'm fine. What drags you out of the office?"

"Arthur's burgers, what else?" Daniels answered with a smile of his own. His eyes landed on Grace and he looked her up and down in a calculating way. That smile changed, turned predatory somehow. She expected a lecherous wink at any moment. "Is this the lady who allegedly saw a murder yesterday?"

Grace didn't like the way he threw the word "allegedly" into the sentence, any more than she liked the way he leered at her.

"This is no lady, Daniels," Ray said, his grin fading. "This is my wife, Grace Madigan."

"Ex-wife," she said automatically.

"Ex," Daniels said with a widening grin. "Yeah, that's what Luther said. Ms. Madigan," he said, turning his full attention to her. "If you need any help during this time of crisis, any help at all, you give me a call." He reached into his pocket and pulled out a business card he placed on the table before her. She got that lecherous wink after all.

"Thank you," she said, glancing down at the card but not touching it. "I have all the help I need at the moment, but if the situation changes I'll certainly call you."

He winked at her again before telling Ray goodbye and heading for the red door.

"What an ass," Ray said, snatching the business card off the table and tossing it atop her unfinished burger.

"A homicide ass I assume, since he works with Luther," Grace said. She made no move to take the card from the remains of her lunch basket.

"Yeah."

She placed her elbows on the table and leaned slightly forward. "I thought Ray Madigan never met a cop he didn't like."

"Daniels is lazy," he said in a low voice. "And stupid."

"Then how'd he get into homicide?"

He laid his eyes on her, hard. Ah, he definitely did not like this line of questioning.

"Daniels wasn't always lazy and stupid. Somehow that makes it worse."

No one knew more than Grace how diligently Ray had taken his career in law enforcement. It hadn't been a job, it had been his calling. He'd loved being a cop. The profession had defined him, it had ruled his life.

"Why did you quit?" she whispered.

He left the picnic table without answering her question. "Come on. If you're late getting back to work Dr. Doolittle will blame me."

She followed him to the car, silent but more curious than ever.

He'd promised to pick Grace up at five-thirty and take her home, since she was obviously still shaky about being alone. Ray wondered how many nights he'd have to sleep on her couch before he ended up in her bed. He was more certain than ever that he would find his way there.

Her question about why he'd quit his job had come out of nowhere, had taken him completely by surprise. She hadn't asked before now, during one of their friendly lunches, probably deciding the question was too personal for the boundaries she'd set.

But last night the boundaries had changed, hadn't they?

He pulled to the curb and looked over the park. In the early afternoon all was well, here. The grass was green, the pond peacefully calm but for the wake of three ducks paddling in the sun. Mothers pushed baby-laden buggies and played with toddlers, men in business suits and women in prim dresses sat on park benches shaded by dogwoods, daydreaming and reading and eating out of paper bags. Women lifted their faces to the sun and a few joggers braved the afternoon heat. It was a tranquil place.

Deceptively tranquil. Right here was where Grace had seen a man jump out of a moving car, the car come to a lurching stop, the driver commit murder.

And then the killer had chased her. That was the one part of her story he couldn't easily explain away. Grace

Madigan wasn't the type of woman to panic. She didn't scare easily, she never overreacted. If she said the man was chasing her and she had to defend herself to escape, it was the truth.

So where was the victim? More than a day had passed. The body could be buried in a basement or a rose garden by now, or resting at the bottom of the Tennessee River. It could be anywhere.

He forgot the murder and the unanswered questions and watched the people in the park. If he and Grace had been able to make their marriage work, she might be one of the women playing in the sun with a baby. He could almost see it, Grace with her hair in a ponytail and wearing jeans and a T-shirt instead of a business suit. Grace laughing and swinging that baby around, without a care in the world. Of course he could see that ideal picture in his mind; he still dreamed about it on really bad nights.

Whenever he got a case of the ''might've beens'' he reminded himself that she was the one who'd left, that she was the one who'd decided the marriage was over. He reminded himself now, as he drove away from the park.

Doris was waiting with messages in hand when Ray walked into his office. He made sure the smile on his face gave away nothing. Nothing at all.

''Did you miss me?'' he asked, winking at his secretary as she came to her feet and grabbed her purse.

''No,'' she said kindly. ''Not at all.''

''You could lie, just to be nice.'' He took the offered messages and scanned them quickly as Doris made her way to the door.

''You have kids, don't you?'' he asked casually, looking down at the messages in his hand.

Doris stopped at the doorway, and out of the corner of

his eye he saw her squint suspiciously at him. "Three boys and a girl."

"Grandkids?"

"Two. Both boys."

"I'm guessing those are the kids in the pictures on your desk."

She rolled her eyes wearily. "Of course." All of a sudden her expression changed, and those all-seeing eyes narrowed. "Where are these questions coming from? You're not thinking about getting married again, are you? And having kids? Heaven forbid." She came toward him, her step solid and practical, her lips pursed. "Ray Madigan, any man who's been married and divorced three times should know better than to try again. You have your good qualities, I'll give you that, but marriage just doesn't work out for you." She nodded her head once in finality.

He gave her a dazzling smile. "Who said anything about getting married? All I did was ask a friendly question about your family, show a little interest in my most valued employee —"

"Your *only* employee," Doris interjected.

"And you go ballistic on me."

Dismissing the uncomfortable conversation, he turned his eyes to the messages in his hand. "Turner called three times?"

"The poor man's meeting with his lawyer tomorrow, and he wanted to know if you'd found anything new."

He'd found much more than Mr. Turner wanted to know, that's for sure. "I'll get what I have together and call him back."

If his own disastrous marriages hadn't been enough of a lesson, his new profession provided a front row seat to the worst side of the institution. Every day he discovered another reason to avoid the trap of matrimonial bliss. He saw adultery, treachery, backstabbing, venomous attacks that never ceased to amaze him. His own divorces had been downright pleasant compared to a lot of what he saw.

But when marriage was good…ah, there was nothing like it. Too bad it didn't last. Not for him, anyway.

"I don't like the look on your face," Doris said softly, her tone reproachful. "Are you absolutely sure you're not thinking of taking on a fourth future ex-Mrs. Madigan?" she pressed. "Huntsville already has enough of that species."

"Of course not. Do I look like I've lost my mind?"

She sighed and turned her back on him. "A little."

Chapter 5

Grace couldn't say she was sorry Ray insisted on coming into the house with her, making a quick check to make sure no one was there, hiding and waiting.

She kicked off her shoes and let down her hair as soon as the door was closed behind her, and slipping off the jacket was a real pleasure. Once his check of the house was complete, Ray stuck his head in the refrigerator, looking for something to eat.

He was already at home in her little house, as if he belonged here. For all her resolve she was getting too comfortable with Ray all over again. Leaning on him, depending on him, had been a bad idea. But how could she stop? When she listened to her heart it guided her to Ray, like it or not.

"I won't eat a thing tonight," she said, heading down the hall to her bedroom. Comfortable old clothes, maybe a pair of shorts and a cool tank top, then an old movie on television, that's what she needed to calm her nerves. "Not after what you fed me for lunch."

"You didn't even finish," Ray shouted as he closed the refrigerator door. "And you don't have anything in your fridge but skim milk and yogurt."

She heard him clearly through the closed door, as she shucked off her work clothes and dug around in her chest of drawers for something to wear. She threw on a pair of dark green shorts and a matching tank top, but after she caught a glimpse of herself in the mirror she added a baggy, off-white camp shirt over it all. The more she wore around Ray, the better. An extra layer of clothing was a flimsy shield, but a flimsy shield was better than none at all.

Looking at her reflection in the mirror, she brushed her hair and pulled it into a high, tight ponytail. While she worked her thick hair up and back she lectured herself silently.

Maybe her heart did lead her to Ray, but her brain knew better than to fall in love with him again. He was a danger junkie who didn't care about anyone, not even himself. He lived for the moment, never thinking about tomorrow, never wondering what his lust for danger did to those who loved him. He was a senseless, selfish, irritating man.

So why did she sometimes feel certain this was a war her brain was going to lose?

When she opened the door she saw him standing there in the hallway, leaning casually against the wall directly opposite her bedroom. Tall, impressive as always, temptingly appealing, the initial sight of him standing there as if he'd been patiently waiting for her to emerge made her heart skip a beat. More relaxed than was natural given the circumstances, Ray's eyes met hers, then flicked past to the neatly made bed covered with blue and cream pillows.

When he returned his full and unnerving attention to her he smiled. Her insides quaked.

"You were taking a long time in there," he explained.

"Sorry," she tried a soft smile that fell dismally short. "It takes me a while to unwind after work, some days."

"You do look a little wound up." He raked his eyes over her from the top of her head to her bare toes.

"So," she said brightly, ignoring the way he looked at her. "What do you want for dinner?"

His wandering gaze stopped when he found her eyes and held them. "Maybe I should just order us a pizza," he drawled.

Grace was no less certain of what she'd seen in the park, and still she knew with all her being that Ray was a more immediate danger to her than the man in the trench coat. Ray was much too tempting, and with enticing glances like this one he threatened to turn her neat life upside-down. She'd worked too hard to get where she was to allow that to happen.

"You don't have to stay," she said calmly, walking past Ray and doing her best to remain calm. "I'm not scared today, not like I was yesterday." As long as I don't *think* about what I saw…

Ray grabbed her arm and pulled her back, spinning her around and drawing her tightly against his chest so she had to tilt her head back to see his face. He wasn't smiling anymore. He definitely wasn't *casual.*

"You always run from me," he whispered darkly. "Why is that, Gracie?"

"I wasn't running…."

"Don't make it worse by lying." His voice remained soft and low, but a trace of fire lurked in his normally placid blue eyes.

She parted her lips to say, *I'm not,* and Ray kissed her,

forcing her lips farther apart, tasting and teasing with his tongue. He rested one hand firmly at the back of her head, holding her in place while he kissed her so deep he took her breath away. Her knees wobbled, her heart caught in her throat, and before she knew what had happened she was kissing him back with everything she had.

Her arms encircled his neck, and she came up on her toes to bring her mouth closer to his. Could she ever get close enough? The taste of him was intoxicating, irresistible, and the way he made her heart beat and her body quiver was impossible to deny.

His mouth was hot and insistent, tender and sweet, and she couldn't get enough of him, no matter how diligently she tried. She nibbled at his lower lip, parted her lips as she tasted deep.

They'd been apart for six years, but at the moment it didn't seem so long. She remembered too well the smell and taste of Ray, the way their bodies fit together, the way he held her when they kissed; close and tender and urgent, all at the same time. He held her that way now.

She felt the beat of her heart all through her body, the warm and insistent rush of blood in her veins, the spreading, mindless need she'd denied for so long. Ray touched the side of her breast with one rocking thumb, and her nipples peaked in anticipation. A catch in the back of her throat escaped, a plea she couldn't contain.

Ray was coming apart, just as she was. He held her tighter, and she felt the deep tremble that shimmied through his body. He touched his knee against her thighs and instinctively her legs parted, just a little. She was falling, far and hard. And so was he.

When he spun her around and steered her toward the bedroom she thought momentarily of protesting, but didn't. She didn't say a word until the backs of her knees touched the mattress and she almost fell onto the bed.

"Ray," she whispered, her reason returning slowly through the haze of desire that clouded her mind. "We can't do this."

He smiled and kissed her again, quickly this time. "Sure we can. We screwed a lot of things up, Gracie, but this is not one of them. We were always good in the sack." He flicked her unbuttoned shirt off, one sleeve and then another, so that it fell to the floor.

Good in the sack? A wave of disappointment washed over her. Here she was, shaking to her bones and terrified of falling in love with Ray again, and he's grinning like always and making light of everything they'd once had.

"Things have changed," she said weakly. "I don't think I can..."

He reached into his back pocket and came up with a foil-wrapped condom between two long fingers. "I'm prepared, Gracie."

A little *too* prepared for her liking. Was this all planned? Every smile a seduction, every touch another well-planned step toward this moment.

"I'm not ready to fall back into a relationship with you." Easy as it would be. "I'm not going to fall into bed with you, either," she added hastily, not giving him the opportunity to tell her that they didn't have a relationship anymore and never would. "We're not married. I don't..." she choked on the finishing words *love you anymore,* but surely he knew what was in her mind.

Ray didn't miss a beat. He ran a caressing hand over her hip, urged her backward so she almost dropped onto the bed, raked his palm over a nipple as he whispered in her mouth. "We don't have to be married. We don't have to be anything but horny."

The haze cleared considerably. She placed a hand against his chest. *Horny?*

"A roll in the hay isn't a relationship, Gracie, it's sex. Pure and simple, uninhibited and flat-out fun." To prove his point he tweaked her nipple and sucked briefly on her neck. Reaching up, he released her hair from its ponytail and ran his fingers through the falling strands. "There doesn't have to be anything more to it than that. Don't complicate matters by thinking so damn much."

She finally collapsed, sitting down with a bounce. Ray placed his knee on the bed beside her hip, urged her backward, touched her cheek with tenderness and passion and longing. Suddenly it seemed that he was all around her, promising everything they both wanted. Comforting her, wanting and needing this coming together as much as she did. Ray encompassed her, surrounding her with his heart and soul.

Her body said *yes,* throbbing insistently when he gently forced her onto her back, tingling as her thighs fell slightly apart. His knee parted them more, working gently up the length of her inner thigh.

Her heart said *yes.* She needed him, wanted him, dreamed of him. When she was alone and in trouble he was the one she went to. Without question, without reserve. Had she ever fallen completely out of love with Ray?

"No," she whispered hoarsely, listening to her brain and ignoring all the rest. "I don't have sex just for fun."

He backed off, raising his eyebrows slightly. "You don't? Darlin', you don't know what you're missing." His eyes darkened, a muscle in his finely delineated jaw twitched. "What have you been doing for the past six years?" he whispered, trying and failing to come off nonchalant. There was too much intensity in his gaze, too much tension in the body he held over hers. "Falling in and out of love in time with your libido? Or do you just like to tease men until they can't think straight and then push them away?" He clenched his jaw and narrowed his eyes. "Is that how you get your jollies these days, Gracie?"

She gave him a gentle shove and he obediently moved away, leaving her and the bed and turning his back to her. Suddenly it was cold in this warm room. Lonely, and Ray hadn't even left yet. Heavens, she was so tempted to call him back!

"I think you'd better go," she whispered.

"I think you're right," he said hoarsely as he walked out of the room without a backward glance. "Dead-bolt the door behind me."

She lay on the bed, trembling, shaken to the core, closing her eyes tight as she heard the front door slam. All of Ray's questions echoed in her head. How could she tell him that there hadn't been any men in her bed in the past six years? That every time she started to get close to a man she found a reason to push him away.

She popped up when she heard the front door open.

"I said throw the damn dead bolt!" Ray shouted, and then the door slammed again.

There was only one woman in the world who had the power to drive him absolutely crazy. He should be running like hell from Grace, not knocking on her door at eight o'clock in the morning.

"Come on, Gracie," he shouted, ringing the doorbell again. "Open the damn door."

He heard the dead bolt move, then the chain, then the lock on the knob. The door opened slowly to reveal mussed dark hair, sleepy eyes, rumpled clothes. The same clothes he'd left her in last night.

"Did I wake you?" he asked, grinning.

"Yes," she mumbled, her voice still hoarse with sleep. "Ray, what are you doing here so early?"

"You run just about every day, right? You missed yesterday, so I figured…"

"It's Saturday," she said, glancing up at him with accusing eyes.

"So it is."

She moved back and allowed him to enter, stepping into her living room. A blanket hung half off the couch, and the pillow there, a soft pillow she'd brought here from her bedroom, still held the indention of a head. He wondered if he'd feel the heat of Grace's body if he sat there. He wondered if she'd slept on the couch all night, unable to crawl into the bed where they'd almost had sex.

If she had, good for her. He had barely slept three hours.

Ray had made good use of his time after leaving Grace yesterday. He'd bought a pair of running shoes, and when he'd gotten home he'd started making phone calls. He hadn't been a cop for years without making a few friends. Alan Chambers, an FBI agent Ray had met during a joint investigation years ago, was going to round up missing persons reports from across the southeast, not just from Huntsville where Luther had promised to check. Chambers had also taken the vague description of the killer and said he'd see what he could find.

One way or another, he had to get this fiasco over and done with. He had to make certain the murderer was caught and Gracie was safe. Hanging around her and pretending he didn't care was killing him.

She made her way to the kitchen, pushing her hair away from her face and yawning, stretching this way and that.

God, he loved the way her body moved, sleek and grace-ful, strong and soft. The world was full of women, pretty and plain, stunning and ordinary, but none of them moved like Grace.

"Coffee," she muttered, reaching into the cabinet above the coffeemaker for the can, silently performing the task she likely performed every morning. When the coffee was dripping into the glass decanter, she turned to him, leaning against the counter.

"I was thinking of getting a treadmill," she said, pin-ning large, dark eyes on his face.

His grin faded. "You're going to let that guy scare you into hiding here? What are you going to do, become a hermit?"

"No," she said, looking down at her bare feet. "Well, maybe. Just for a while."

Dammit, how could Luther think she was making all this up? "No," he said.

She lifted her face to look at him.

"You can't hide, Gracie."

"I'm not hiding, I'm just being cautious. That's all."

He lifted one foot to show her his new shoes. "You mean I bought these for nothing? The guy in the sporting goods store told me these were the best, that even I could run in them."

That got a small smile out of her. "You're not exactly dressed for running." She took in his jeans and T-shirt, the baggy denim shirt he wore loose to conceal the pistol at his spine.

"It'll do," he said softly.

They had coffee and toast, and he sat on the couch while Grace curled up in her favorite chair. Yep, the couch was still warm, and he could actually...he closed his eyes briefly...he could smell her, that scent of soap and shampoo and skin that was uniquely Grace. He wondered if she'd tossed and turned here all night, the way he'd tossed in his own bed.

Grace didn't hurry, even had a second cup of coffee. But eventually she excused herself and disappeared down the hallway. Tempted as he was to follow her, he remained on the couch.

Just a few minutes later she stepped into the living room dressed for her morning run in white shorts and a baggy gray T-shirt, her hair in a ponytail, her socks white against tanned legs. Damn, she had great legs.

He came to his feet. "Take it easy on me," he said. "I haven't done this before."

She passed him and opened the front door.

"I guess you could say," he said softly to her back, "I'm a virgin."

She didn't look back.

"Don't hurt me," he added as she began to stretch on the front porch. "I'm fragile."

She cut her eyes to him as she stretched to the side. "If you don't stretch you will hurt yourself."

He stretched a little, copying her, watching the way her sleek muscles moved.

Yep, the world was full of women. Why did he want this one so bad? Because he'd had her once and lost her, maybe. Because she had great legs. Because he still remembered how it had been with them. Had they really been so good together, or was his memory faulty?

She bent over double, legs spread, and touched the flat of her hands to the ground.

Nope, there was nothing wrong with his memory.

She took off running and he followed her, keeping a short distance between them. He kept his eyes on her shapely back, on her fine backside, on her great legs and the curve of her neck and the way her ponytail bounced as she ran. And he tried to tell himself that's all she was. A great body. His mind whispered differently.

Whenever he thought about confessing everything to Grace, telling her how he really felt, out-and-out asking her why she'd walked out on him six years ago, he remembered the way she'd left. How she'd leave again when things didn't go her way.

She'd wanted him last night. He'd felt her heated response in every move she made, had seen it in her eyes, tasted it in her lips. They would end up in bed together, sooner or later, and it would be on *his* terms. No false promises, no pretty words. Just sex.

Grace glanced over her shoulder and smiled, and something in his chest constricted.

Just sex.

With Ray behind her, Grace didn't worry about being on the street. He was right. She couldn't let what she'd witnessed change her life. Knowing he'd been seen, surely the murderer had left town. He was probably in Mexico by now. Or Canada. She didn't care where he was, as long as he wasn't here.

Ray made a show of disdaining all physical activity, but he must be doing something to stay in shape. He didn't lag behind, or ask her to slow down or stop. He kept a steady pace directly behind her. Some virgin.

She didn't run her usual route through the park, but turned on the next street over and ran in the shade of ancient oak trees. From here she could see the park, the flowering trees and the expanse of grass, but she couldn't see the corner where the man had been murdered. She didn't ever want to see that place again.

There were a few other runners out this morning. Two

women jogging slow, talking and laughing. An older man
walking his two black labs. A muscular man with short-
cropped blond hair ran straight ahead. He wore shorts that
fit much too tight and a shirt with ripped-out sleeves.
Showing off for the ladies, no doubt.

There was no menacing man in a trench coat, no squealing tires.

It took her a while, but she finally relaxed, enjoyed the
run, tried to forget that Ray ran right behind her.

But she couldn't forget, and to be honest she didn't want
to. Not yet.

They made a circle around the block and headed for
home. As she neared her driveway, Ray sped up to jog
beside her.

"That's it?" he asked, a touch of disdain in his voice.
"I haven't even worked up a sweat."

She maintained a steady jog and glanced sideways to
see his face. "Yes, you have."

He grinned at her. She fought the urge to grin back. She
had a sinking feeling he was about to suggest they shower
together. She had a sinking feeling that if he asked at just
the right moment, in just the right way, she'd agree that it
was a fine idea.

But suddenly his focus changed. He wasn't looking at
her anymore, he stared straight ahead. His smile disappeared and he moved past her. "That's Luther's car in
your driveway."

They both sped up, running faster than before. They met
Luther as he was returning to his car.

"Where the hell have you been?" Luther snapped. "I
was just about to call someone down here to bust your
door in. Both cars in the driveway, no answer at the door."
He narrowed his eyes and glared at them, first at Grace,
then at Ray. "You were *running?*"

"Yeah," Ray said, all business. "What's up?"

Luther took a deep breath and stared Grace dead in the eye. There had been a time when she could read his expressions almost as well as Ray's. No more.

"We have a body."

Chapter 6

Luther paced, cutting his eyes to Grace as she placed coffee mugs on the counter then glaring at Ray with eyes that were somehow accusing.

"His name was Carter Lanford. Forty-two years old, married, no kids. Owned a local software company. Made a lot of money in the past seven years, but because of his family connections he's always been wealthy. Big in charity, local government, donated money and computers to a number of school programs. Sounds like a great guy," Luther said with a grimace. "Early this morning his car was found at the foot of Justin Mountain, Lanford in the driver's seat. He's been dead a couple of days."

"Neck broken?" Ray asked tersely.

Luther nodded. "It looks like his neck was broken in the crash. It'll be a couple of days before I have the medical examiner's report, but…"

"His neck wasn't broken in the crash," Grace said calmly.

Luther ignored her. "A couple of kids out searching for arrowheads at the crack of dawn found the car. It was pretty well hidden from the road by trees, so if those kids hadn't found the car it might've been winter before it was spotted."

"Making it very hard to tell exactly how he died, I would imagine," Ray said.

He wondered if Luther felt guilty for doubting Grace. Luther didn't look particularly guilty, but then as he'd grown older he'd gotten pretty good at hiding his feelings. Hadn't they all.

"Now what?" Grace asked, bringing them both coffee. Luther's black, his with a little sugar. After all these years, she remembered.

"I'd like you to take a look at some photographs of the victim, just to be sure he's the one you saw."

Grace nodded once and turned her head away, not wanting either of them to see that she was disturbed by the thought of those photographs. Too late. Her emotions, her fears and uncertainties, were there for the world to see.

"Then I'd like you to meet with a sketch artist."

"I guess we need to do all this at the office," she said, sipping at her own coffee.

Ray watched Grace, noted the way she didn't look directly at him or at Luther. She had always called the detectives' pit an office, never "the station" or "downtown," as if giving his former workplace an ordinary name would somehow make it ordinary.

"If you don't mind," Luther said.

She excused herself to take a quick shower, and Ray immediately placed himself in Luther's face.

"You owe her an apology."

"I do not." Luther didn't back down.

"You didn't believe her."

"Well, I'm here now."

Luther finished his coffee quickly and placed the empty cup on the kitchen counter.

"Who did it?" Ray asked, watching Luther's back.

Luther shrugged his shoulders and reached into the pocket of his dark blue jacket for a piece of hard candy. "I don't know. The wife didn't seem overly bereaved when I broke the news to her before coming here. There's a definite possibility she was involved."

"Why didn't she report him missing?"

"Said he was supposed to leave town Thursday morning. A business trip to D.C. They'd had a tiff before he left, so when he didn't call..." Luther shrugged his shoulders. "Sounds like a convenient excuse but I can't prove she's lying."

Luther roamed the room, picking up this and that, peeking behind pillows, shaking the snow globes. Ah, old Luther was fidgety. He might not admit that he owed Grace an apology, but he did feel guilty. Just a little.

"She's certainly not the one Grace saw," Luther said as he picked up a small snow globe and shook it gently, "but the man who did the dirty work could be a boyfriend, a relative, an accomplice of some kind."

Ray's heart lurched. "Gracie could be in serious trouble."

Luther didn't seem concerned. "We don't know for sure that Lanford is the man Grace saw killed. All we know right now is that he's dead."

"Of a broken neck," Ray added.

Luther shrugged, conceding ungraciously. "Let's say Lanford is the man she saw murdered. It's possible the wife isn't involved at all. I haven't checked into Lanford thoroughly yet. Who knows what kind of dirt we'll dig up? The killer could be a thousand miles away by now."

"Maybe," Ray muttered. Grace entered the room from the hallway, her hair slightly damp and hanging around her shoulders, her shorts and T-shirt traded for a pair of khakis and a white button-up blouse. She'd put on a little makeup, some pale lipstick and a touch of mascara, but that was it.

She looked a little scared, more than a little nervous. "Let's get this over with."

Freddie watched them drive away, the three of them in two cars.

If they looked back they might see him leaning against the tree, then bending over to tie his shoe. They wouldn't pay him any mind, just as the woman and the one who'd run with her this morning hadn't paid him any mind on the street.

But they didn't look back. Dammit, they were intense, in a hurry, and that one cop, the one who had been running with her, had hovered over the witness protectively as he'd escorted her to the car.

The body had been found, or else someone had reported Lanford missing.

It was a complication, but not an insurmountable one. People who had threatened to testify against him in the past had met untimely deaths, freak accidents and out-and-out executions. The woman wouldn't be any different.

He made yet another mental note of the address he'd followed them to, studied the front door and the placement of the windows. As he jogged away from the house he was already making plans. An accident would be best. Would cause less commotion; attract less attention. And if that didn't work he'd burn her house to the ground or put a bullet through her head. Made little difference to him. He had time. Lots and lots of time.

An attractive, fair-haired woman jogged past him, heading in the opposite direction. He smiled at her and she smiled back.

Freddie made a U-turn in the street and pulled up alongside the blonde. She was tall. He liked that. Her blond hair was cut too short for his liking, almost like a man's cut, but on her the style looked classy. And she didn't turn her nose up at him the way that redhead had.

"Hi."

"Hi yourself," she said, glancing coyly to the side.

"Nice day for a run."

She nodded, smiled again. One of those secret, female smiles that drove him wild. Someone classy like this, she probably had a husband, or a boyfriend. Maybe both. She was too pretty to be on her own. Still, nothing ventured, nothing gained.

"Who's Martha?" she asked, grinning as she nodded at his tattoo.

"An old girlfriend," he admitted, cursing himself for his youthful foolishness. One day he was going to have the damned thing removed. "She's been out of the picture for a long time."

"Oh," the blonde muttered.

"I'm new in town," Freddie said, not bothering to waste her time or his with more pleasantries. "My name's Jimmy."

She looked him over, taking in the tattoo and the muscled arms he worked so hard to sculpt. Apparently she liked what she saw. "I'm Gillian."

"What a beautiful name." He smiled at her again, and she blushed. "I don't know many people in Huntsville, and I was just wondering…what are you doing tonight, Gillian?"

* * *

Grace didn't protest when Ray insisted on coming inside with her. He made the usual quick rounds while she fastened all three locks on her front door.

Seeing the pictures of the dead man had made this all too real again. Going over every detail of the killer's face with the sketch artist had brought back too many memories of that morning.

What she really wanted to do was pack her bags, load up the car, and head back to Chattanooga. Returning to Huntsville had been a really bad idea. She was definitely not working Ray out of her system, as she'd hoped, and now this. Yeah, coming back had been a *really* bad idea.

"So," Ray said calmly as he exited the hallway. "Do I move in here or are you coming to my place?"

"What?"

"Just until we ID the man who killed Lanford. You shouldn't be alone when we have no idea what we're dealing with."

"We?" she said, ignoring the question. "You're not on the force anymore, and since this is an open investigation you have to stay out of it. Right?"

"Right," he said with a sarcastic edge to his voice. "I'm going to sit back and wait."

"There's nothing you can do."

He lifted his eyebrows, silently challenging her. "Can I borrow your phone?"

She grabbed the portable phone from the handset on the kitchen wall and handed it to him. He dialed the long-distance number from memory.

"Chambers," he said, turning his back to her. "I know you haven't had time to find anything yet, but I have an update. We've found the victim. Carter Lanford, local muck-a-muck, lots of money, not-so-grieving widow."

There was a pause, and while he waited Ray paced. "I know the description of the suspect I gave you is sketchy, at best, but to narrow it down…" He spun and faced Grace, looking her square in the eye. "Look for a pro. A hit man who's maybe done business in the south in the past. It's too early to tell, but this definitely smells like a professional job."

Ray answered a few questions, gave the man on the phone her number in case he wasn't at home or in the office, and his beeper number in case there was no answer at either. He ended the conversation with a promise to call again on Monday.

"You're trying to scare me," Grace said softly as Ray returned the phone to its hook.

"No, I'm just trying not to hide anything from you."

"What makes you think the killer was a hit man?"

Ray fidgeted. A situation like this one, not knowing what had happened or what would happen next, always put him on edge. "For one thing, Lanford had a lot of money. When there's money at stake, anything's possible. His wife didn't seem too sorry to see him depart this earth, but we know she didn't kill Lanford herself. It makes sense to at least consider the possibility that she hired the murder out. And the crime scene was squeaky clean. This guy didn't leave a single clue behind."

"Except for me," Grace said softly. Ray nodded once.

The idea that she might have faced a professional hit man and escaped by surprising him with pepper spray and a well-placed kick made her go weak in the knees.

"I can leave town," she said. "Maybe stay with friends in Chattanooga for a while."

Ray quit pacing and stared at her. "And give up your great job with Dr. Doolittle?" he deadpanned.

"It's not working out exactly like I'd planned," she

admitted. Nothing had. "Besides, it's not fair to ask you to put your business, your whole life, on hold while you baby-sit me. I'm not your responsibility." *Not anymore.*

"Yes, you are." Ray took the two steps that separated them and placed his hands on her face, forcing her to look up at him.

His hands were large, warm and comforting, and still demanding. Making her face him, making her look him squarely in the eye. She fought the temptation to lean into one of those hands, to turn her head and kiss his palm and beg him not to go.

"You came to me," he said softly. "When you were scared, when you didn't know where else to go, you came to me. Do you think I can turn my back on you now? Pretend nothing has changed?"

"Nothing has changed," she said weakly, trying, so hard, to mean what she said.

"Gracie Madigan," he whispered, his mouth moving toward hers. "Everything has changed and you damn well know it."

Ray kissed her, long and deep, soft and gentle. But he did not push, he didn't steer her toward the bedroom or let his hands roam enticingly over the body he knew too well. He just kissed her, his mouth brushing across and then lingering on hers, and she loved it. She wallowed in it.

"So," he said as he reluctantly took his mouth from hers. "Your place or mine?"

With his feet propped on Grace's coffee table and the laptop sitting on his thighs, Ray began his own investigation. A narrow cord ran from her kitchen phone to the computer, where he searched the Internet for information on Carter Lanford.

He'd brought a few things from home, including the

Lyle Lovett CD that played softly on Grace's stereo. She'd been in her room for an hour now, since just after ten, and was no doubt sleeping like a baby.

His mind was only half on the task at hand. Gathering information was a dull but necessary part of any investigation, but he had to start somewhere. Who, besides the rich widow, might want Carter Lanford dead?

The name was not entirely unknown to Ray. Lanford's Huntsville-based business had grown quickly and had made him very wealthy at a relatively young age. He was on the board of the Children's Hospital Charity, employed over three hundred people in the Huntsville area and played softball on an over-forty league. Ray pulled up old newspaper articles about Lanford, as well as a feature that had run last year in a national financial magazine.

There weren't that many reasons for murder. Money. Love and the baggage that came with the damnable sentiment. Hate and the jealousy and delusions that came with it. Self-preservation.

Lanford had money and lots of it. Any successful man of his age had surely had his brush with love and hate and all that went with those emotions. Was there a girlfriend out there? A jealous husband? A business rival who'd been pushed over the edge?

Ray cursed beneath his breath as he read the articles. Lanford's PR was good, you had to give him that. His skeletons, if he had them, were still in the closet, waiting to be uncovered.

"Lyle Lovett."

Ray turned to watch Grace as she stepped from the hallway and into the room. Covered with a blue terry-cloth robe that hung to the floor, she looked smaller than usual. Vulnerable. Scared.

"I Love Everybody."

She cracked a small smile. "I know."

"That's the name of the CD," he clarified. *"I Love Everybody."*

"I don't remember it," she said, stepping close to peer over his shoulder to the screen.

"I didn't have it when we were married. I got it after you left."

"Oh," she said, her voice small.

He turned off the computer and closed the cover, then unceremoniously dropped the laptop to the cushion beside him. He wasn't getting anywhere, anyway. "If the music's keeping you awake..."

"No," she interrupted. "I just can't sleep." She sat in the fat chair to his right and curled her legs beneath her. "My mind is spinning, and every noise I hear, every car that passes on the street startles me."

She smiled at him, a sad, small smile, and he knew in that instant what he had to do.

He wanted Grace in his bed, he craved her to distraction, sometimes. She'd crawled into his head and she stayed there, keeping him awake at night, teasing him during the day when he should be thinking of a hundred other things. He needed her beneath him, he needed her to wrap her legs around him while he buried himself inside her. Only then...only then would he get her out of his head.

As hard as he tried to convince himself of that, he knew what he wanted from Grace was much more than her willing body. He wanted things to be the way they had once been, and that wasn't going to happen. Not ever. She'd left before. If he got involved with her she'd leave again. Hell, he'd barely survived the first time.

And she was right, dammit. They couldn't have *just sex* without it becoming more. The emotions that flowed, unacknowledged, between them were intense and complicated. He didn't want complicated, not from her, not from anyone.

But Grace was his weakness. He wasn't strong enough to push her away again and again. Not if she kept looking at him this way, not if she kept kissing him back when he lost control and went to her. She had to maintain the wall between them, she had to fight him tooth and nail. She had to understand that they had no future together. He knew just how to make sure she got that through her pretty head.

"I'm taking the job in Mobile," he said.

Grace's eyes got big, but she said nothing.

Ray plowed forward, knowing what he had to do. "I'm going to call Stan tomorrow and let him know, but I'm also going to tell him that until this thing with you is taken care of I'm not available."

Her lips trembled, just a little. Her eyes went soft and vulnerable. Dammit, she wasn't supposed to look hurt. Like his leaving was a betrayal, like he owed her something more.

"Don't stay for me," she whispered. Unshed tears made her dark eyes sparkle dangerously. "I can…I can…"

"You can do what?" he interrupted. "Hide? Run? Hire a full-time bodyguard?"

She shrugged her shoulders. "All three, maybe."

"No," he insisted. "This is the way it's going to be, Grace, and I don't want any argument from you. We're going to catch this guy. Until then, I'm going to watch over you like a hawk." He nodded his head, left no room for argument. "Before this mess is over you'll be so sick of me you'll probably offer to buy me a bus ticket to Mobile." He tried a smile but it was weak, more of an effort than he wanted to admit.

"What if we never know who it is?" she asked softly.

"What if you never find him?" He could see the fear in her face, fear of the never-ending nightmare of a killer waiting...patiently waiting...

He wondered which she was more afraid of. Never catching the killer, or living indefinitely in this painful limbo, caught between the past and the future they didn't have.

"We'll get him."

"And then you're moving to Mobile to go into narcotics again. Undercover?"

"Yeah."

"What if Stan can't wait?"

Knowing that he couldn't have Grace, no matter how much he craved her, put a damper on the evening. Right now he just wanted her to go back to bed where he didn't have to see her. Where he didn't have to look her in the eye and pretend that he'd forgiven and forgotten the way she'd left.

"He'll wait," Ray said, reaching for the laptop.

Chapter 7

Grace had tossed restlessly half the night. She'd dropped into bed disheartened and exhausted, but for what seemed like an interminably long time her mind refused to be still. When she had finally fallen asleep she'd had the dreams, the nightmares she thought she'd finally gotten rid of. In her nightmares, Ray was dead and there was nothing she could do to save him.

She woke weary, unrested but unable to go back to sleep. Ray was going back to undercover work, would probably already be on his way to Mobile if not for the murder she'd witnessed and the fact that when she ran from trouble she ran to him.

It was too early to be up and about on a Sunday, but she rolled out of bed, dressed in figure-concealing sweats, and combed her hair with her fingers. Coffee, about two pots, would make her feel better. Maybe.

Ray was sprawled on the couch, his body too long for the makeshift bed, an arm thrown over his eyes to cut off the morning light that shot through the part in her living room curtains. And still he slept, dead to the world and apparently without a care.

Grace started the coffee. While the coffeemaker coughed and sputtered, she stepped outside to collect the Sunday paper from her front walk, then quickly reentered the house and locked the door behind her, her gaze landing on Ray as he opened his eyes.

"Dammit, don't go outside by yourself," he said gruffly, still more asleep than awake.

"You're kidding, right?"

"No." He closed his eyes again. "I never kid with you, Gracie."

If she had any doubts about falling in love with Ray again, his determination to go to Mobile killed them all. She couldn't afford to give in, no matter how tempting surrender would be.

He'd been working undercover the second time he'd been shot. Luther had shown up at her door in the middle of the night and she'd known before he said a word, she'd *known,* that Ray had been hurt again. Just like the first time, she'd imagined the worst as Luther drove her to the hospital. Just like the first time, she'd arrived to find him wounded and doped up but still the same old Ray. Smiling. Laughing. Holding her hand and telling her everything would be all right as she'd perched on the edge of his hospital bed and cried.

Someone had made him, that time, and all hell had broken loose, the way he told it. He'd caught a bullet in the leg, but was pretty lucky, all things considered.

All things considered.

She'd died a little that night, deep inside in a place that didn't heal easily. The fear had stolen part of her youth, her hopes, her innocence. She'd never been able to make Ray understand that.

Grace unfolded the paper to see the murder victim's picture on page one. Carter Lanford looked surprisingly different in the posed photograph; alive, unafraid, handsome in a cultured kind of way. She turned the paper over to take a glimpse at the bottom fold, and found herself staring at a familiar face.

"Ray," she said softly, then louder, when he didn't respond. "Ray!"

He opened one eye, rolled up, and ran sleepy fingers through his hair. Anyone, *everyone,* should look disgusting waking up, but not Ray. He looked like a man should in the morning, a little coarse but still appealing. Invitingly warm and deceptively innocent. Long and rough, tall and solid. Somehow mussed hair and stubbled chin were attractive on Ray. Oh, she was such a putz!

"Do you have any idea what time I got to sleep last night? This morning, actually," he grumbled.

"I know her." She held the paper up, grasping it with both hands and thrusting it forward so he could see the bottom half of the front page. "The widow. We're in the same exercise class."

"You know her?" He was instantly awake.

"Not let's-have-lunch know her, but say-hi-in-the-locker-room know her. Yeah."

She didn't really enjoy putting a familiar face to the not-so-distraught widow Lanford. It made her queasy. Louise Lanford, the paper said. Grace couldn't remember ever exchanging anything more personal than first names, usually just commiserating over a tough class now and then. Louise was a few years older than she, but not many. Late thirties, she imagined.

"What are the odds?"

Grace shrugged her shoulders. "Huntsville's not that big a town. I see the same people all the time, in the grocery store, in class, on the road, in the office. Is it really such a stretch that I'd know her?"

"Not really." She had finally grabbed his interest. "What's she like?"

She tossed Ray the paper and plopped down in her chair, thinking. Pondering. "She strikes me as being tough. One of the steel magnolias you hear about. A real lady on the outside, hard as nails on the inside."

"Interesting. Do you think she's tough enough to commit murder?"

"I don't know. Maybe." Grace tried to remember the words they'd exchanged, the woman's attitude and facial expressions. "She's very confident. False smile. Calculating eyes. Let's put it like this. I wouldn't want to get in her way."

She had Ray's full attention. He didn't look sleepy anymore. "Did she ever talk about her marriage?"

Grace shook her head. "No, we talked about crunches and heart rates and body aches, not personal stuff." Not that she had any personal stuff to talk about, these days.

Ray glanced over the article, then lifted his head and stared at her. "Wait a minute. Exercise class? You run four or five days a week and you go to exercise class, too?"

"Yes," she said, lifting her chin a little and trying not to sound defensive.

"Why?"

Gotta do something. "What difference does it make? I like to exercise. It makes me feel good."

She expected a quip about new and improved methods of exercising and *feeling good,* along with a friendly wink, but she got neither. She didn't even get a heart-stopping promise-filled grin.

"Whatever turns your crank," he muttered, returning his attention to the newspaper.

A Sunday afternoon drive was pleasant enough, with Grace beside him and the sun shining bright.

She'd taken a long shower and emerged with her hair twisted up and a touch of makeup on her flawless face. Her navy blue pants were creased and conservative, and the pale blue lightweight sweater she wore was just a little baggy. Except when she moved just so and unknown to Grace her fine shape was momentarily revealed.

"I could've stayed home," she said, not for the first time.

"She might be more inclined to talk with a woman there," he said, not willing to tell Grace that he wasn't ready to leave her home alone. Not yet. "You know, do the girl thing and give her a hug and listen while she spills her guts."

"That's so cold," she admonished.

"Welcome to my world," he muttered.

The Internet was a fine place to start, but for a murder investigation it was definitely inadequate. Ray had spent the morning on the phone, talking to people who knew Lanford. Luther would have his hide if...*when* he found out, but that certainty hadn't bothered Ray for any longer than it took to punch seven numbers into the telephone.

He had to find out who murdered Carter Lanford, put the guy Grace had seen in jail, and get the hell outta Dodge.

You just couldn't find info like this on the Net. Carter Lanford was, to all outward appearances, a decent man. He was not only on the board of the Children's Hospital

Charity, he'd founded the charity along with a doctor friend. He was generous with his money, contributing to several other charities and schools as well. Look at the public man and you saw only what the man wanted to be seen. You had to talk to people who knew him to get the dirt.

By all accounts Lanford hadn't been exactly charitable at work. The guy was a shark. Maybe that's what it took to make it big in business, but it was no way to make friends. It was a great way to make enemies.

Heather Farmer, Lanford's secretary, had been Ray's last phone call this morning. He hadn't gotten much out of the conversation, but he'd sensed potential there. Heather had been so distraught she could hardly speak over the phone. When Ray had suggested a face-to-face meeting, she'd quickly agreed. Anything to catch the man who'd killed her boss, she said.

The secretary was more distressed by the murder than the widow. Did that mean anything?

"You'll have to let me buy you lunch," Grace said, staring out the window. "To celebrate."

"To celebrate what?" he asked, his eyes on the road.

She turned her head to look at him and smile. "Your birthday. Don't tell me you forgot your own birthday."

"No. I was just kinda hoping everyone else had."

"Thirty-four's not so old," she teased. "You're not quite ready for a walker and a bad toupee."

"See?" he said, taking one hand from the wheel to shake a censuring finger at her. "This is why I'd just as soon you'd forgotten."

She ignored him. "I was going to get you one of those sporty car hats, the kind little old men wear when they drive, but I just didn't have time to get to the department store. I'll pick one up this week. Promise."

"Very funny," he muttered.

"Houndstooth, I think," she mused.

"You're merciless."

"Or would you prefer a solid lemony yellow? You know, something people will see from miles away."

"Don't make me pull this car over," he warned.

An awkward silence filled the air where seconds earlier there had been joy and lighthearted teasing.

In years past Grace had teased him more than once to the point where he'd threatened to pull the car over. And he had, a couple of times, pulled off a country road or into a quiet park. And things had gotten...hot. That had happened long ago, though. It wasn't going to happen again. Dammit.

Fortunately he saw his turn ahead, and moments later they were driving down a peaceful residential street, looking at the numbers on the mailboxes.

"She makes good money, for a secretary," Grace said, studying the tall brick houses that lined the curving street. "You said she was single, right?"

"Yep."

Ray pulled into a circular driveway. This was one of the nicest houses on an upscale street. Yellow brick, wide double doors, professional landscaping. Heather Farmer was twenty-seven years old, had gone to college but hadn't finished, and had been working for Lanford for three years. Lanford was a savvy businessman; he did not overpay his employees.

"Wow," Grace said as she stepped from the car. "I shoulda been a secretary."

Heather answered his knock quickly, as if she'd been waiting and watching for them. She had short cinnamon hair and a strikingly pretty face, and she was dressed for a quiet Sunday at home, in pastel plaid flannel pants and a pale yellow cotton blouse. Her green eyes were red and swollen from crying. At least someone was mourning poor Lanford.

"Miss Farmer, I'm Ray Madigan. We spoke on the phone."

Her eyes swept past him to Grace.

"This is my wife, Grace."

"Ex-wife," Grace corrected in a low voice.

"You said you were an investigator," she said suspiciously. "Cops don't take their wives along when they work. Who are you?"

"*Ex*-wife," Grace muttered.

Ray ignored her, as he reached into his back pocket for his ID. "I'm a private investigator." He offered his ID and Heather studied it carefully.

"I don't know if I should be talking to you...."

She shouldn't be, he knew that. Luther wouldn't like this, not at all. "The police haven't spoken to you yet?"

She shook her head.

Luther would probably be by bright and early in the morning. Boy, would he be pissed when he found out Ray had beaten him to the punch.

"They will," he said. "I'm just trying to gather what information I can about the murder. If I find anything of importance I'll turn it over to the police immediately."

It was clear that Heather wanted to talk, she wanted to vent and grieve and cry. Maybe she was tired of crying alone.

"Well, I guess it won't hurt anything to talk to you," she said, stepping back and opening the front door wide.

The interior of her house was as classy as the exterior. The furnishings were simple and expensive, classic and elegant. She used lots of white in her home, accented with pale pastels and gilt-framed artwork. The real thing, to

Ray's eyes. Two oil paintings and a piece of alabaster
sculpture were placed near the front door, a first-class welcome.

"You and Mr. Lanford were close," Ray said as
Heather led them into the cream-and-white living room.

She nodded her head and sniffled as she curled up in a
fat chair and motioned to the couch.

"I know who killed him," she said softly. "It was that
witch he was married to."

Grace lowered herself to the couch and he sat beside
her. Well, Miss Farmer didn't believe in wasting time,
that's for sure.

"What makes you say that?" he asked.

She laid wide, teary eyes on him. "I just know," she
whispered. "In my heart I *know* she killed him."

"If you're right, she didn't work alone," he said. "A
man was seen with Mr. Lanford at the time of his death."
He didn't want to point Grace out as a witness. The less
people who knew of her involvement, the better.

"If she didn't do it herself she had someone do it for
her." Heather sniffled and brought a tissue to her weeping
eyes. "Did she tell you that Carter wanted a divorce?" she
snapped, her eyes turning hard. "That she's been sneaking
around behind his back for years? She did it and she had
help. You tell the police *that*."

Looking at the grieving secretary, Ray had a suspicion
that Mrs. Lanford had not been the only one sneaking
around. "I'll make sure they know."

"He'd asked her for a divorce, but she was being difficult. She didn't want to give him up." Heather angrily
wiped away a tear. "What she didn't want to give up was
his money. She didn't love him."

"Not like you did," Grace said gently.

Heather pinned her eyes on Grace, and her whole face

changed. It softened and fell. "I did love Carter, and he loved me. We were going to be married as soon as he got rid of that wife of his. She was a horrid woman," she said venomously. "Hateful and vindictive. She didn't want Carter to be happy."

"That's very sad for you both." Grace leaned forward, toward Heather. The move appeared to be intimate and comforting.

Damn, she was good at this. Sympathetic and trustworthy and appealing, in a down-to-earth kind of way. If she ever decided to leave Dr. Doolittle he'd give her a job in a minute.

Except he was moving to Mobile, Ray remembered with an unpleasant jolt.

He nodded, trying to shake off his personal thoughts and return to the matter at hand. "You said Mrs. Lanford was fooling around. Do you have a name? Names?" It was too much to ask for.

"You bet I do," she said, with more than a touch of her own vindictiveness. "There were two of them, one new lover and an old flame who kept coming back. And I can do much better than provide a couple of names. They'll both be at the Charity Ball on Friday. I can point them out to you. Introduce you. I hope you find out which one of them was involved in Carter's murder and the courts send him *and* Louise to the electric chair for what they've done."

It was Grace who asked, her voice soft and calming, "How did you know about these two men?"

Heather sniffled again. "Carter told me. He knew all about his wife's lovers, had known for a long time. She didn't care that he knew." She placed a stilling hand over her face, as if to stop more tears from falling. "What am I going to do?"

Ray felt truly sorry for her. She seemed lost, confused, truly desperate. Maybe she really had loved poor Lanford.

She gulped and wheezed, apparently close to panic. "I'll have to sell the house. I'll have to look for another *job*. Carter said he was going to pay the mortgage off in a few months and then I wouldn't have to worry, but he hadn't done it yet. I can't keep up the payments on my own."

So, was Heather distressed about losing the house or Lanford? It was difficult to tell.

Heather gathered her strength, pushed away the threatening panic and lifted her chin defiantly. "I want to help, if I can. I'll get you two tickets for the ball next Friday. Louise will be there, and so will both her lovers. Ben McCann is the newest love of her life, and Elliott Reed is the old beau who keeps turning up. Do you need to write that down?"

Ray shook his head. No, no need to write those names down. Ben McCann had been Carter Lanford's right-hand man, and Elliott Reed was an assistant district attorney.

The ride back to her house was silent, without the banter and subsequent awkwardness they'd experienced on the drive over to interview Heather Farmer.

How did Ray do this all the time? Delve into the private lives of others, dissect their lives until you had the bare bones of it laid before you like a buffet? And that was what he did, whether it was a murder case or a divorce case or uncovering an insurance scam. He picked people apart until he found the truth.

She still didn't know what the truth was, who might've killed Carter Lanford. Not Heather Farmer, that's for sure. She was grieving the loss of her fine house. To think, she'd actually felt sorry for the woman for a while, until she'd realized that Heather wasn't crying for a man she loved, she was crying for the *things* she was going to lose.

Thinking about the murder and the people involved was easier than dwelling on her inappropriate thoughts about the man sitting beside her, but again and again her mind turned in that direction.

When Ray had threatened to pull the car off the road her heart had just about stopped. The way the conversation had suddenly ceased, she knew the moment had been awkward for him, too. She closed her eyes and reminded herself of all the reasons they wouldn't work, his determination to go back into undercover work being at the top of the list. But no matter how hard she tried to tell herself this would never work, all she saw was Ray leaning over her, touching her, promising her everything.

Everything but love.

She opened her eyes and steeled her heart. Maybe she should run again. Pack a bag while Ray was sleeping and just leave. There were always jobs to be had, new places to discover. There was always a place to hide.

That's what she'd been doing when she left Ray, wasn't it? Hiding. Burying her head in the sand and pretending, for six long years, that what she felt and wanted and craved didn't matter. That loving him wasn't as important as surviving unhurt. That if she wanted badly enough to stop loving him, she would.

And now here she was, back at the beginning again.

"Ray, I don't know that car," she said, when they turned onto her street and she saw a red Mustang parked in her driveway.

He cursed, low and foul. "How about let's keep driving? You didn't buy me that birthday lunch yet. There's this great little Italian place in Nashville...."

"Ray," she interrupted. He obviously recognized the

car. "Who is it?" A cop? Someone who knew what he'd been up to and was here to make sure he stopped?

He pinned his eyes on her. "That's Trish's car."

Great. "I'd love to meet her," she said, when in fact Nashville, a good two hours away, sounded pretty good right now. Sandy and Nell Rose had provided all the pertinent details about Madigan wives number two and three, but Grace had never met either of them face-to-face.

Ray pulled the car to the curb and gave her an apologetic glance. Before he could say anything the blonde knocked on Grace's window.

Trish had a wide smile on her face. Her hair was teased up, big but not too big, her makeup was there but wasn't too much, and her pink outfit was feminine without being overdone. And Grace wanted, with all her heart, to hate Mrs. Madigan number two.

Trish backed up as Grace opened the car door, and tossed a wide grin to Ray as he left the car. "I was wondering when you two were going to get home."

"How did you find me?" Ray asked with a smile that was a little bit forced.

"We went by your place and you weren't home, so I started calling around. Doris about bit my head off and told me to page you, but Luther told me where you were." She looked at Grace, curious but without anger. "So you're Grace. I always wanted to meet you."

"You said *we,*" Ray said tiredly.

About that time Grace saw the dark-haired woman sitting in the single porch rocker. Great. Both of them at once?

"Why didn't you just page me like Doris suggested?"

Patty stood as they reached the porch. "Now what kind of a surprise would that be?" she asked, her voice deeper than Trish's, more Southern, somehow.

"I hate surprises," Ray mumbled.

"You do not!" Trish slapped him playfully on the arm. "You love surprises."

"No," he insisted. "I could just never convince you of that fact. I hate surprises. They give me gray hair."

"You don't have any gray hair."

"That's because everyone but you knows I hate surprises."

Grace unlocked the front door and pushed it open. "Y'all come on in," she said, Southern hospitality coming to her with some difficulty. "I'll make us some coffee."

"I'll get the cake out of the car," Trish said.

"Cake?" Ray asked.

"Yeah, happy birthday," Patty said, leaning over to kiss Ray on the cheek.

Grace started the coffee, wishing she'd said *yes* when Ray had suggested lunch in Nashville.

A shapely blonde carried a big cake from a red Mustang to the front door, and someone else—not the witness, not the man who'd been with her since that day—opened the door for her. Freddie shook his head. Was the woman never going to be alone again?

"Should I be jealous?" Gillian, who jogged beside him, asked.

He looked down at her and grinned. "Sorry. I have a thing for Mustangs."

"You were looking at the *car*."

"What else?"

He'd spent the night with Gillian last night, would spend tonight, too, though she didn't know it yet. He'd convince her, somehow. It wouldn't be difficult.

She'd been surprisingly eager when he'd taken her home from their romantic dinner. She'd invited him in, offered him a drink, and fifteen minutes later they'd been making out on the couch. Thirty minutes after that they'd been in her bed. He hadn't given the witness a thought after that, until the morning.

Gillian lived one street over and a few houses down. Just recently out of a long-term relationship, she was lonely. She needed to feel attractive and desired and she was tired of being alone. He couldn't have planned it any better. Besides, she definitely gave him something to do while he waited for things to calm down.

She'd keep him busy for a while, a few days, a week at the most. But eventually he was going to have to finish up and move on. If an opportunity didn't present itself soon, he'd make his own opportunity.

Just to make sure he had it right, he again silently repeated the Mustang's license plate number in his head. He pictured it, planted the image in his mind so he wouldn't forget.

"Jimmy," Gillian said, seduction in her voice.

He was already accustomed to his false name, but then he was an adaptable man. Had to be in this business.

"What's on your mind, sugar?"

"You can stay over again tonight, if you want," she said, as if she didn't care one way or another. "Staying in a motel can't be very comfortable. You can stay with me as long as you want."

He smiled. "That would be great."

Ah, she was already getting that gleam in her eyes, that mushy, clinging, frantic look women sometimes get when they fall in love. If he was going to be around for more than a few days he might worry about that gleam.

"I can call in sick tomorrow and we can have the whole day together, if you can manage it," she added.

He'd told her he was in town for a few weeks, visiting

clients, making sales, covering his territory. That he might, if all went well, settle in the area. When she'd asked what he sold, he'd told her computer parts. Hardware. Lanford had been in computers, and that had been the first thing to come to mind. Fortunately Gillian didn't know squat about computers, so they hadn't talked in any detail about his career.

"I can manage it," he said with a smile, already looking forward to tonight.

Chapter 8

It was every man's worst nightmare; three ex-wives sitting around, eating cake and drinking coffee and talking. About him.

Trish did most of the talking, but Patty provided the occasional barb of her own. Grace didn't say much, but she certainly did listen attentively.

Ray stood back and watched, his spine to the bar that separated the kitchen from the living room, a cup of coffee cradled in his hands. "I'm in the room," he said. "Y'all are talking about me like I'm not even here."

"Well face it, Ray," Patty said with a smile. "You make an interesting topic, and the three of us *do* have a few things in common. For one thing, we all put up with you, for a while."

Trish mentioned how he snored when he was really tired, and Patty did a quick, and totally inaccurate, impersonation that had them all laughing. What had he done to deserve this?

Patty was right about one thing. The three of them had a lot in common. There was one very important difference, though no one knew it but him. He liked Trish and Patty, but he'd never loved them. That's why it was so easy to remain friends with them—because in truth they'd never been more than friends. It was harder with Grace, because sometimes he looked at her and he wanted to shake her and ask her why she'd ruined everything.

He'd loved being married to Grace. Life with her had been exciting and fresh and wonderful. After she left, after he'd quit killing himself wondering what had gone wrong, he decided he could, by God, be happy without her. If he'd had a good marriage with Grace, he could have a good marriage with someone else. Anyone else. He'd found out the hard way that it wasn't that easy.

He wished he could be friends with Grace, just friends. That he could laugh with her about her boyfriends and promise to attend her wedding knowing it wouldn't hurt to watch her take another man as her husband.

After Grace had left he'd made damn sure he kept his relationships with women on a shallow level. Even when he'd gotten married again. Sex. A few laughs. Maybe a shared interest or two. Nothing more. What he needed to do now, what he had to do, was keep his relationship with Grace on that same level. Skin deep.

"And he has such a lovely singing voice," Grace said with a wide smile, finally getting in on the let's-bash-Ray fun-fest.

He cringed.

Patty and Trish stared at Grace like she had lost her mind, and number one's smile faded.

"In the shower," she added. "Lyle Lovett, always, and occasionally just a little off-key."

"Ray," Patty said accusingly. "You *sing?*"

It wasn't easy, but he gave her an I-don't-care smile. "I used to sing in the shower, on occasion. It was a youthful quirk I outgrew a long time ago."

Trish nodded. "I never heard him sing, but the man does love Lyle Lovett, doesn't he?"

Patty nodded. "Yeah. I never quite got it, myself."

Trish wrinkled her nose. "Me neither."

Grace pinned her eyes on him, questioning, wondering maybe…damn, she saw too much.

Ray clapped a hand over his wounded heart. "I can't believe y'all would say that. My next wife," he added with a forced grin, "will be required to pass a Lyle Lovett trivia test *and* sing a song of her choosing in its entirety."

Trish spoke up quickly. "I thought you said you were never getting married again."

"I'm not, but just in case I change my mind in a moment of weakness…"

Grace no longer stared at him. She gazed into what was left of her coffee as if something fascinating floated there. As if she wanted to jump in and hide there while Trish and Patty went on and on. Hell, he'd like to dive in and hide with her.

Finally Trish and Patty rose to leave. Ray told Trish again that he would gladly attend her wedding but would not give her away. She pouted, but he didn't change his mind. It just wasn't right.

Patty said she had to get back to her place to get ready for an early dinner with her doctor boyfriend.

He had never been so glad to see Trish and Patty prepare to leave.

At the door, Trish wished him happy birthday again and kissed him briefly on the lips. Patty did the same, absently delivering the quick smack of a friend in a hurry. Both kisses were amicable and pleasant enough, but executed almost as an afterthought.

He closed the door, took a deep breath and turned to face Grace. She had come to her feet and stood before the couch, her eyes wide, her cheeks flushed.

To survive this, he had to keep his relationship with Grace on the same friendly, shallow level he called upon for his other ex-wives. He had to be able to kiss her and feel nothing, to care about her without remembering what it had been like to love her. To *like* her; nothing more.

"What about you," he said, nonchalantly closing the distance between them. "Aren't you going to wish me happy birthday?"

"I already did," she said in a small voice.

He raised his eyebrows and reached out to touch her chin with the tips of his fingers. "Not properly." Before Grace could protest, he leaned down and gave her a quick kiss, no more than a brush of his lips over hers.

In an instant, he knew he'd made a mistake. That quick caress was not enough, so he kissed her again. Quickly, softly, his mouth barely touching hers. She held her breath and closed her eyes and he kissed her yet again. Deeper this time, with a hunger he couldn't conceal.

His arms wrapped possessively around her and she fell against him, warm and soft, yielding and sinfully tempting. No one felt like Grace, no one smelled like Grace, no one tasted like Grace. One kiss and she was in his blood, singing her own song, making him half-crazy.

Her arms encircled his waist and she held on tight, as if she might fall if she didn't. Her lips parted for him, when he tasted her bottom lip with the tip of his tongue, and when he slipped his tongue into her mouth a little moan slipped out.

More than anything in the world, he wanted her. Here

and now, fast and furious. He needed to be inside her, he wanted, more than anything, to watch her come apart beneath him. She was his in a way so primal he couldn't explain it. His body was drawn to hers, after all this time, as if there was no other woman on the planet who would do. After he'd made love to her, would he break down and ask her why she'd really left? The question was on the tip of his tongue, teasing his mind.

But if he asked she'd know it mattered to him, she'd know that he still cared more than he should.

Skin deep.

He slipped his hand beneath her sweater and trailed his palm over bare, warm skin. She gasped, but didn't take her mouth from his to tell him to stop. He unfastened her bra with a twist of his fingers, and moved the undergarment aside to cup her bare breast. Firm, soft and warm, she filled his hand. He teased her pebbled nipple with the tips of his fingers and his thumb, kissing her, touching her, all the while edging closer and closer to a complete loss of control.

Skin deep. Nothing more.

He grasped her hip and pulled her against him so she could feel his arousal pressing into her flesh. She was his one weakness. If he couldn't walk away she would have to. And he knew just how to make her run.

"How about it, baby?" he whispered hoarsely into her mouth. "A little birthday present?"

Grace stiffened, dropped her arms and tried to back away. He held on tight, for a moment, and then let her go so that she fell onto the couch.

Tempted as he was, he didn't fall with her.

A little birthday present! Grace fumed, her face hidden behind a section of the Sunday paper while Ray watched television without comment. She was such an idiot. Ray kissed her, and she started thinking impossible thoughts. She remembered too well how it had been, once. What she'd dreamed of for them. She remembered what it had been like to love him.

And Ray, master of the poetic that he was, told her without reservation that all he wanted was a roll in the hay or a little birthday present.

She snapped the paper into her lap. "You know, I think you should leave."

"No," he said, never taking his eyes from the evening news. Shea was doing the weather forecast, promising them a beautiful Monday.

"It's not a good idea…"

He turned his head and pinned intense blue eyes on her. "It's the sex thing, isn't it?" he said emotionlessly. "Okay, I'll drop it."

The sex thing. She shook her head. "Sometimes I think I don't know you at all."

"Maybe you don't," he said softly, and as if he didn't care. He stared at her hard, though, and there was no trade-mark Ray Madigan grin to break the seriousness of the moment. "Six years is a long time."

"Yes, it is."

"And there's nothing wrong with sex just for the sake of sex. People do it all the time."

"I don't," she said quickly.

His eyebrows shot up. He crossed his arms over his chest and stared at her hard. She felt that stare to her bones. She knew this look, determined and tenacious. Devil-may-care Ray could be obstinate, when it suited him, and he was definitely being obstinate now, as he studied her with calculating eyes. He found something in her, saw something that made a muscle in his jaw twitch. His entire body seemed to grow rigid.

"Gracie, honey, when was the last time you had a tenth date?" His voice was ominously and falsely serene.

She brought the paper up so she couldn't see his face and he couldn't see her blush. This was not a conversation she was comfortable having with anyone, least of all Ray! Her sex life, or lack thereof, was nobody's business but her own.

She didn't hear him move from the couch, but without warning a finger appeared at the top of the page, and Ray slowly pushed the paper down. He was right there, unsmiling, blue eyes burning, evening stubble on his finely shaped jaw making him look rough and untamed. "Gracie?"

"None of your business," she said crisply.

"Everything about you is my business," he said in a low voice. "Everything. We can pretend that's not so, we can deny it out loud when things get complicated, but we both know the truth."

She looked at him and knew he was right. Ray was still a part of her, and that's why she hadn't been able to move on, that's why there hadn't been any other men in her life. She needed to get him out of her soul, to exorcise him once and for all. Somehow she had to get past the myth to the truth, she had to replace memories she surely saw through rose-colored glasses with cold, hard facts.

"Six years," she whispered.

His eyebrows lifted only slightly, but she saw the surprise in his eyes. The questions. Surely he wouldn't ask. Surely not....

"Why? You were never shy about sex, you even seemed to like it well enough. Why'd you give it up?"

He made it sound as if it would have been easy to move

on, to replace him with someone else. Of course he thought it was easy. He'd managed quite well to replace her.

If she did have sex with Ray it would probably be awkward. They'd fumble around like a couple of strangers and it would be over too quickly and she'd wonder what all the fuss had been about. She'd see Ray for what he was. Just a man. And then she'd be able to go on when he moved to Mobile.

"I didn't intend to give my sex life up, it just happened that way."

"Don't you miss it?" he whispered.

"Sometimes," she admitted.

He didn't back away, didn't ask another personal question. He just stared at her, studied her as if he hadn't ever seen her face before.

If he'd make another crude suggestion she could easily push him away, as she'd been doing since he came back into her life. But he didn't. Instead he reached out a hand and touched her cheek, brushing his thumb lightly against her mouth.

He was right here before her and, as always, all he had to do was touch her and her heart leapt into her throat. A hand on her cheek made her body grow warm. The thumb on her mouth teased her with the memory of the way he kissed her. She could smell him, taste him, feel him all around her. All she needed was one good look into those clear blue eyes of his and she dismissed all her reservations.

With an easy motion of his hand he removed the pins that held her hair up and tossed them aside. "Why do you insist on wearing your hair up?" he asked, his eyes on the strands as they fell around her shoulders. "You have beautiful hair." Tossing the paper aside, he knelt before her, spread her legs slightly so he fit between them, and leaned forward to kiss her. His hands wound through her hair, his mouth working wonders that clouded her mind and affected her body to the core.

"Ray," she whispered as she took her mouth from his. She saw in his eyes, in the way his face hardened, that he expected her to push him away again. She should. What he wanted was so much less than what they'd once had. Instead of pushing him away, she reached out to touch his jaw, leaned forward to kiss him again.

The kiss was soft and promising, a little more tentative than the last one. This was a big step, a *huge* step, and they both knew it.

Ray's mouth swayed and tasted and skimmed, but never left hers. He rose slowly, pulling her to her feet. Their mouths parted only briefly as they stood, coming together easily as they stood chest to chest, knee to knee.

"Let's get one thing straight," Ray whispered. He narrowed his eyes, crinkling the corners. "I should rephrase that. Let's get a couple of things straight here."

She smiled and placed a hand on his neck. "A couple of things?"

"You're not going to get me halfway home and change your mind again."

She shook her head. "No, I won't." Her mind was made up.

"And if you're expecting a quickie on the couch, a wham-bam-thank-you-ma'am, you're in for a surprise." He kissed her mouth again, barely brushing his lips across hers. "A woman who's been without for six years deserves to have it done right."

Her whole body quivered in anticipation. Sex just for the sake of sex, he said. No prettying up what was about to happen with fantasies about love and happily ever after.

No false promises to be broken in the morning. "You won't get any complaints from me."

He speared his fingers through her hair, resting his hand at the back of her head. He looked her dead in the eye, serious and passionate and apparently every bit as bewildered as she was. "And, Gracie, don't make this more than it is."

"I won't," she whispered.

He pulled her sweater over her head, the action smooth and almost cautious. As if he was afraid she might break. And he looked at her, watching his hand as it played across her shoulder, as it skimmed down her side. There was nothing hurried in his touch, nothing rushed. When he kissed her his lips were gentle and still demanding, the kiss exacting and intimate.

And she was already lost.

Again he unfastened her bra with a simple flick of his fingers, slipped the straps off her shoulders and dropped the garment to the floor, and while he continued to kiss her his fingers brushed and cupped and caressed her breasts.

Purely for physical pleasure, Grace thought as Ray so easily roused her deepest passions. This encounter had nothing to do with the heart, she reminded herself. It was sex for the sake of sex, right? She untucked his T-shirt and slipped her hands beneath to touch Ray's warm flesh as she wrapped her arms around him. This felt so good, so right. Amazingly powerful. She dismissed the certainty that there had to be more between them than just the physical.

He shrugged off the unbuttoned shirt he wore over the T-shirt and dropped it to the floor, and they began to walk, still kissing, still touching, toward the hallway. She kicked off her shoes one at a time, and Ray removed the gun from its place at his spine and left it on the occasional table by the hallway entrance. He unzipped her trousers and pushed them down, and she kicked them aside as she reached for his zipper.

So far nothing about this surrender was awkward. Their movements were slow and deliberate, smooth and effortlessly intimate. She knew Ray well, his body and his mind. Together they still felt right. More right than anything she'd ever known.

By the time they reached her bedroom they were both naked. They tumbled to the bed and lay side by side, kissing, reveling in the feel of one eager body against another. Grace lifted her leg and wrapped it around Ray's, instinctively searching to bring herself closer to him. His arousal touched her thigh, and she swayed against him.

"Not so fast," he whispered, rolling her onto her back and hovering above her.

The hallway light lit the room softly, so she saw his face and body well. She ignored the scars on his chest, close as they were, and concentrated on his face. At least she knew without doubt that Ray wanted her. She could see the passion in his eyes, feel it in his heartbeat.

He kissed her, deep and tender, and she spread her thighs so that he fit there just right. She trembled to her bones, quaked to her center, throbbed all over.

Ray moved his mouth to her neck, kissed her there while his hands explored her body as if she were a stranger. As if he didn't already know every inch. No, she thought hazily, as if he knew every inch and was relearning every one. Slowly, with loving fingers. Grace closed her eyes and savored the feel of those hands everywhere.

His mouth came to hers again and again. He kissed her gently while his palm raked tenderly over her breasts, down her ribs. There was no urgency in his kiss or in his airy, arousing touch.

When he took a nipple into his mouth she almost cried aloud, the pleasure was so great. She threaded her fingers through his hair while he caressed her there, while he sucked her sensitive flesh into his mouth.

He slid one slow hand up her inner thigh to touch her intimately, to stroke her gently while he suckled. She shuddered deeply, closed her eyes and welcomed the rush of pure pleasure through her body.

Ray slowly slid his body lower to kiss her belly, then slipped his hands beneath her thighs to cock her legs up and kiss her where she throbbed for him. He teased the sensitive flesh at the back of her knees, trailed his fingers down the backs of her legs, and then he made unrelenting love to her with his mouth, slow and torturously easy, light and teasing until her entire body shook.

She had to hold on to *something* to remain earthbound, anything, so she reached behind her and grabbed the headboard, grasping tightly as Ray heightened the gentle assault. She closed her eyes and lifted her hips as he slipped a finger inside her, bringing her to a climax that made her shudder deep and cry out softly.

Still weak, she didn't move as Ray kissed her inner thigh, her belly, and then, again, her breasts. She closed her eyes and clutched him to her, knowing she had made a terrible mistake. Awkward? Not as good as she remembered? How could she have been so stupid?

They fit together perfectly, they moved in sync and always had.

She expected Ray to enter her quickly, but he didn't. He very gently rolled her onto her stomach and began to feather kisses down her spine. His hands gently kneaded her buttocks and trailed down her thighs.

"You have a great back," he said.

She smiled into the pillow.

"You have a great front, too," he said, a hint of teasing in his voice.

He spread her thighs slightly and touched her intimately. Grace rocked slightly against his hand. Amazingly enough, she not only wanted Ray inside her, she *needed* him. Was incomplete without him. He kissed her neck and her spine, continued to touch her tenderly. On the ebbing waves of one climax, she could already feel the growing urgency of another.

She saw his arm reach past her to the bedside table. He opened the top drawer and took out a foil-wrapped condom. With her face still against the pillow, she heard him rip open the wrapper.

"How did that get in my drawer?"

"I put it there," he whispered, nuzzling her neck.

"When?"

"Yesterday," he admitted, apparently unashamed. "You're not going to hold that against me, are you?"

How could she? "No."

He rolled her onto her back and spread her thighs wide with his knee. "There's a dozen in there."

She wrapped her arms around his neck and lifted her hips to bring him closer. "Good," she whispered.

Ray fit himself to her, then thrust to fill her waiting body. Her body stretched and yielded to take him, and Grace closed her eyes in sheer delight, in wonder at the unexpected pleasure that shot through her body.

He stroked her and she rose to meet each gentle thrust. Ray was all around her, inside her, above and beneath her. He filled her, he completed her. He made love to her. He could tell her not to make too much of this, he could claim it was just a roll in the hay or a hop in the sack if he wanted, but there was love here; she felt it.

There was nothing in the world but this moment, the sway of their bodies and the way Ray made her feel, their hearts beating in time and their bodies dancing. She wrapped her legs around his and held on tight, as he thrust deep and completion claimed her again. She cried out; his name, a wordless cry, a moan.

While her body still shuddered he found his own release, then sank down slowly to cover her.

His head rested against her neck. She threaded her fingers through his hair and held on, not yet ready to let him go.

There had been nothing awkward about their encounter, nothing fumbled or less than perfect. While he'd loved her, she'd had no doubts, no fears at all. She'd taken and given with complete abandon, and so had he. In this way, physically, they were made to go together. Surely they were meant to be.

"I'd forgotten," she whispered, stopping before she caught herself and gave away too much. There would be no confessions in the dark, no pleading for what could never be.

"Just like riding a bike," Ray said breathlessly.

"Uh-huh," she murmured, stroking his head and the wavy strands there. Holding Ray against her while she still could. He thought this was simple, unfettered sex, but she knew better. She also knew there was nothing she could do to get Ray out of her system. She couldn't confess that terrible secret, not now. Not ever. But she would take what she could get.

"And I'm happy to see you're still a nice guy," she teased.

Ray raised his head and smiled at her, and her heart skipped a beat. He was big and warm, wonderfully heavy. "Nice guys finish last," he said, and then he kissed her.

Chapter 9

Ray woke slowly to morning light and an odd surge of contentment. He slept on his stomach, his face half buried in a soft pillow, his legs spread to take up most of the bed. The sheets over and around him were tangled, the arm that rested on his back was warm and familiar.

Grace.

He turned his head slowly so he could watch her sleep. Her arm draped familiarly over him, her face was inches away from his shoulder. She looked...damn, she looked good. Eyes closed, dark hair across one cheek, face pressed into the pillow, she was beautiful.

And still naked.

He touched her and she sighed and slithered closer to him. Last night had been incredible, better than he'd remembered, better than he'd imagined it could be. There had been no questions about the past, no second thoughts, no annoying moments of uncertainty on her part or his.

Knowing she hadn't been with anyone since she'd left

him had broken down the last of his labored restraint. In that moment he'd realized that she was still his, in at least one elemental way. He hadn't been able to grin and scare her away, to pretend that he didn't need her in ways he'd never needed any other woman.

So he'd allowed himself to give in, he'd allowed her to give in, rationalizing with every step down the long hallway that what was happening meant nothing more than any cheap one-night stand. She was a woman, he was a man, there was nothing more sinister or meaningful than that in the sexual equation. One night, he'd reasoned, wouldn't change anything.

His hand settled on her hip and stayed there, resting comfortably. Why had he thought sleeping with Grace would somehow end things, make his demons go away? She haunted him still, would likely bedevil him more insistently than ever, now that he had the feel of her strengthened in his memory, the scent of her fresh on his skin.

Her eyes drifted open, landing on him immediately. She smiled, soft and sleepy, and he smiled back. He'd tried for six years to forget her, to replace her. Unsuccessfully. He wanted, more than anything, to believe she was back for good, that when she'd returned to Huntsville she'd been coming home to him.

His fanciful thoughts were short-lived. In an instant Grace's apparent satisfaction disappeared. Her smile vanished. Her eyes widened and she scooted away from him, taking the sheet with her.

"I can't believe we did what we did."

"Believe it, Gracie," he said as she left the bed, taking the sheet with her and wrapping it around her luscious body.

A shy man would reach for the quilt on the floor and cover himself, especially since touching her had him aroused and ready for another round, but Ray had never been shy. He didn't move.

She turned her back on him and looked at the clock. "I'm late for work," she snapped nervously. "Didn't the alarm go off? I always have it set for six."

"You turned it off at four," he said, silently daring her to turn around. "After the last time we…"

"I know what we did," she interrupted tersely. "You don't have to remind me."

"Well, you seemed to think you'd be in no shape to make it to work this morning."

She hugged the sheet more tightly to her. "I don't know what I was thinking."

"You were probably thinking it was four in the morning, and we were both exhausted, and after a night like last night…"

She went to the chest against the far wall and, still holding the sheet so that it covered as much of her lovely body as possible, reached into a drawer for underwear, a pair of sweatpants and a matching sweatshirt.

As Ray watched, his smile faded. Of course she had regrets. Didn't she always? Maybe now was the time to ask her why she'd left. He'd promised himself he wouldn't, but watching her right now he wondered more than ever what had gone wrong.

"Gracie…"

The phone rang, and she jumped like she'd been shot.

"That's probably the office," she said, turning to reach for the bedside phone, very pointedly not looking at him as she dropped her sweats onto the bed.

As she lifted the receiver the doorbell rang. "Put on some clothes and answer the door," she said. Adding, when he didn't immediately jump to do as she asked, a very softly whispered, "Please."

Ray rolled from the bed as Grace said hello and the doorbell rang again. He smiled as he left the room. Grace was trying to explain why she wasn't at work, and would also no doubt have to explain exactly *who* had to put on clothes and answer the door.

He grabbed his jeans from the hallway floor and stepped into them quickly, and snagged his pistol from the table at the end of the hall. The doorbell rang again, only this time it turned into a long, continuous, annoying peal that vibrated through the house as whoever was at the front door pressed continuously on the buzzer.

"I'm coming," he shouted, and the ringing came to an abrupt stop. He looked through the peephole and sighed when he saw who stood there.

"You are in so much trouble," Luther said before the door had opened a full foot.

"What else is new?"

Ray moved back as Luther stepped into Grace's house. "You've been talking to people you have no business messing with, Ray."

"Just because you're slow getting the job done..." Ray began.

Luther looked around the room with narrowed eyes, taking in the undergarments and clothing and shoes scattered about the room, the very clear trail to the hallway. "For God's sake, Ray," he muttered. "Jesus..."

"Let it go," Ray said, an undisguised warning in his voice. "If you want to talk about the case, I'm all yours. Right now everything else is off-limits."

"Why is it that your personal life is always so much more fascinating than something so common as murder?" Luther grumbled.

"Maybe because you don't have a personal life of your own," Ray said with a tight smile.

Grace, wearing her baggy sweats, her hair hanging straight and uncombed past her shoulders as she walked into the kitchen, didn't try to rush around and pick up the evidence of last night's activities. She headed straight for the coffeepot.

"Morning, Luther," she said softly.

"Morning," he said, a touch of resentment in his voice.

"Detective Malone, are you armed?" Grace asked as she reached for the coffee grounds.

"Yes."

"Would you shoot me, please?"

Luther hesitated before muttering lowly, his back to Grace so she couldn't possibly hear. "With pleasure."

Ray quickly gathered the scattered clothes from the furniture and the floor and offered Luther a seat. The detective sat, shaking his head in unconcealed dismay.

Amy, who worked the front desk for Dr. Dearborne, smiled widely when Grace came in several hours late. It was almost lunchtime. Grace didn't know if she was most embarrassed because she was so late, or because Amy had heard her hiss to Ray to get dressed and answer the door. After that, making lame excuses to Amy would've been a waste of time.

And to top it all off, it had been Luther at the door! Disbelieving, sour, dagger-eyed Detective Malone, who might be irresistible to *some* women, had really been getting on her nerves, lately. Why did she care what that malcontent thought of her, anyway?

Because he'd been her friend, once upon a time. Because he had been with her during some of the best times, and all of the worst.

"I'll work late," Grace said as she passed Amy on the way to her office.

Once she was in her office she closed the door, something she rarely did, shrugged off her navy blue jacket, and plopped into her chair.

Ray had dropped her off and watched her walk into the building, and he'd promised to pick her up at five-thirty. He'd be here early, as usual, and she'd likely have to work after hours to make up for her late start. He wouldn't leave her here alone, either, after the rest of the staff had gone home. It had taken all her powers of persuasion to convince him that she didn't need him hovering over her twenty-four hours a day!

Last night had been a mistake. She'd been so certain, when she'd given in, that Ray's roll in the hay for old times' sake would be awkward and less than perfect, common enough to convince her that she did not need him in her life, that her memories of him were false.

She hadn't expected to get so lost in physical sensation that she forgot everything else. She hadn't expected to wake up, look into Ray's face, and be certain, for a moment, that she still loved him and he loved her.

He had never really loved her, she thought angrily as she pulled up the payroll files on her computer and tried to turn her mind toward the day's work. If he had loved her at all he wouldn't have tortured her the way he had, he would've chosen her over a dangerous career that threatened his life every day. When she'd asked, when she'd *begged,* he should've listened to her.

Why had he quit? The question he'd refused to answer had plagued her since she'd heard the news. Why? He'd loved his job so much. More than that, he hadn't been willing to quit for her, to save their marriage. So what had happened? She forgot the payroll, pulled up her Internet connection and began to do a little investigating of her own.

*   *   *

Luther's warning about interfering in the investigation had been halfhearted, at best, so Ray had no qualms about pulling into the parking lot at Lanford Systems.

Why was a homicide detective more concerned about who his ex-partner slept with than anything else? Luther had been annoyed that Ray had questioned Heather Farmer, but he'd been really ticked off to find him in bed with Grace.

Like Ray couldn't handle his own personal life, thank you very much. He wasn't a kid anymore, and he wasn't about to let a woman—any woman—throw him into a tailspin again.

Ray dismissed his thoughts of Grace and last night and looked at the redbrick building before him. The place smelled of money and power, it had an air of exclusivity about it. With his jeans and T-shirt and cotton button-up open down the front, he wouldn't blend in here, that's for sure. Ray stepped from his car with a smile on his face. He'd stir 'em up a little, that's all. See what floated to the surface.

Ben McCann was first on his list of possible suspects. Not only would getting rid of Carter narrow the romantic field where Louise Lanford was concerned, his position at Lanford Systems had improved overnight. McCann was the one people were answering to, now. He was the one stepping into Carter Lanford's shoes. The move was a temporary one, a necessity to keep the business running, but with Louise Lanford's backing McCann was definitely first in line to take over a very successful company.

Lanford's shoes and his bed. Now, *that* was a motive.

Lanford Systems ran like a well-oiled machine, inside and out. No slackers here, Ray imagined as he approached the main receptionist's desk. The woman eyed him suspiciously, but after she spoke to Heather over the telephone her expression and her attitude changed. She sent him right up, with a smile.

On the fourth floor, where the main offices were located, Heather was waiting for him when the elevator doors opened smoothly.

"You got here just in time," she said softly. "Ben has a very important meeting in fifteen minutes."

"Life goes on, I guess," he said as she led him toward a corner office.

She sighed tiredly, maybe agreeing with him. Maybe not.

"So, are you working for McCann now?"

"I'm the only one who knows how Carter had everything set up," Heather said softly. "His files, his calendar, I took care of them all. So yes, I'm working for McCann. If he's given this position permanently I imagine I'll be out on the street." She glanced over her shoulder and grimaced. "I know too much. Might get messy."

Ben McCann was a tall, widely built man wearing an expensive dark blue suit and a burgundy tie. He looked every bit the harried businessman.

"Mr. McCann," Ray said with a smile. "I'd like to ask you a few questions about Carter Lanford." Not about Louise Lanford. Not yet.

McCann appeared to be startled that his office had been broached by a commoner. "I don't have time…"

"You have five minutes," Heather said. She got a cutting glance for her trouble.

"Two," McCann grumbled. He pinned dark, suspicious eyes on Ray.

"I understand you worked very closely with Carter Lanford," Ray said in a nonthreatening tone.

"For several years," McCann said testily.

"Did you spend time with him personally? Play golf, go out to lunch, grab a beer after work..."

"No," McCann snapped.

This man was going to give away nothing. He was stonewalling already. "Who would want to kill such a swell guy?" Ray asked with a straight face.

McCann's eyebrows shot up. "You're no cop."

"I'm private."

"Then I don't have to talk to you." McCann swiped a manila folder off his desk and headed for the door, side-stepping Ray and Heather to escape.

"Miss Farmer, show this gentleman out."

Heather sighed as they watched McCann step into the elevator. "Well, that was a waste of time," she muttered.

"Sorry."

Ray wasn't so sure. He needed a face-to-face feel for the players in this game, a reading on all the suspects. Was McCann capable of murder? Most likely.

"Is everything all right, Heather?" A young man wearing wire-rimmed glasses and a gray suit came out of his own office. He was slender, pale, and his fair hair was cut short and precise. A geek.

"Everything's okay, Hatch," she said in a voice that made it clear nothing was okay. "Mr. Madigan, this is Christopher Hatcher. He was Carter's right-hand man when it came to technical matters. If you want to know about the business, talk to Hatch." She smiled sadly. "He's the one who keeps this place running."

Hatch blushed and cast a shy smile at Heather. "I'll be happy to help in any way I can."

"You two can talk while I get you those tickets for Friday night," Heather said, turning about and heading for her desk.

"You're going to the Charity Ball?" Hatch asked. His

eyes flicked to a retreating Heather, and his smile faded. "With Heather?" Hatch's gaze went moony, for a second.

"Yes and no," Ray said casually. There was no need to share more information than was necessary. He wanted everyone to be relaxed Friday night. Heather could keep a secret, but he wasn't sure about Hatcher. "I'm going, but not with Heather. The old lady's been hassling me to take her somewhere nice." Ray rocked back on the heels of his boots. "Heather was nice enough to suggest the Charity Ball."

Hatch's countenance changed. "The ball is always quite grand. I'm sure your...old lady will have a wonderful time."

Ray nodded toward the man's office. "I'm counting on it," he said. "Heather said you were the man to talk to if I wanted to know how this place works. Do you have a few minutes?"

Grace waited calmly until Ray was inside and everyone else was locked out. She'd assured Dr. Dearborne and Amy that she wouldn't stay too late, and that Ray would remain with her. They didn't know she'd witnessed a murder, Ray had been adamant that only those who *had* to know be told, and still they were a little concerned about her being in the office all alone at night.

She likely wouldn't get much work accomplished, though, she thought as Ray followed her back to her office. Her mind was shooting off in too many different directions to concentrate on work. Besides, Ray had some serious explaining to do.

"How was your day, wild thing?" he asked softly, his voice teasing and seductive.

She glanced over her shoulder as she entered her office. He was right behind her, a wide grin on his face. She was

too old to blush, but her cheeks flushed warm as he reminded her how she'd lost control. If she hadn't already
known that last night was a mistake…

"My day was fine," she said almost primly.

Ray looked around her plain office, at the desk and the
chairs and the blue carpeted floor. "We have the place to
ourselves, Gracie. You don't really have work to do, do
you?" He closed in and wrapped his arms around her, laid
his lips on her neck and sucked softly. "You locked me
in the office to have your way with me in the dentist's
chair, didn't you?"

She could hear the humor in his voice, but he held on
to her as if he were deadly serious.

Grace didn't panic and push him away. Fighting Ray
never did any good anyway, unless you fought on his
terms.

"You quit your job over a hooker," she whispered.

Ray's body stiffened and he stepped back, releasing her.
Withdrawing from her so completely and effectively she
felt a sudden chill. His face was no longer relaxed and
smiling. There was no humor in his eyes.

"I did not quit my job over a hooker," he said tersely.
"What did you do, Gracie, call your friend the part-time
weather girl and ask her to poke around and see what kind
of dirt she could dig up on me?"

Grace shook her head. "No. I found most of what I
needed on the Internet, in old articles from the local newspapers. The rest I just reasoned out for myself." She
cocked her head and glared at Ray, tried to read the stony
expression on his face. "Did you think that just because
you didn't want to tell me what happened I couldn't find
out if I wanted to know?"

The expression on his face didn't change. "I really

didn't think you cared enough to go to all the trouble,''
he said coolly.

Grace tried to remain as calm as Ray was, as distant. It
was so hard, when what she really wanted was to scream
at him.

''Was she a friend, this Emily Buck?'' He must've cared
about her very much to go so far, to lose control completely. It was so unlike him. Ray Madigan, who never
cared enough about anyone to lose control, had thrown his
career away. He must've cared for the woman. ''What was
she to you, Ray?''

His face was rigid, his eyes like chips of ice. ''Emily
Buck was a nineteen-year-old mixed-up kid,'' he said, his
words crisp. Harsh. ''You want to know what she was to
me? I'll tell you everything. I arrested her twice, and both
times I tried my damnedest to get her off the drugs that
had completely screwed up her life.''

Grace looked at the floor and closed her eyes. She
should've known.

In an instant Ray was standing before her, his hand on
her chin as he forced her to look up.

''No,'' he said lowly, a coarseness she was not accustomed to in his voice. ''No more hiding. No more turning
your head or closing your eyes when you don't like what
you see. You go digging around in my life, you want to
know what happened, when I tell you the truth you will
damn well look me in the eye and listen.''

His eyes bored into her. ''Emily Buck was a nineteen-
year-old crack addict who prostituted herself to support her
habit. She wasn't a bad person,'' he whispered. ''Her family loved her, and cared for her, and tried to help. They
were good people who never understood what had happened to their only daughter. One night her boyfriend—
her *pimp*—killed her. The people in the apartment next

door found her body, obviously dead, on the concrete steps outside their door.'' He took a deep breath but did not release her. ''They called the police, but first they called *investigative reporter* Sam Morgan's hotline, so they'd get the fifty bucks he pays for juicy, exclusive information.''

He leaned in close, and for the first time since she'd met Ray she felt threatened by him. He was so much bigger than she was, so much stronger. His strength had never frightened her before, but right now he was furious, dancing on a dangerous edge. His cruel mouth looked as if it never smiled.

''Emily's mother heard about her daughter's death on the ten o'clock news. *Known prostitute Emily Buck,* Morgan called her, while he showed a tasteful shot. All Emily's mother saw was a bloody bare foot in the background.''

Grace swallowed hard. ''That's why you...''

''That's why I broke Morgan's nose. Smug S.O.B. deserved that and worse.''

''I'm sorry,'' she whispered.

''Yeah. Everybody's sorry. Emily's pimp was sorry he left his fingerprints on the knife. The neighbors were sorry they hadn't called the police first, once the money Morgan had paid them was gone.''

She had never seen Ray so tense. The muscles in his face and neck were tight, his eyes flashed, hard and bright.

''Luther was sorry he didn't get there faster, to stop Morgan before it was too late. The Captain was sorry when he told me I could resign or be fired because the station owner was going to sue the city if I remained on the job. Morgan's still sorry his face isn't quite as pretty as it used to be.''

The fingers holding her chin tightened, just a little, and

he stared into her eyes. "What are you sorry about, Gracie?"

Her heart caught in her throat and she couldn't answer.

"Sorry you left Huntsville? Sorry you came back?" He bit out the harsh words. He moved forward, slanted his head and kissed her, but there was no passion in the kiss. No love. "Sorry about last night?" he added, his voice a whisper.

She wanted to say yes. Yes to all three. But instead she laid her hand on Ray's cheek and kissed him. A real, tender kiss this time. Something to say *I'm sorry* without words, without awkward explanations.

Ray relaxed as he took his lips from hers, laid his forehead against hers and closed his eyes. "As for me? I'm not sorry for what I did. I'm just sorry I couldn't save Emily. She was a kid, Gracie. Just a kid."

She threaded her fingers through his hair. "I know you tried. It's not your fault, Ray. You can't save the whole world." It was what he tried to do, wasn't it? The reason he'd always been the one at the front of the action, the reason he'd taken risks with his life. Risks he could live with and she could not.

"I wasn't trying to save the whole world," he whispered. "Just one kid."

Somehow she doubted that. "There have been others, haven't there? Other kids."

"Sure."

"And you were able to help some of them, I know it."

"Maybe…"

"No maybes, Ray."

He looked her in the eye, and she could see the pain there, a pain she'd never seen before. A barrier between them had crumbled, leaving them both raw. Exposed. She'd never seen Ray like this before.

"You tried to help her, you did your best. That's all you could do." Tentatively, wondering if he would push her away, she laid her hand on his cheek, stroked him there before lowering her hand to touch her palm to his chest.

He didn't push her away; he didn't step back or crack a joke or turn his back on her.

"I never told you that I had a sister."

It was the last thing she'd expected to hear. "A sister?"

"Yeah," he breathed his soft answer. "But when I was twelve and Crystal was sixteen, she died of a drug overdose. She was at a party, and it was…it was a mistake. She was experimenting, joining in with the group, having fun. One minute she's there, in the next room over and yelling at me about leaving my clothes on the bathroom floor or eating the last of the chocolate chip cookies, the way big sisters do, and the next minute she's dead."

Grace laid her head against Ray's shoulder and closed her eyes. She didn't know what to say.

Ray's body tensed, he balled his fists at his sides and took a deep, cleansing breath. When he spoke, his voice was low, as uncertain as she'd ever heard it. "I looked at Emily and I saw Crystal, and when Emily died I knew why I'd always been so determined to make a difference, to…to stop what was going on. And I knew, that night, that I'd been wasting my time. I threw away half my life for nothing."

"Not for nothing," she assured him.

"For nothing," he whispered.

She rested her hand on his side, needing the connection, trying to give him her comfort. He had comforted her more times than she could count. He'd never needed consolation himself until now.

"Why did you never tell me about Crystal?"

He threaded his fingers through her hair and held on

tight. They stood there, joined here and there, holding on as if to let go would mean to fall apart.

"Habit, I guess," he finally answered. "It was so painful, after Crystal died we didn't talk about it. She was just gone, and we never mentioned her name or talked about what happened." A finger rocked gently, absently against her back. "Six months after Crystal died, my mother left home. Packed her bags, said she couldn't take it anymore, and left. I haven't seen her since. My father and I got real good at pretending everything was fine, everything was great. We ignored the unpleasantness and the pain and went on as if nothing had happened."

Grace leaned into Ray, wanting to dissolve and melt through the floor. Ray's need to wage his own war went too deep for her to fight. Of course he would go to Mobile when this was over, of course he would continue to throw himself into the middle of his own personal war. There was nothing she could do to stop him.

"It was more than that," he added, his voice so low she could barely hear him. "I didn't tell you about Crystal because you were my place to hide. I didn't want to bring any of the crap in my life home to you. I wanted to forget with you."

She'd always felt guilty for leaving Ray the way she had, for wimping out and walking away without telling him, face-to-face, why she had to go. Knowing about his sister's death and his mother's desertion when he'd been so young made her feel even worse. Ray didn't need to be deserted again, he didn't need the people he loved walking away from him.

She wanted to hold him like this all night. There was nothing she could do to change the past, to make up for leaving him, and she had no illusions that they might have something lasting.

But she still wanted to hold him, to have him for as long as she could. When he left—and this time he would be the one to do the leaving, she knew—it was over. Until then...

''Ray,'' she whispered against his shoulder. ''Take me home.''

Chapter 10

He shouldn't have told Grace so much, and wouldn't have if she hadn't caught him off guard by asking so coldly about Emily Buck's death and all that came after. *What was she to you?*

Most of all he regretted telling Grace why he'd never told her about Crystal before. His place to hide, his refuge, his sanctuary...what sentimental hogwash.

Ray stared up at the ceiling and listened to Grace breathe, deep and even. She'd been asleep for a while now, but he...hell, he'd likely never sleep well again.

He tried to turn his mind to the case, to the surly Ben McCann and the merry widow and the grieving mistress. There were still too many possibilities to consider, too many people who might've wanted Lanford dead.

Unplanned, unwanted, his mind returned to Grace. Until this was over, until she was safe and he left for Mobile, they'd be together. He knew it, she knew it. They hadn't talked about this new aspect to the situation, it just was.

And when this was over he'd leave for Mobile and smile when he told her goodbye, no matter how much it hurt.

They wouldn't talk about the inevitable leaving, either.

He reminded himself that no matter how disgustingly sentimental he occasionally got where Grace was concerned, he had to keep his relationship with her on a superficial level. Sex. A few laughs. No more heartfelt confessions that laid his heart open.

"Aren't you asleep yet?" she asked sleepily.

"No."

All the lights in the house were out and the curtains were closed tight, shutting out the moonlight and the glow of the streetlamps. Grace was a shadow, a warm, indistinct shape at his side. She rolled into him, slipped her arm around his waist, and sighed. He felt her sigh and her heartbeat—savored them. He waited for her to ask what kept him awake and tried to think of an innocent answer that wouldn't reveal too much.

But she didn't ask. She cuddled against him and stayed there, silent and soft. And not quite still. Her fingers brushed his side. Her foot rocked gently back and forth against his leg. When she raised her head and lightly brushed her lips against his chest, he put his hands in her hair and lifted her, dragging her body against his until they were firmly mouth to mouth. Her hand skimmed down his side, over his belly, until she reached out to touch him, to wrap her fingers around his arousal and stroke gently. Too gently.

He cupped her breasts and lightly brushed a nipple, and she shuddered, the quiver shaking her from head to toe. Her every response to his touch, every tremor, was deep and complete. Intoxicatingly so.

She hadn't been with another man since she left him. He was the only man who had ever touched her this way, who had ever laid with her and whispered in the dark and made love as the sun came up. She was his, only his. Why did he have to remember that now? Why couldn't he just enjoy the sex and forget the rest?

"Did you miss me, Gracie?" he asked as he rolled her onto her back and spread her thighs with his knee.

"You know I did," she whispered.

He kissed her neck, sucked gently beneath her ear where she was so sensitive. She sighed and turned her head to give him greater access to her slender throat, and arched her back slightly so her breasts pressed against his chest. He licked and nibbled his way down her neck, and she raked her hands slowly down his back, her fingers exploring, touching, loving.

In the dark he could not see her nearly well enough. He knew her face, though. He knew it too well. He could close his eyes and see her lying beneath him as he loved her, he could see her lips part, her eyes shine dark and tender. He could see her hands when they reached for him, her pale body pressing against his.

He could see the shape of her, lean and rounded, soft and strong. The shape of a woman who came to him the way a woman comes to a man. Open and naked. Giving and taking.

Ah, he was much too tenderhearted where Grace was concerned. He'd warned her not to make more of this temporary relationship than it was, and here he was fantasizing while he touched her in the dark. *Skin deep.*

"What do you want, Gracie?" he whispered as he ran his hand down one long, slender thigh.

"You know what I want."

"Tell me." He kissed her, hard and fast and deep, before she could speak. He thrust his tongue into her mouth and devoured her while his hands roamed over her body, touching what he remembered. What he saw in his mind. A curve here, a dimple there.

She kissed him back, and that little catch in her throat when he took his mouth from hers told him exactly what she wanted.

"What do you want?" he asked again, parting her legs wide with his hand on her thigh, his fingers almost touching her intimately.

She wrapped her hands around his neck and held on tight, trembling soft and deep. "I want you to make love to me."

Ah, that request was phrased too prettily, much too fancifully. "Tell me plain, Gracie," he insisted softly as he touched her, parted her legs wide and stroked her where she was already wet for him.

She rocked gently against him, sighing and shuddering. "I want you inside me," she whispered, so softly he could barely hear her words.

He reached for the bedside table, throwing open the drawer and reaching inside to grope about for a condom. Tempted as he was to immediately give Grace what she wanted, what he wanted as well, he couldn't forget how and why they were here. They were temporary, he was nothing more than a passing fancy. There would be no mistakes made, no reminder nine months from now that Grace was the one woman in the world who could make him lose control.

"At this rate I'm going to have to make another trip to the drugstore soon," he said as he slipped the condom on.

"Yes," she whispered, not arguing, not denying their days together that were still to come.

He pushed inside her and she released a moan that tried to stick in her throat. While her hips rocked against him he made love to her slowly, holding back, wishing for enough light to see her face. Imagining wasn't enough, not anymore.

Darkness blanketed them. Ray kept his thrusts gentle and incomplete, teasing them both, making this encounter last. Grace swayed against him, wrapped her legs around his hips and surged to meet him. Her hands were in his hair and on his back, her breath, coming harder now, caressed his ear.

He didn't have many perfect moments to remember. Most of them, maybe all of them, included Grace. In his best memories, she was there. If he died happy he would die with the memory of her face behind closed eyes. He tried to memorize the way she felt right now, under and around him, moving against him. Wanting him.

Thrusting hard he filled her and held himself deep inside her. As soon as he was there, complete, she began to pulse around him, to shudder in his arms, and he didn't know anything else. There were no memories, no thoughts at all, just the feel of Grace shattering in his arms. He pumped hard, again and again, and she moved with him and cried out softly.

His release came on the waning waves of hers, while her inner muscles squeezed him and she shuddered and whispered soft words he couldn't quite understand.

Who was he kidding? He could never have a shallow relationship with Grace. They had too much history, he'd loved her too much. She'd hurt him too badly.

Her arms remained possessively around his neck, but her body was relaxed. Depleted. She breathed deep and not so easily, and seemed in no hurry to disentangle their bodies.

He'd sworn not to ask. He knew this was a terrible idea. But he lifted his head and looked down at her. He was tired of looking at a shadow, so he reached out and turned on the bedside lamp.

Grace blinked against the harsh light, but smiled at him, anyway. He didn't smile back.

He brushed the hair away from her face. "Why did you leave?"

Grace's smile faded. Not now, please not now. "I told you, years ago."

"No," Ray snapped. "You didn't."

He pinned her to the bed, hovering directly above, all around her. There was no escape.

"You asked me to quit my job," he whispered. "I said no and less than a week later you were gone. It was nice of you to hang around until I was on my feet again. I never got the chance to thank you for that."

"Ray, I told you a thousand times…"

"You told me nothing."

She had explained, hadn't she? Ray watched her and waited, and she didn't know what to say.

"Never mind," he said, rolling away and leaving the bed quickly to head for the hallway and the bathroom. "I don't know why I asked. Must've been some kind of bizarre afterglow backlash."

Grace sat up and reached for the bathrobe on the floor at the side of the bed, where she'd left it hours ago. The pink silk was frivolous and feminine and sexy. She'd bought it on impulse three years ago but she hadn't worn it until tonight. It didn't cover much, but if she was going to confess to Ray as he had confessed to her…well, she couldn't sit here naked and do it. She was still wondering if there was time to get completely dressed before this confrontation when Ray came back into the room.

She wished she could read his mind, that she could look

into the face she'd loved and know what he was thinking. He'd become too skilled with the nonchalant mask he wore to keep his thoughts from others. Sometimes he could even fool her.

Saying not a word, Ray crawled into bed and pulled the sheet to his waist, positioned himself with his back to the headboard and his eyes pinned on her. It would be easiest to turn her back to him, to bury her face in a pillow. She didn't though. Instead she scooted up to sit beside him; close but not touching.

"The third time you were shot," she said without preamble. "I was sitting at home watching some silly sitcom. I remember which episode, I remember the dialogue that was being spoken when the doorbell rang."

Ray said nothing, just stared at her and waited.

She turned away, staring straight ahead as she continued. "When I saw Luther, I knew what had happened. I knew that you had jumped into the middle of someone else's mess and gotten yourself shot again.

"But I was smarter than I had been the first two times, or so I thought. This time I was not going to panic. I was going to be calm. Mature. *Reasonable.*" She took a deep, calming breath. "I took the time to get dressed and brush my hair, even though Luther shouted for me to hurry. After all, I'd made a fool of myself the first two times, showing up at the hospital in my nightgown and a coat and untied tennis shoes. Worried half to death while you sat there and…and laughed with your buddies and flirted with the nurses."

Her heart lurched. She didn't want to remember. "On the way to the hospital, Luther assured me, as he always did, that you were going to be fine. He said it again and again, and I didn't notice that there was anything different in his voice. Not until later, when I thought about it while

I sat in the waiting room and waited for you to get out of surgery.''

"We don't have to relive this," Ray said gently, surely regretting his impulsive question.

"You asked," Grace snapped. She felt him next to her, saw his form out of the corner of her eye, and still she couldn't make herself look directly at him. "Now you can damn well listen."

"Yes, ma'am."

She stared straight ahead, not wanting to see his accusing eyes. "You were out of it, so I'm sure you don't remember much, if anything, about those first few days. The doctor didn't give you much of a chance to make it. He thought it was a miracle that you didn't arrive DOA." Her voice shook, just a little. She wanted to reach out and lay her hand on Ray's sheet-covered leg, for support. For comfort. But she didn't.

"The first two times you got shot were bad enough. I always felt like someone had reached inside and yanked out a part of my soul that I'd never get back. Afterwards I always felt…less whole, less safe."

She finally turned her head to look at Ray, and her eyes fell on the scar high on his chest. She reached out and touched it. For the first time, she purposely laid her hand on the evidence of that devastating wound. "You almost died and it nearly killed me. I don't know how I got through that week, I really don't." She stroked the scar one last time and then let her hand fall away. "We'd been talking about having children then, remember?"

He nodded his head once.

"My period was a few days late," she whispered. "It was too soon to be sure, too soon even to mention, but I thought of it that night while I waited for you to get out of surgery. I didn't know if I was pregnant or not, but I wondered while I waited to see if you would survive this latest shooting. And I wondered how I was going to get by without you, how I was going to raise a child without you.'' Tears stung her eyes and she willed them not to fall. ''Luther kept saying that everything was going to be all right. He said it until I wanted to scream and slap him until he just shut up. Nothing was all right. I felt like someone had taken me apart and put me together again all wrong.'' A too-familiar hysteria welled up inside her. ''My heart was battered, my brain was mush. I knew I couldn't go through that again, and you refused to quit. What was I supposed to do?''

''I was a cop when you married me,'' he said defensively. ''You knew what I did.''

''But I didn't know you were a hotdog who felt compelled to be at the front of every battle, a danger junkie who would regularly risk your life without a second thought.'' She understood now why Ray felt compelled to do what he did. It didn't make any difference. In fact, it made things worse. This wasn't something he could walk away from.

''I didn't know you were so damn delicate you couldn't weather a few bad times,'' he said harshly, refusing to understand. ''I didn't know you were going to run at the first sign of trouble.''

''First sign?'' She shook her head in wonder at his incredible density. ''I lived in absolute fear for three years of the six we were married. After the first time you were shot everything changed. If you were five minutes late I started imagining all the terrible things that might've happened. When you were working undercover and I didn't know when you might come home it was even worse.''

''Things got too rough for you and you left,'' he said casually. ''You've told me all I wanted to know. You didn't care enough to stick it out when things didn't go your way.'' He shrugged his shoulders as if he didn't care at all.

''And you didn't care enough to choose me over your job.'' She breathed deeply, painfully. All along she'd known there wasn't a chance for them, and still it hurt to face the truth head-on. ''You didn't even care enough to come after me.'' She would've gone home with him if he had. If just once she'd opened the door and it had been Ray standing there…

He turned his head and pinned his eyes on her. ''Would it have made any difference?'' he asked, dark and caustic.

Yes. She wanted to scream at Ray, she wanted to make him understand. But screaming at him wouldn't fix anything. They were beyond repair. ''Would it make any difference if I asked you not to go to Mobile?'' she whispered, knowing what the answer would be.

''Well, that settles that,'' he said, throwing the sheet aside and reaching for the clothes he'd tossed to the floor hours earlier. ''I think I should just settle on the couch for the duration. We may be good in bed, darlin', but beyond that what we want is too different. Nothing's changed in the past six years.''

''No,'' she said. ''Nothing's changed. I can't go through that again, Ray. I just can't.''

He stepped into his boxers and then his jeans, his back to her the whole time. Why did they always go so wrong? Just when she thought things were beautiful, that everything was going their way at last…

But she hated to give up so easily. ''I can't fall in love with you and then live the rest of my life waiting for you to get killed.''

Ray glanced at her from the doorway. ''Nobody's asking you to, Gracie. We're not married anymore.'' He said it as if he was reminding himself, not her. "All we are now is…" he shrugged his shoulders. "I scratch your itch, you scratch mine."

She grabbed his pillow and threw it at him. Hard. He caught it and headed for the couch.

Freddie lay in the bed with his hands behind his head, as the sun came up. It hadn't taken him long to dig up the information he needed, while Gillian had worked yesterday. He knew everything he needed to know about the woman who'd witnessed the hit. Grace Madigan, divorced, parents retired to Florida, one older brother she saw once a year, if that. Decent income, small savings account, and until she'd come to Huntsville, no social life.

Ray Madigan was the one he'd have to worry about, when the time came. The P.I. was always armed, and he hadn't left his ex-wife's side since the hit, as far as Freddie could tell. He spent the night at her place, drove her everywhere, watched her like a hawk.

The witness wasn't Madigan's only ex-wife. There were three of them. Freddie had to wonder if the man was as protective of his other ex-wives as he was of Grace. Only one way to find out.

"I made breakfast," Gillian said, coming into the bedroom wiping her hands on a towel.

He took one look at her and smiled widely. "Call in sick again."

"I have to go to work today, Jimmy," she said, looking as if she regretted the necessity as much as he did. "I missed Monday this week. If I call in sick again I might lose my job. But we can have breakfast together before I go."

Freddie dismissed his unpleasant but necessary thoughts of all the Madigans. He liked Gillian, he liked her a lot.

He was in no hurry to finish his business in Huntsville. "Come home early," he said as he sat up and reached for her.

She'd been curious about Ray's new business, so she didn't object when he said they'd be stopping by his office on the way home from Dr. Dearborne's on Wednesday evening. Anything to delay the inevitable tense and uncomfortable evening in her much-too-small house.

Last night he'd driven her to exercise class, in the hopes that the widow Lanford would be in attendance. He'd waited for her in the parking lot, refusing to leave for even an hour. Of course, Louise had not been there...not that Grace would've had a clue as to what to say to her if she had been.

"My goodness, you *do* still work here," the middle-aged woman behind the desk said as Ray led Grace through the door. "I was beginning to wonder."

"Hello, Doris," Ray said with a smile. "Messages?"

"A good-sized pile." Doris lifted the stack of messages, but kept her eyes on Grace. "New client?"

"Doris, this is Grace," Ray said, sighing as if he knew what was coming and knew just as well that he wouldn't like it much.

"Number one," Doris said with a wide smile as she came to her feet.

Grace noted that the solidly built Doris was not very tall, probably no more than five feet in height. Her eyes sparkled with intelligence and humor. No wonder Ray liked her. "Most people just call me Grace."

Doris rounded the desk and slapped the messages into Ray's hand. "I'm late getting out of here. Again." She rolled her eyes. "Ray, if you're not going to be around you need to hire some help. There are three new possible clients in that stack of messages. If you don't call them back they'll find someone else.'' She reached up to pat him on the cheek, a warm maternal gesture delivered just a bit too soundly.

While Doris grabbed a sweater from the coat tree she looked Grace up and down, scrutinizing. ''I like her better than the other two,'' she said bluntly. ''She's got class.'' Doris looked Grace square in the eye. ''Are you sure you were really married to this lug?''

''Once upon a time,'' Grace said, trying to keep her voice carefree.

Doris grabbed her purse and left, mumbling about getting dinner on the table. The office was oddly empty once she was gone.

Ray locked the door behind his secretary and sat at her desk to peruse the messages. ''She runs the office,'' he said without looking up.

''I'm sure she's very capable.''

''She is.''

He laid the messages aside and leaned back in Doris's chair. ''I guess I should call these new clients and refer them to someone else,'' he said absently. ''I've got my hands full with the Lanford case, and after that . . .'' he shrugged his shoulders.

''You won't be here.''

''I won't be here,'' he repeated softly.

The Lanford case was driving him to distraction, she knew that. He ran into one dead end after another. Sometimes he told her about what was going on. More often he did not. They lived together, he took her everywhere she went, and still they rarely spoke.

''Ray.'' She approached the desk, feeling safe here in this office. This was neutral ground. They hadn't kissed here, they hadn't made love here. There were no memories to cloud her mind.

"What?" He leaned back in the chair, feet on the desk, eyes neutral and still.

"Things are kind of a mess right now." In more ways than one. "But I do want us to be friends."

He made no move, said nothing. His face was completely passionless.

"I don't know if we can," she added softly. "But maybe if we tried…"

"Friends shouldn't have to *try,*" Ray interrupted, his eyes growing hard. "I'll be honest with you, Gracie. I don't think I can be your friend. It's too damn hard."

She nodded, and turned her back to him while he finished reading through his messages. She almost managed not to cry at all.

Chapter 11

From her seat at one of the round tables on a raised platform in the middle of the restaurant, Grace nervously glanced toward the restaurant door and the sunlit sidewalk beyond the glass doors and sparkling windows. A newly arrived couple wearing expensive suits and carrying leather briefcases waited to be shown to their seats. The usual Thursday clientele laughed and talked too loud, the waiters and waitresses bustled to please the lunch crowd, and in Grace's sweeping line of vision there was no sign of the killer or Ray.

Ray would have a fit if he found out she was not having lunch in her office, as he'd ordered her to do. Like he had a right to order her to do anything! Right now she needed a friend or two, she needed to forget, for a while. She needed to forget the killer *and* Ray.

"Are you all right?" Nell Rose asked, leaning forward to get a better look at Grace's face. Her chin-length blond hair danced as she dipped her head to the side. "You're downright pale."

"She's right," Sandy said, her South Alabama accent more of a true Southern drawl than Nell Rose's. She flipped her pale brown hair over her shoulder. "Have you been sleeping?"

"Not very well," Grace admitted.

Before they could ask her to elaborate, their waiter arrived. They all ordered the usual: chicken salad with honey-mustard dressing and iced tea.

The three of them had a standing rule. They didn't talk about work and they didn't talk about the old days. Anything else was fair game. As the waiter moved away Nell Rose began a spiel about her oldest son's latest exploits on the baseball field. Grace had to smile, since little Kyle was all of four years old. Sandy asked if either of them had seen the latest Antonio Banderas movie, and when they said no she gave them a detailed rundown of the plot.

And then they both turned their curious eyes to Grace.

"You sure are quiet today," Sandy said softly. "What's up with you?"

Grace started to shake her head, then capitulated too easily. She needed someone to talk to. "I found out what happened to Ray," she said, "I know why he quit."

Sandy and Nell Rose exchanged a quick glance.

"The girl," Grace added. "The reporter with the broken nose."

"I guess we shoulda told you ourselves," Nell Rose said. "But it just seemed senseless to drag the whole mess up at this point. It's over and done, and I didn't know how you'd react. I mean, the whole thing made me so mad I wanted to go punch that Morgan guy out myself, and I was never married to Ray. It was just so unfair."

"Yeah," Sandy added. "Billy and Earl tried to go to

bat for Ray, but it didn't do any good. I mean, you wave a lawsuit in front of the mayor's nose and you know what happens.''

"How'd you find out?" Nell Rose asked.

"I found some of the story in old articles on the Internet. The rest Ray told me himself.''

Sandy's eyebrows shot up. "He did? Grace, are you and Ray…I mean…are you two…'' Her fingers danced restlessly.

"Grace," Nell Rose snapped. "Are you and Ray together again?''

Grace felt the warming rush of a blush in her cheeks. "No." After all, they hadn't slept together since Monday night, and Ray had barely spoken to her since then, except to tell her that they couldn't even be friends. It was apparently too *hard.* But he was always there, watching over her.

"Yes," she whispered. Like it or not there was something going on, something unresolved. "I don't know," she finally added.

They were silent while the waiter placed three tall glasses of iced tea on the table, but as soon as he was gone Nell Rose leaned over the table and whispered, "What do you mean you don't know? You are or you're not. There's no in-between.''

"There's a lot of in-between," Grace said softly. "And that's where we are. In-between.''

Sandy leaned forward, too. Her mischievous eyes sparkled. "Are you sleeping with him?''

Grace nodded. Then she shook her head. Nell Rose slapped her gently on the arm.

"Honey, when it comes to sex there's no in-between. You did or you didn't.''

"Did," she whispered.

After a moment of what could only be stunned silence, her two friends leaned back and smiled.

"I predict a June wedding," Nell Rose said smugly. "No matter what you said, I always knew you and Ray would get back together."

"May," Sandy said with a widening smile. "They're not going to wait until June."

Grace's heart lurched, her insides tightened. Nothing was so simple. "We are not getting remarried," she said decisively. "I can't go through that again. Besides," she added, drawing on her reserve of serenity and strength. That reserve was drawing low, and she needed it now. "Ray's moving to Mobile. He's going back into narcotics and I'm going to stay here and...and..."

"And what?" Sandy asked, her smile long gone.

"I don't know," Grace said softly. "I honestly don't know."

The investigation was moving too slowly to suit him. Ben McCann had been uncooperative during his brief interview. Hatcher had filled in a lot of the business blanks where Lanford was concerned, but couldn't add any personal dirt.

Ray hadn't been able to get close to the assistant D.A. who had once had an affair with Louise Lanford. The grieving widow had not attended the Tuesday night exercise class he'd driven Grace to.

Friday night was the key. They would all be there Friday night, at the Charity Ball for the Children's Hospital. Ray didn't want to wait even one day. The more time that passed, the harder a resolution would be.

The intercom on his desk buzzed and snapped. "It's the FBI," Doris said. "At least, that's what the man says. I don't buy it. An Alan Chambers. I don't think he's FBI. He sounds perfectly normal..."

"It's about time," Ray grumbled into the phone as he snapped the receiver up and brought it to his ear.

"You're welcome," Chambers said sarcastically. "I did a little digging around and I came up with three possibles. I'm sending you a fax. These three guys are pros that fit your general description. It's a long shot, but this is all I've got."

It *was* a long shot, and Ray knew it. Whoever had had Lanford killed could've hired a bartender or a friend or a bum to do the murder. He didn't think so, though. The job was too clean not to be professional. He gave Chambers his fax number, and seconds later the fax machine came to life, spitting out pages.

"For your sake, I hope none of these are your guy," Chambers said. "There's not a teddy bear among them. You have an army standing by?"

"Am I going to need one?"

"Maybe. I wouldn't want to go up against any one of these guys without an army of my own." Chambers sighed. "There was a time when I would've loved to go up against any one of them, preferably alone. Hell, who wants to share the glory?" He sighed tiredly. "No more. I guess I've spent too many years behind a desk. I used to like chasing bad guys, when I was young and full of adrenaline."

"Well, I've still got a little adrenaline left," Ray muttered into the phone, Grace's words about him being a danger junkie coming to mind.

"Be careful."

"Thanks," Ray said as he rolled his chair back to collect the first page.

"Just keep my name out of this," Chambers insisted.

"Unless you find out that one of these is your man. Then I want to know. I *have* to know, you got it?"

"I got it," Ray said halfheartedly.

"If one of these hit men is after your witness, I'll...I'll send somebody down," Chambers said before he hung up the phone.

Ray laid the three pages, pictures with stats beneath, on his desk. All bad guys, all fitting Grace's vague description and the rough sketch that had been drawn from her description. He picked up the phone and dialed Dr. Doolittle's number.

The receptionist answered the phone with a professionally crisp, "Dr. Dearborne's office."

"Hi, put me through to Grace," he said.

"I'm sorry, Grace is out to lunch. Can I take a number and have her call you back?"

"She's taking her lunch break in today though, right? This is a personal call. You can put me through."

A short, warning pause put Ray on alert. "No, she's not here. A friend picked her up a few minutes ago."

Ray saw red, but his fury didn't come through in his voice as he asked, "When do you expect her back?"

"Not for about forty-five minutes," the receptionist said.

"This is her hus...her ex-husband, Ray. We met the other day. It's Amy, right?"

"Oh yeah," she said brightly. "You've been around a lot lately."

"That's right," he said calmly. "Amy darlin', do you know where Grace is having lunch?"

They were finishing their salads when Ray strolled into the restaurant. Shoulders squared, head high, he looked like a soldier sauntering into battle. His eyes landed on her immediately, as if he'd spotted her the moment he walked in the door. Maybe before. At the foot of the stairs he planted his feet and glared at her, looking oddly fierce for a man in blue jeans and a blue-checkered shirt.

"There you are," he said, bounding forward, taking the steps to the center platform two at a time. There was no hostility in his voice, but she could see it in his eyes. A flash, and then it was gone.

Sandy and Nell Rose smiled widely and greeted Ray like the old friend he was, and he did the same, telling them both to say hello to their husbands, Sandy's Billy and Nell Rose's Earl. He was his usual charming self.

But when his eyes landed on Grace they were cold as ice. "We have to go."

"The waiter hasn't brought our checks yet," she said, not anxious or even willing to let Ray rush and bully her out of the restaurant.

He reached into his pocket, impatiently pulled out a twenty-dollar bill and handed it to Nell Rose. "This should cover it."

"I'm not quite finished with my tea," Grace said, not looking at Ray as she swirled what was left in her glass. The ice clinked loudly. She held her breath.

Ray placed his hands on the table and leaned in. He smiled, placed his cheek on hers, and whispered softly in her ear. "You can stand up and walk out of here with me right now, or I can toss you over my shoulder and you can leave that way."

"Ray," she said, trying to remain calm, not succeeding. Her heart beat too fast, her knees shook. "You can't…"

"Feet on the ground or ass in the air," he breathed. "Your call, Gracie."

He backed away and she stood slowly, collecting her purse from where it hung on the back of her chair. Blushing, she was sure, she told Nell Rose and Sandy goodbye. They both tried, unsuccessfully, to hold back wicked smiles. Like they thought this was entertaining and charming and adorable. Ray was many things, but *adorable* was not one of them.

Grace did not hurry to the exit, even though Ray looked like he was about to explode as he took her arm and hurried her along. His grip on her arm was too tight, and he hovered over her protectively.

He didn't say another word until they were outside the restaurant. "Didn't I tell you to stay in the office? Dammit, you're just asking for trouble. You're actually going out looking for it."

"It's been a week," Grace said calmly, "and there's been no sign of the killer. He's probably left town."

He opened the car door for her, and slammed it shut after she sat down. When he dropped into the driver's seat, he reached into the back seat and grabbed three sheets of paper he tossed at her.

"Do any of these guys look familiar?"

She looked at the first picture and quickly dismissed the possibility. The man's face was too round and he was too old. The man in the second picture was too small, too dark. His eyes looked black in the poorly reproduced photo.

But the man in the third picture…his hair was different, paler and longer, and he was wearing wire-rimmed glasses. But…but…

"This is him," she said, handing the sheet to Ray.

Ray studied the sheet intently. "Freddie Potts." He muttered something filthy and shook his head. "This guy is a pro. The FBI's been after him for years." He scanned the small print beneath the grainy photo. "There have been witnesses in the past."

"So someone else besides me can ID him?" Grace

asked hopefully. She did not want to come face-to-face with the man again, didn't even want to be in the same building, the same *city* with him. If someone else could identify him...

Ray shook his head, then lifted his eyes to glare at her. "No. He killed them all. Some at the scene. Some days, even weeks or months later. Always well before trial."

Potts wasn't a man to give up easily, then. *Months?* "You think he's here somewhere, don't you?"

Ray nodded his head. "I do." For the past few days he'd made it a point not to touch her. It was too dangerous, too *hard*. But right now he reached across to grab the back of her head and pull her close. "But Potts is not going to get you," he said softly. "I won't let him."

"I know," she whispered, glad for the closeness just this once.

"We'll take this information to Luther, and he'll have every cop in the city combing motels, hotels, boarding-houses...the guy has to be sleeping somewhere. They'll put this on the news, too. Television and newspaper. Somebody's seen him. He may be good but he's not a ghost." His thumb rocked absently on her neck. "The FBI will be here, too. They'd love to get their hands on him."

Grace nodded, and Ray placed his forehead against hers. "And the next time I tell you to stay put," he said gently. "Do it."

The hand at the nape of her neck was comforting and strong. And she wished with all her heart that everything was different, that she could tip her head and kiss Ray and tell him that she was scared, but not nearly so scared as she would be if he wasn't here.

"Would you really have carried me out of the restaurant if I hadn't gone willingly?" she asked.

"You bet your pretty little ass I would have."

He let her go, dropping his hand and moving slowly away from her.

"Here are the rules," he said as he started the car. "Call the office and tell them you won't be in tomorrow. Next week is iffy."

"Ray, I can't…"

"You can work on your computer or my laptop, and once we catch this guy you can work eighty hours a week to catch up, if it suits you. Until he's off the street you're not going to be where Potts might expect you to be."

"He doesn't know where I work or where I live," she argued. "Does he?"

"He might. We're not taking any chances." He glanced at her as he stopped at a red light. "We're moving into my apartment for now, until a more secure place can be arranged."

"Ray…"

"Don't worry. You can have the bed, I'll take the couch. I'll try to have something more comfortable set up by tomorrow night."

She slunk down in her seat. "It sounds a little extreme," she said softly.

"Extreme?" he snapped. He took one hand from the steering wheel to grab the sheet with Potts's picture on it. "Take a look at that face and read the notes beneath it and tell me I'm trying too hard to keep you from getting killed."

She glanced at the photo, but didn't bother to read the details beneath. "You're right," she said. "I'll do whatever you say."

"Promise?"

She nodded. "Where are we going?"

"To see Luther."

* * *

They were lying in bed watching the ten o'clock news and eating popcorn when Freddie saw his face on the screen. It was an old picture, taken when he'd been younger and leaner and stupider. His hair was long and a shade darker than it was at the moment. But it was him, he knew it and so would anyone else who looked closely.

He thought about trying to distract Gillian, kissing her, maybe, making love to her again so she wouldn't pay attention to the television. But if it was on TV now it would be in the papers tomorrow and on every station in the area by tomorrow's noon newscast. He couldn't watch her every minute of the day.

Besides, it was too late. She turned to look at him, scrutinizing his face. "That guy looks kinda like you, Jimmy," she said, her voice hesitant.

"You think so?" he asked, flicking another kernel of popcorn into his mouth. "I don't see it."

The photo was gone from the television screen now, they'd moved on to another story. Without that picture to compare him to, Gillian's doubts faded away.

"You're much more handsome than that guy." She laid her head on his shoulder. "And a lot sweeter, from what they said. A hit man. I always think of hit men being in big cities, not quiet towns like Huntsville."

"I know what you mean," Freddie said, kissing Gillian swiftly before rolling from the bed.

"Where are you going?" she asked, sitting up.

In the doorway he turned and smiled at her. What a shame. What a waste. "I thought maybe you'd like a glass of wine."

Gillian returned his smile and settled herself against the pillows. "That would be great."

* * *

She had slept too well in Ray's bed, on the sheets that smelled faintly like him, on the mattress where he laid, most nights. Sipping at coffee and munching on toast, Ray appeared to have actually slept just as well on his lumpy couch, a piece of furniture that looked as if it belonged in a landfill somewhere.

Ray's apartment was small, basically two rooms and a bathroom. The kitchen was no more than one corner of the main room, and most everything in the place looked as if it could be trashed without significant loss—well, everything but the sound system. The stereo, complete with CD and cassette player as well as a working turntable, was the only thing of real value in the place.

That and the extensive Lyle Lovett collection.

Luther had not been happy to find out that the man she'd seen was a professional hit man who was certainly still in the area. The homicide detective was even less thrilled when Ray insisted that he had no choice but to call the FBI and tell them Potts had been identified. He didn't want the federal jerks in his jurisdiction, he'd said adamantly.

Ray insisted on taking care of her, watching out for her, even when she tried to insist that it wasn't necessary. She could probably get federal protection, and since Potts had been identified, Luther could no longer insist that she'd been living in a fantasy world. It wasn't Ray's job to look out for her. Not anymore.

But whenever she tried to convince Ray of that fact he stopped her with a stare.

She sat on the couch beside him, her own coffee cup in hand. "So, what's the plan for today?" she asked casually.

"We find a place to stay and we go shopping," he said without looking directly at her.

"Shopping?"

He shrugged his shoulders. "For tonight."

"We're still going?"

He rotated his head to glance at her. "Of course. What are we supposed to do? Sit in a hotel room somewhere and play gin rummy all night?"

"Luther's on it," she said. "And the FBI..."

"We're going," Ray insisted.

Grace propped her feet on his scarred coffee table and stared at her running shoes. With everyone working on the case, surely Potts would be in custody soon. And then...and then Ray would have no more reason to stay in Huntsville. Would he?

"Have you called Stan?" she asked casually.

"Not yet," Ray said tersely. "I keep meaning to, but one thing and then another..."

She took her frightened gaze from her shoes and stared openly at Ray's profile. At the cut of his jaw and the stubble there, at the strength in his neck and his arms and the softness of his lips. Heavens, she loved the way his hair curled over his neck, the set of his shoulders and the strength and tenderness in his hands.

What an idiot she was. Ray was wrong for her, they had nothing...but she did love him. She would always love him, no matter where he went, no matter what he did. No matter how many times he broke her heart.

Leaving him had been a mistake, one she couldn't take back. She couldn't convince him that they still had a chance, a future, but she could heal some of the hurt, couldn't she? Didn't she have to try?

What would it take to bring him back to her completely, just for a while?

"Shopping," she said softly, and with a slow smile.

Chapter 12

"**W**ow," Ray said appreciatively as Grace stepped into the main room of the two-bedroom suite they'd moved into this afternoon. Neither the hotel nor the room was fancy, but it was comfortable and clean and spacious, and no one but Luther knew they were staying here.

Grace's red, floor-length gown hugged her body, showing off her fabulous shape. It was cut low enough to show the globes of her breasts, but not so low that she was in danger of revealing too much. *Too bad.* When she walked, the slit on one side of the blood-red skirt danced so a long bare leg was partially revealed. A black strappy high-heeled shoe showed off that leg to its best advantage.

She often wore her hair up, and tonight was no different. But the style was softer, and a few curls fell to her shoulder in an artlessly elegant fashion.

"You look great."

She smiled, almost bashfully. "So do you. I've never

seen you in a tux before. I should've known you'd go for something different.''

He grabbed the lapels of the white jacket. "Has kind of a forties look to it. At least, that's what the girl who rented it to me said.'' His outfit for the evening consisted of a perfectly fitted white dinner jacket, black creased trousers held up with white suspenders, white shirt and black bow tie. "I feel like I should light up a filterless cigarette and start calling you doll.''

Grace smiled, a real, wide smile that made his heart thud hard in his chest. For the past several days she'd been shy, skittish. Asking nervously if they could be *friends*. She didn't look at all skittish right now. She looked…enticing, seductive, willing and able. And contented.

"The shoulder holster really finishes off the look, big guy,'' she said in a husky voice.

His gut tightened.

Potts's name and face had been all over the news, on television and in the newspapers. So far they'd been able to keep Grace's name out of it. Luther was making sure no one knew of her involvement, unless that knowledge was absolutely necessary. Only a handful of cops and the district attorney had been told that she was the witness.

Nothing on Potts had turned up in the hotel search, but there were a lot of hotels in the area, not enough manpower, and too many hotel clerks who apparently never looked directly at their clientele. The search continued.

For all they knew Potts might've identified the witness as Grace. He could be watching her house or his apartment, but he surely wouldn't be at the Charity Ball tonight.

Unless he was there to meet the man or woman who had hired him. Unless he showed up to take care of the only other person in Huntsville besides Grace—his client—who could ID him. Things had gone very wrong for

Potts. He might decide to wipe the slate clean and get out of town.

"Maybe we should stay in and order pizza," Ray suggested as the doubts nagged at him. Grace would be safe in this hotel room. "Or you can stay here and I'll go on alone and scope out the shindig."

"No way," she said confidently. "I bought a new dress, you rented that tux, and you know whoever hired Potts will be there tonight. This is our chance to mingle, to get close and gossip and see what we can find out." She smiled as she neared him. "Besides, Louise Lanford won't give you the time of day, no matter how charming you might be. But she'll talk to me because she knows me. You need me, Ray."

Poor choice of words, but he didn't dare mention that fact.

"What makes you think I can't get the widow Lanford to talk to me?"

"You're not her type," Grace said, brushing his cheek with one finger as she passed him. "Louise Lanford goes for money and power, not boyish charm."

"Ouch," he muttered, watching her walk away.

The front of Grace's dress might not be indecent, but the back certainly was. It plunged to her waist and beyond. He saw and appreciated the shape of her spine, the way the soft muscles in her back moved when she walked.

She glanced over her shoulder and her smile widened.

What was she thinking?

"Assistant D.A.s don't make that much money," he said, unwilling to tell Grace that the offered view of her back was making him break into a sweat. "Louise and Elliott Reed were apparently together for almost two years," he argued.

"Family money and lots of it," she said as she gathered

her small black purse from the table by the long blue couch. "That's why he'll be there tonight, too. His mother is a bigwig in the Children's Hospital Charity."

"How do you know all this?"

"I did a little more searching on the computer. I borrowed your laptop last night, after you went to sleep."

"You can't find…"

"If you know where to look," she said softly, her smile all knowing, "you can find anything."

"Not personal information, not without…" The smug expression on her face stopped him cold. "You're a hacker."

"Purely an amateur, I assure you."

"My own wife…"

"*Ex*-wife," she said softly. "I checked into McCann and Reed a little, so I'll know what to say and what not to say if I get close to either of them tonight."

"I don't want you getting close to anyone but the widow, you got me?"

"We'll see," she said, unperturbed by his order.

There would be no stopping her, would there? And to be honest, she might be able to get information he couldn't. She had good instincts, sharp eyes and ears.

"If you get close to Reed or McCann, you play it safe, you hear me?"

"Yes, sir."

He looked Grace up and down audaciously. Hell, a woman who wore a dress like that one was begging to be ogled. His eyes lingered on the swell of her breasts, then fell to follow the curve of her waist and her hip…and back up again.

"Gracie Madigan," he said softly. "You're not wearing any underwear."

She *did,* at least, have the good manners to blush. "I see your radar is still in good working order."

"Radar my ass," he grumbled.

"The dress is cut too snug through here," she explained unnecessarily, barely touching her hip. "I can't go to a fancy ball with panty lines, now can I?"

Ray looked her up and down again. Slowly. Grace was wearing that red dress and a pair of shoes. Nothing else. His mouth went dry. He swallowed with some difficulty.

She was torturing him, wasn't she? Flaunting what he couldn't have in front of him as if to say *Skin deep? Think again.*

He made himself grin at her. "What would Doris say? She thinks you have such class."

She didn't take the bait, just wrinkled her nose at him and turned away, giving him a too-fine view of her backside and bared back.

Ray closed his eyes and groaned low in his throat. Torturing him? Hell, the woman was trying to kill him.

Inside the main Civic Center ballroom the lights were dim and the big band on the stage played "String of Pearls" while well-dressed people danced. Some danced well, others did not. But they all did their best.

Grace wrapped her arm through Ray's, growing nervous for the first time. From a distance it had seemed like an adventure, coming here to search for whoever had hired Freddie Potts. In the moment, though, it was…frightening. Ray was the investigator. Not her. He was the danger junkie, she was timid. Maybe she'd been timid for too long.

Flaunting herself at Ray was as nerve-racking as facing a room full of potential murderers, but she tried to remain cool. As far as she was concerned bringing Ray around was just as important as finding Potts and the person who'd hired him. More.

"The widow Lanford is hobnobbing with the mayor at a table to the left," Ray said softly. "McCann is talking to Heather Farmer in the far corner, and Elliott Reed is dancing with his mother."

"I see him," Grace whispered.

Ray led her to the dance floor and took her in his arms. His hand lay against her bare back and he looked her squarely in the eye as they began to dance. She didn't look away, she didn't draw back when he pulled her close. Yes, she'd been timid for too long.

He tilted his head down to whisper in her ear. "Dammit, Gracie, what are you doing to me?"

"Nothing," she whispered.

"Nothing." He pulled her head against his shoulder and held her there. "How am I supposed to dance with these blue-haired ladies all night in this condition?" He held her so close his *condition* was more than apparent.

"You'll manage," she said softly against his shoulder. He always did, didn't he? Nothing ruffled his feathers for very long.

She lifted her head and looked up at Ray. The way he gazed down at her she thought that maybe, just maybe, this had become simply a dance for the two of them. Just this one dance, just this one precious and private moment before they began their investigation. She realized too soon that he was leading her toward Reed and his mother.

But for the moment she allowed herself to enjoy the way Ray held her, the feel of his hand at her back and his fingers over hers, the brush of his body against hers. And she wished, for the thousandth time, that things were different for them.

"I'll bet they don't play one Lyle Lovett song all

night," Ray grumbled, blatantly trying to change the subject.

"You're probably right. Of course, we could always get closer to the stage and yell out, 'Don't Touch My Hat,' 'Her First Mistake!'"

Ray didn't laugh, he didn't smile at all. His hands tightened and he pulled her closer.

"Are you sure you want to do this?" he whispered as they neared Reed.

No, she wasn't sure about anything. But she nodded once.

The music ended and they joined the crowd in clapping politely as the big band began another number.

"Mrs. Reed," Ray said, turning on the charm as he addressed Elliott Reed's mother. She had the look of the grande dame, elegant and polished, cold and perfect, from the gray hair piled on her head to the champagne-colored gown to the pointy tips of her toes. "I was so hoping for the opportunity to dance with you."

The older woman smiled, properly flattered, and Reed backed away. Ray threw a glance at the assistant D.A. "I'll even let you dance with my wife if I can have your mother for a few minutes. Elliott Reed, right?" he asked as if trying to remember. "This is Grace Madigan."

Reed seemed annoyed, until he turned to Grace. He looked her up and down like a coyote surveying fresh kill. She should have known this dress she'd chosen for Ray's benefit would bring unwanted attention. Had she thought no one would look at her tonight but Ray?

"It would be my pleasure," Reed said with a grin.

Elliott Reed was a fine dancer, though he held her too close for comfort. When Ray had held her close it felt warm and right. This was just creepy.

"Good band," she said, trying to start a casual conversation that might make Reed take his eyes from her cleavage.

"Yeah," he said, lifting his head to look her in the eye. "If you like this old crap."

She raised her eyebrows and drew back slightly. He continued to try to hold her too close. "If you don't like the music, why are you here?" she asked.

He grimaced. "My mother commands it."

"And you always listen to Mother?"

His eyes darkened and he sighed tiredly. "I find it easier to get by if I keep her happy."

Beatrice Reed probably kept a tight rein on the purse strings, Grace decided. "That's very sweet," she said with a smile. "Going to so much trouble to keep your mother happy. You're a good son."

He hummed noncommittally. "Well, now that I've met you, I'm glad I came. Maybe your husband will dance with Mother all night and I can have you."

For once, Grace didn't quickly correct the mistake by muttering *ex*-husband. She'd just as soon Reed believed her to be taken. If Elliott Reed behaved this way when he thought she was a married woman, what would he do if he knew she was single? She'd rather not find out.

They drifted steadily away from Ray and the elderly Mrs. Reed, and as soon as they were at a decent distance Elliott laid his hand on her rear end. Casually, lightly, but definitely inappropriately.

"Mr. Reed," she said in a lightly admonishing tone. "Behave yourself."

He smiled, moved his hand to a proper position, and spun her around to the squeal of a trumpet. "Can't blame a man for trying, Mrs. Madigan."

Grace found herself facing Louise Lanford, who sat at a small table with the mayor and a tall drink. Louise didn't look like a woman whose husband had been dead a week, in her diamonds and bright blue gown that was cut nearly to her navel.

Reed's eyes traveled that way, too, just for a moment.

"Isn't it a shame?" she asked softly.

"What's that?"

"What happened to Carter Lanford. That's his widow, isn't it?"

He stiffened, just slightly. "I don't think it's a shame. The man was a world-class jackass."

Her eyes widened. "You knew him?"

"I'm afraid so," Reed muttered, leading her toward the center of the dance floor once again.

"Everything I read about him made him sound like a really good man," she said innocently.

Reed's gaze went distant, detached. "There was nothing *good* about Carter Lanford but his bank account."

Grace smiled warmly. The man was going to open up right here on the dance floor. He was going to spill his guts.

He didn't get the chance.

"Excuse me," a familiar voice interrupted, with a sigh and a tap on Reed's shoulder. "I believe this dance is mine."

Grace sighed herself as Luther, in a traditional dark tuxedo, stepped into Reed's place. He held himself stiffly, distant, and so did she.

"Luther," she said softly.

"Grace," he grumbled her name. "What the hell are you doing here?"

"Same thing you are, I imagine."

He was a lousy dancer. She almost told him so.

"Dammit, Grace, this is not *The Thin Man Meets the Hit Man*." Luther snapped as he stepped on her toe and

quickly stepped back. "You and Ray can't run around trying to solve the mystery yourselves like it's some kind of
game. This is a seriously dangerous character you're messing with."

Luther had been her friend once, but he'd been nothing
but nasty to her since her return to Huntsville. She'd tried
to understand, but right now she was simply annoyed. As
if she didn't have enough trouble!

"If we thought there was the slimmest chance *you* might
find Potts, we wouldn't be here," she said coolly.

"I could have you arrested," he threatened.

"You won't," she said with confidence.

Her new dance partner swung her around clumsily. His
eyes scanned the room as he steered her toward the edge
of the crowd. They left the dance floor, and Luther grabbed
her wrist and half led, half dragged her toward an exit. He
pulled her through a door and she found herself in a
brightly lit and deserted hallway, her back against the wall,
Luther scowling at her with his face just inches away.

"I'm only going to say this once," he hissed. "Ray
doesn't need you flitting in and out of his life, turning him
upside down and inside out and then disappearing when
the mood strikes you. You screw with his head again and
I will throw you in jail. Don't ask me what for, I'm sure
I can find something. If I can't I'll manufacture something," he warned lowly. His face was rigid, his eyes dark.
"Why the hell did you come back?"

His eyes didn't dance like Ray's, they smoldered. Dark
and condemning. No matter what he said or did, she
couldn't be mad at Luther any longer. He obviously had
Ray's best interest at heart. Tough as nails, seemingly can-
tankerous, he would go to the ends of the earth for a friend.
And Ray was his best friend.

"Just between us?" she whispered.

"If that's the way it has to be," he snapped.

She didn't talk to anyone about Ray and what had happened between them. Not her parents or her friends. She didn't trust anyone with her heart.

But something had to give. "I came back because I never got Ray out of my blood, because I could never make myself fall out of love with him. For six years I tried, and I just…couldn't."

Luther's face softened. "You never should've left."

"I know that."

"It damn near killed him."

She closed her eyes. God, she didn't want to know how hard her leaving had been for Ray. She wanted to believe it had been easier for Ray. It made her guilt less, somehow.

"Me, too," she whispered.

"Dammit, if you leave him again…"

"I won't," she said, opening her eyes, trying to look at Luther so openly and honestly he would know without doubt she was telling the truth. "This time, Ray's going to leave me."

It was for the best, she'd decided. She wasn't going to run; she wasn't going to let Ray push her away. She was his completely for as long as he wanted and needed her. Until he left for Mobile.

Luther cursed, low and profanely, as he backed away.

"So," Grace said, relaxing and even taking Luther's arm as they headed for the ballroom. "How have you been?"

He cut a sharp glance her way and grimaced. "I'm fine."

His answer for everything.

"Did you ever get married?" Luther was a handsome man, sweet when it suited him, a good guy like Ray. She couldn't believe he'd never found the right woman.

"Nope."

"Why not?"

He stopped with his hand on the door that would open into a crowded ballroom. The music was muffled, still, but would blast them when the door was opened. Muted laughter met her ears.

"If you and Ray can't make it," Luther said softly. "I don't have a chance in hell."

Before she could respond he threw open the door and dragged her through the doorway.

Ben McCann was an attractive man with meticulously styled dark hair and soulful brown eyes that made him look more like an artist than a businessman. In spite of his athletic build, Grace half expected him to start spouting poetry at any moment.

"Are you a big supporter of the charity?" Grace asked. Heather Farmer had introduced them, and had then suggested that her new boss dance with her "friend." He had grudgingly obliged.

"The company has connections with the Children's Hospital," he said. "I had no choice but to be here tonight." His eyes wandered about the room until they found Louise Lanford. "To be honest, I'd rather be at the hockey game. They're in the playoffs, you know."

"Huntsville has a hockey team?" she asked, genuinely confused.

"Yeah. Not on the NHL level, of course. It's a minor league team." He almost broke into a smile. Almost. "You didn't know? Where have you been?"

She smiled. "In Chattanooga for the past six years."

"Ah," he said. "Well, you don't know what you're missing."

Again his eyes found and lingered on Louise. Those

eyes went dark and deep and sad, while Louise laughed
with a supporter who leaned too close and blatantly peered
down her dress.

"Hockey," she said. "I have never been to a hockey
game."

"You should give it a try. One game, and I promise
you'll be hooked."

"Do you go to all the games?"

"Most of them." He looked her in the eye, fearless,
nothing to hide. "To be honest, with my new position at
work I don't know if I'll ever make it to another game.
There's so much involved. Traveling, working late. The
responsibility for everything falls in my lap, now."

"I thought men liked that sort of thing," she said with
a small, comforting smile. "Power. Money. Everything
that comes with it."

"I'd rather be back where I started, designing games."
He grinned. "I had to grow up to discover that games are
a lot more fun than business. The kids have it right. We
should play every chance we get."

"I don't play much anymore, I must admit."

"You should," he said, looking again for Louise. "We
all should."

Ray cut in while Grace was dancing with an old fart
who kept stepping on her toes. She'd been working diligently all night. Rescuing her was the least he could do.

"Having fun?" he asked as he swung her around.

"A blast," she said sarcastically. "I didn't know there
were so many bad dancers in Huntsville, or that they'd all
be here."

He'd been watching Grace most of the night, keeping
an eye on her, never losing sight of her for more than a
few minutes at a time.

"What do you think?" he asked softly. She'd danced with Reed twice and McCann three times, and from a distance she'd looked gorgeous and charming and he'd wanted, too much, to cross the room and cut in.

She sighed thoughtfully. "I don't see McCann involved. The change at work has been a tremendous pressure. I don't think he really wants that position. Besides, he seems like a nice guy."

Ray lifted his eyebrows, and Grace smiled widely.

"You know what I mean." Her expression went soft. "I think he really does love Louise, though. The way he looks at her…"

"Does he love her enough to kill for her?" Ray asked softly.

She hesitated. "Maybe. But I think if he'd wanted Lanford dead he would've done it himself. He seems like a hands-on kinda guy."

"And Reed?"

She didn't hesitate. "Definitely not a nice guy. I can see him hiring a hit man to do away with someone he doesn't like, and Mommy's got the money. Poor little rich boy never had to do without anything he wanted, and if he wanted Louise and couldn't have her, I think he'd kill to clear the field."

"I don't know," Ray said, glancing around the room and spotting all three suspects and, a good distance away, a nervous Heather Farmer. While he watched, Christopher Hatcher, Lanford's bespectacled assistant, approached Heather with a glass of champagne. She took it and gave the man a small smile. "Maybe you think McCann is innocent because he's *nice,* and you think Reed is guilty because he keeps grabbing your ass."

"Well what do you think?" she asked.

"I think it's Reed."

"Why?"

"Because he keeps grabbing your ass."

He spun Grace around and smiled down at her, and let his own hand drop to rest low on her hip. His fingers gently caressed silky red fabric and the firm, bare hip beneath. He expected a reprimand, but got a smile.

"People are watching," she said softly.

"I don't care." He spun her around again.

Her body skimmed his, close and yet not close enough, so near he could smell the hint of perfume she wore and the fragrance in her shampoo. More than that, he smelled *her*. The scent of her skin. The warmth of her passion.

He bent his head and nuzzled her ear. "You're driving me crazy."

"Am I?" she asked, innocence and seduction, the forbidden and the inevitable rolled into one irresistible package. She didn't just dance with him, they moved together in a way that was undeniably sexual. He didn't want to let her go, not now, not ever. Difference be damned. How could he go on without her?

For a while, for a few precious minutes, he forgot the murder and the hit man and Mobile. He closed his eyes and held onto Grace as they moved to a slow and easy melody that crept under his skin. The perfection didn't last long, but while it did he let himself get lost.

The music stopped. Over Grace's shoulder, Ray could see that the old fart who'd been stepping on her toes was headed their way. Now was not the time to take her face in his hands and kiss her, now was not the time to ask her why she was trying to kill him.

There would be time for that later.

"Have you talked to the widow yet?"

Grace shook her head. "Every time I get close she

moves away. I don't want to chase after her. That would be too obvious."

"She's headed to the ladies' room."

Grace gave him a dazzling smile. "I think I'll go powder my nose."

She turned and walked away, and while he watched and admired the view the old fart sidled up to him.

"I don't appreciate being horned in on, young man," the old guy said, almost primly. "I was making some progress with the lady, I tell you."

Ray looked down at the white-haired man. "You were making progress with my *wife?*"

The man blushed, from the roots of his thin white hair to his jowls. "I apologize. There was no ring, so I naturally assumed she was unattached."

Ray kept his eyes on Grace as she disappeared into the hallway that led to the rest rooms. Watching her walk away was painful, and it had nothing to do with the snug cut of her gown or the bare back or the knowledge that beneath she wore nothing. Nothing at all.

Okay, maybe that caused part of the pain.

"No," he said confidently and with just a touch of despair. "My Gracie is definitely not unattached."

Chapter 13

Grace looked at her reflection in the mirror and reapplied her lipstick, her eyes flitting occasionally to the woman beside her. Louise Lanford was checking the straps on her gown and leaning toward the mirror, scrutinizing her own face as she turned it this way and that.

Would Louise recognize her out of the setting where she normally saw her? Would she look this way at all? The woman was totally self-absorbed.

Louise pulled a lipstick out of her own black purse and quickly and expertly swiped her pouting lips with a daring shade of red.

"What a lovely dress," Grace said absently as she lifted a hand to her hair and turned her head slowly, as if checking for strands that might have gone astray.

"Thanks," Louise said, and then she turned her head. "Oh, hi." She flashed a small smile. "I didn't recognize you." She returned her attention to her own reflection. "It's Grace, right?"

Grace nodded and smiled. "And you're Louise?"

"That's me." She squinted, checking out a small imperfection. "I didn't see you at exercise class this week."

Grace poked at a nonexistent flaw in her swept-up hairdo. "I only made it once," she answered. "Tuesday. I didn't see you there."

"My husband's funeral was Tuesday," Louise said, wrinkling her nose in distaste. "I couldn't get away in time for class."

It was a pretty cold and emotionless statement.

Grace quit pretending to preen and turned to face Louise Lanford. "I'm so sorry," she said, trying to sound sincere. "How awful for you."

Louise finished with her own repairs and straightened to look at Grace. "Thanks, but to be honest it wasn't so awful. My husband and I hadn't had much of a marriage for a long time." She looked, for an instant, almost sad. "I lost the man I married years ago, first to his business and then to his young and disgustingly bubbly secretary." Her eyes went hard; the smile she flashed was obviously false. "I'm not going to pretend to mourn a man I quit loving years ago."

"I'm sorry," Grace said again, meaning it this time.

"Don't be," Louise said sharply. "You know what the worst part of it is? The bubbly secretary is actually here tonight. We've been very careful to be on opposite sides of the ballroom at all times." She flashed a false smile. "It's all very civilized, the way Carter liked things to be when he was with us."

"Sounds uncomfortable," Grace said, realizing the truth in Louise's statement. She hadn't seen Heather and Louise stand close to one another tonight, they had never acknowledged the other's presence in even the smallest way.

She wondered if it had been the same before Lanford's death.

"So," Louise said brightly, dismissing her problems. "What about you? Why did you only make it to class once this week? You're there almost as much as I am."

"Husband problems of my own," Grace said in a soft voice. "Well, ex-husband problems. He's been...hanging around a lot lately."

"Sounds interesting," Louise said as she snapped her purse shut and checked her reflection one more time, pulling in her stomach, thrusting out her breasts. "Do you *like* him hanging around? It's hard to tell by the tone of your voice."

"I haven't decided yet," Grace muttered as she followed Louise to the exit.

Louise laughed lightly. "I know the feeling." Before they joined the crowd, she turned to Grace again. "Men. I swear, sometimes I think we'd be much better off without the opposite sex. Other times I'm sure I can't live without them."

"Or a particular one," Grace said softly, thinking of Ray.

Louise gave Grace a sympathetic nod of her well-coifed head. "Oh, you look like you've got it bad."

"You don't know the half of it." She didn't have to pretend to be distressed. All she had to do was call on her deepest feelings.

Laying a comforting hand on her arm, Louise leaned in and said softly. "If you're really having a problem with the ex, I can give you the name of a wonderful man to help you out. He was a lifesaver for me."

Grace's heart almost stopped. It couldn't be this easy. Was Louise Lanford about to recommend her own personal hit man? "Really? I'd appreciate it."

"Dr. Wendell Wells is a great couples therapist. He tried to help us, when things first went wrong, and he did help me." For a second Louise looked like she was no older than Heather. Sad and a little lost. "When I was confused he tried to help me see where I was going and why…and why I couldn't make things work no matter how hard I tried. I haven't seen him for years," she said thoughtfully. "Maybe I should give him a call."

"Thank you," Grace said.

"Good luck," Louise said before putting back on her false face to join the crowd.

"They're playing our song," Ray said as he swooped in and saved Grace from yet another aging Romeo. He gently dragged her onto the dance floor and into his arms, swinging her around in time to the slow, jazzy tune.

"'Makin' Whoopee'?" she said with a smile. "Our song is 'Makin' Whoopee'?"

"Why not?"

The crowd had begun to thin, as the evening headed for a close, so they had a large portion of the dance floor to themselves. It gave him room to swing Grace around, to dance with her unrestrained, without worrying about running into another couple. He twirled her across the dance floor, wanting to make her head whirl the way his did.

"What did you find out?" he whispered in her ear as he stopped spinning and pulled her close.

"I don't think Louise had anything to do with it," Grace said softly.

"What, she didn't grab your ass?"

Grace pulled back and glared up at him. "Be serious," she admonished. "You asked me what I thought and I told you. I don't think she needed to kill him. They'd been married a long time, so if there was a divorce she wouldn't have exactly been left penniless. She said they fell out of love a long time ago. I'd be more likely to think her guilty if she was putting on a show of mourning when she so obviously didn't love him anymore.''

"So, what is the trick to getting past the Grace Madigan test? Is our bad guy someone who's putting on a show of mourning the dearly departed Lanford, or the most inno-cent-looking man in the room?" He lowered his voice. "I know who we should check out next. The little old man who kept stepping on your toes," he teased.

"I'm serious," she admonished. "I told Louise you were driving me crazy, and she tried to send us to coun-seling. The tough gal is an act, I think, no more substantial than the gown she's wearing.''

Ray ignored the bit about driving her crazy. After all, turnabout was fair play. Right? "So, we're back to Reed."

Grace sighed and laid her head against his shoulder, easily, comfortably. "I don't know. Maybe we're looking in the wrong direction. I just can't see any one of them having Lanford killed.''

"You're too tenderhearted," Ray said, trying to ignore the way she felt against him. Yielding and seductive. "Too gullible. You'd make a lousy detective.''

She didn't argue with him, just rested her body against his and relaxed. He closed his eyes and spun her around, easy this time. Wherever he led she followed, smoothly and without an ounce of resistance.

"I'm tired," she whispered, her breath warm against his shoulder. Her body lay soft and smooth against his, flesh and red silk and nothing else. "Maybe in the morning some of this will make sense.''

"Maybe," he said, not yet ready to lead her from the dance floor.

Holding Grace this way led to those impossible

thoughts. He knew when they got back to the hotel tonight he'd have to smile and tell her good-night and head for his own room as if letting her go wasn't killing him. He didn't want to, though. He wanted to hold her all night. And tonight, tonight she wouldn't resist him any more than she resisted the way he led her around the dance floor. But what about tomorrow?

Whenever he felt like he was on the verge of falling in love with her all over again, he reminded himself that when the going got tough, Grace got going. She'd said it herself. She couldn't take who and what he was. It was too hard to work through the bad times for the sake of being there when the good times rolled around.

That didn't make her any less his. It just…hurt a little.

He couldn't be her damned friend any more than he could maintain the skin-deep relationship he craved and needed. Having a purely sexual encounter with Grace sounded like a good idea, it made perfect sense. He just didn't think he could pull it off anymore.

When the song ended he stepped back and gave her a small smile that would tell her nothing of what was in his mind. "I think we've done all we can tonight. Reed and McCann are both gone, the widow Lanford is gathering her bag and saying good-night to a few friends as we speak, and Heather is walking out the door. Looks like Hatch is driving her home."

"Good. She's still too shook up to drive, if you ask me," Grace said. "And she's been drinking."

"So have you."

She grinned. "A little champagne, that's all. For social purposes only, I assure you."

He wanted to kiss her here and now, in the middle of the room, in front of all these people. Instead he brushed back a silky strand of dark hair that brushed her cheek. "Let's get out of here."

He took her arm and led her toward the door. Once they were outside, where the night was cool and pleasant, he spotted Luther standing across the street, in front of the parking garage. Waiting. As they crossed the street Luther straightened, scowled and crooked a finger at Ray.

"I'd like a word with you," Luther snapped.

"Fire away."

"Alone." Luther turned his back and started walking toward the park.

"I'll wait here," Grace said, leaning against a lightpost.

"I won't go far," Ray promised.

She smiled, tired and trusting, and he walked to where Luther waited impatiently. Ray circled around so he could see Grace over Luther's shoulder. He watched, fascinated, as she leaned against the lamppost and closed her eyes.

"What?" Ray snapped, his eyes remaining on Grace.

"Don't make me arrest you," Luther snapped. "I want you, no, I'm *ordering* you to step back and stay out of this case. No more talking to my suspects, no more talking to anyone who knew Carter Lanford. If I so much as catch you looking at his first-grade teacher I'll haul you in and lock you up."

Ray grinned. "No, you won't."

"Yes, I will," Luther promised darkly. "Jesus, you and Grace deserve each other, you know that? She said the exact same thing when I told her to back off. This is a murder investigation, Ray, not a game of Clue."

"You told Grace to back off?" He'd seen them dancing, briefly, and neither of them had looked too happy. Right after that, Beatrice Reed had started introducing him to all her friends and he'd lost sight of his friend and his wife. *Ex*-wife, he reminded himself.

"For all the good it did me," Luther snapped. "Keep her out of it, too, for God's sake. She has less business than you do nosing around this case."

"She's your only witness. I'd say she has every right."

"Witnesses do not investigate the crime, Madigan."

Luther only called him Madigan when he was really pissed, so Ray backed off. A little. "Okay, Malone. I'll take it easy for a while." He wasn't having much luck, anyway. "But if you don't find something soon…"

"I will," Luther interrupted. His face changed, softened a little. "You know, with all that's happened I can get the okay to post security on Grace. There's no reason for you to put everything aside to be her bodyguard until this thing is finished."

"That's okay." Ray planted his eyes on Grace again. She looked like she was about to fall asleep, there against the lightpost. She was completely relaxed, soft and sexy in her red dress in the circle of light. Lean and delicate, strong and smart, she was everything a man could want in a woman. After all they'd been through, how could she still be so tempting?

If he was smart he'd take Luther up on his offer and hand Grace over. No more wanting her and knowing he couldn't have her, no more moments of weakness when he knew without a doubt that she was his woman and always would be. No more painful nights tossing and turning because he knew, deep in his gut and in the portion of his brain that continued to work properly, that Grace wasn't his anymore.

No, he wasn't that smart. "I farmed out a couple of cases that couldn't wait, and put the rest on hold. I can't walk away from Grace now."

"She's not your wife or your responsibility anymore,"

Luther said sensibly. "This is going to lead to trouble, I know it, I can feel it in my bones."

"You and your bones," Ray said with a smile. Unfortunately Luther's bone-deep feelings were usually right. Grace was trouble, but he still couldn't walk away from her when she needed him. "I'll be fine."

"I hope you're right," Luther grumbled.

The car turned slowly from Clinton onto Monroe. What caught Ray's attention was that the headlights were off. Some drunk trying to find his way home on a Friday night, probably. Too many beers or too much champagne had dulled the driver's senses. That was all it was, right?

His heart did a funny flip in his chest. The hairs on the back of his neck stood up as the dark car stopped in the middle of the road. The engine revved once, and then it began to roll forward. Slowly, at first, then a little bit faster. The direction of the rolling car changed subtly, the nose pointing not straight down the street, but turning toward the lamppost.

Ray took off running at full speed; the driver of the car floored it.

"Grace!"

At the sound of his voice she opened her eyes and smiled at him sleepily as he continued to race toward her. Her smile faded as he reached into his shoulder holster and withdrew his gun.

Grace heard the roar of the gunned engine and spun to face the approaching vehicle. The car was headed straight for her, gaining speed, hugging the curb. Flying toward her faster than was possible. She jumped out of the way just as the bumper of the speeding car scraped against the lamppost with the screech and howl of a metal bumper on a concrete column. Mere inches away from being run over, Grace hit the sidewalk and rolled away. The car swerved and the back fender glanced off the lightpost with a grinding crunch and kept going, picking up speed.

Ray took a shot at a back tire and missed. Luther did the same. As people came running from the Civic Center to see what the noise was about, some of them placing themselves in the line of fire, Luther and Ray both lowered their weapons. Seconds later the car that had tried to run Grace over was gone.

And Ray shook all over.

He holstered his weapon and knelt down beside Grace. Her arm was scraped, seeping blood; tendrils of dark hair fell around her face. Her gown had ripped a little, there at the slit up the side. And she trembled as thoroughly as he did. More.

"Are you all right?" he asked, brushing the hair away from her face.

She nodded her head slowly. "I think so."

Luther joined them, finishing up a cell phone discussion with dispatch, as he described the car. He broke off the connection with a flick of his thumb, and dropped to his haunches beside Grace. "That was a close call."

"A close call," Ray snapped angrily. "He aimed his car at her and damn near ran her over. The S.O.B. was waiting for us."

"It could've been a drunk," Luther said sensibly, "or some kids on a joyride who lost control, or…"

"It was him," Grace said, looking not at Luther, but directly at Ray. "I saw his face. Just for a second, and he looked a little different, but it was him. He was staring right at me when he tried to run me down. If the lightpost hadn't been in his way he would've followed me onto the sidewalk, I know it."

"We're already looking for the car," Luther said, not bothering to argue with her. "We'll find it."

"In the morning," Ray said as he helped Grace to her feet and placed his arm around her. She needed the support, and so did he. "You'll find it in the morning. It's a stolen car, and there won't be any prints."

"What makes you so sure?"

Dammit, he didn't want to hear another word of Luther's nonsense. His blood boiled, his heart pounded so fast he could feel it. He couldn't hold on to Grace tight enough. "Because this guy is a pro," he snapped. "He's probably already ditched the car."

"But…"

"Not tonight, Malone," Ray said as he led Grace down the steps into the parking garage. "We'll talk tomorrow. I'm getting Grace out of here."

Freddie pulled into the bar and took a deep breath as he leaned back in the driver's seat, trying to calm himself. Again he'd failed to kill the witness. A hit and run might've looked enough like an accident to suit him, but he'd missed and the woman had seen him. Their eyes had locked for a split second, and he'd seen the spark of recognition.

She wasn't staying at her place, or at her ex-husband's apartment. Freddie cursed himself. He should've been patient tonight and followed them back to where they were staying and done the deed there. He could have taken his time and made sure there were no more mistakes.

But seeing her stand there, alone and unprotected, had been too much of a temptation.

Oh well, he'd pick them up in a day or two.

This job had been nothing but wrong. The woman had seen his face and she'd been able, somehow, to ID him. The body had been found too soon. His picture was all over the news. Bad luck, all bad luck.

There was another problem. The client was not stalwart enough to suit Freddie. If the man who had hired him was interrogated he would crack, no doubt. And he knew too much, way too much. More bad luck.

He'd kill them both and get out of town. The witness and the client. He could do nothing else.

Freddie stepped out of the car and straightened his jacket. He'd changed his look again. His hair was black now, his eyes dark blue. The inserts between his lower back teeth and cheeks changed the shape of his face, just enough. The suit he wore was expensive—no more bicycle shorts and tank tops for him—and the diamond stud in his left ear gave him a roguish look.

He hated that everything on this job had gone so wrong. Most of all he regretted being forced to kill Gillian. She'd been fun. He'd really liked her.

The bar was dark enough to suit him, and the music was too loud. Rock and roll. His eyes scanned the crowd until they landed on the woman at the bar. She was cute, but not actually pretty. Short and shapely, maybe a little heavier than was fashionable, but pleasant, nonetheless. Her brown hair was inexpertly styled, her clothes were too dark and plain for this meat market.

From a shadowed corner he watched her for a few minutes. She fidgeted, she glanced nervously around like a lost puppy. No one joined her, no one so much as waved at her. Yes, she was alone. She was grabbing her purse from the bar as he joined her.

"You're not leaving, are you?" he asked, smiling down at her.

"Yeah, I guess so," she said softly.

Freddie gave her his most charming smile. "But I just got here."

She reclaimed her seat and placed her purse back on the

bar. "Do you come here often?" The question was followed by a blush. "Oh, that sounds awful, like some kind of pick-up line." She blushed again.

He ignored her agitation. "I've never been here before."

"Me, neither." She sighed. "And I never should've come here. I'm not...I'm not very good at this," she said, dismay in her voice.

Freddie cocked his head. "Not very good at what?"

She smiled. "Being social. I'm kind of a homebody. I'd rather be at home with a good book."

Ah, but she wasn't at home with a good book tonight, was she? She was out looking for something. Excitement, maybe. An undiscovered passion.

"Something soft on the stereo," he added. "Maybe a fire in the fireplace, if the night is cool enough."

Her smile widened. Her eyes danced.

"Can I buy you a drink?"

"Why not?"

"My name's Hank," he said, offering his hand.

"Jenny."

He held her hand just a little too long, looked deeply into her eyes. Cute Jenny practically melted in his hands. She licked her lips nervously and, judging by the sparkle in her eye, dismissed thoughts of a boring evening alone by the fire.

Hotels were too risky right now, but Freddie needed a safe and quiet place to stay. If Jenny didn't have her own digs, he'd move on to someone who did.

Chapter 14

Grace perched on the edge of the couch in the main room; she couldn't stop shaking. She'd been sitting here for several minutes, trying to pull herself together while Ray thoroughly checked out each of the rooms in the three-room suite.

Potts had tried to run her over, and if Ray hadn't called her name, if he hadn't seen and come rushing toward her...she closed her eyes. Heaven above, she could still hear the roar of the engine, still see Potts's determined face behind the wheel.

Satisfied that all was clear in the suite, Ray approached with a damp washcloth and sat down beside her, pulling her back, making her relax against the back of the couch instead of perching on the edge. He'd loosened his tie so it hung, untied, around his neck, and he'd removed the top stud from his tuxedo shirt. Still, he didn't look at all relaxed. He was wound so tight she could see the tension in his neck, in the set of his mouth.

"You shouldn't cry," he whispered, gently wiping her cheeks with the warm washcloth.

"I'm not crying," she said, and then she sniffled once as he washed away the tear tracks.

"I know you're not," he joined her in her denial as he laid the washcloth on her scraped arm and tenderly washed away the dirt. "Does this sting?"

"Just a little," she admitted, watching the gentle movement of his hand on her arm. The way his long fingers looked so dark against the white washcloth, the way the tips of those fingers brushed her bare arm. A hand so large and masculine and strong shouldn't be so tender, should it? The simple touch shouldn't feel so good. She shouldn't want that touch so much.

"I guess I thought he was gone," she whispered as she watched the easy movements of his hand. "Gone back to New York or Miami or Chicago or wherever hit men go when they're not working. Silly, huh? For all we know this guy lives in Decatur."

"I'd hoped he was gone, too." Ray's voice was low, no more than a whisper as he ran his hands over her arms, checking her for scrapes and scratches he'd missed. He hadn't missed anything, but she didn't tell him so. She was afraid he'd stop if she did.

She shook her head slowly. "Trying to figure out whodunit was turning out to be fun, when I'd convinced myself Potts was gone. That it was just a game." That it was just an excuse to stay close to you. "But he was here all the time, watching and waiting for his chance."

"When I get my hands on Potts I'll make him wish he'd never set foot in this town," Ray grumbled.

"Stay away from him," she insisted, her heart skipping a beat. She didn't want Ray anywhere near that killer! "Let Luther and the FBI handle it."

"I don't run from trouble, Gracie." He didn't say *That's your way of handling things,* but she heard it in his voice, anyway.

"That doesn't mean you have to run headlong into it."

He lifted his eyes to hers. "We're not going to talk about this anymore tonight."

She nodded her agreement.

Ray dropped the washcloth on the end table. "Better?" he asked.

"Better."

He took her face in his hands and searched her eyes, his own eyes so blue it almost hurt to look at them. "You scared me half to death."

"I know," she whispered.

"When I saw that car headed for you..." He shook his head. "It was like my life flashed before my eyes."

She nodded, understanding all too well.

He continued to hold her face in his warm hands, coming closer to plant a kiss high on her cheek. "But you're okay," he whispered.

"Yes."

He kissed the other cheek. "I wish you would stop shaking."

"Me, too." But right now she felt like she'd never stop trembling.

Ray leaned forward and tenderly brushed his mouth against her forehead, then he closed his eyes and rested his forehead against hers, there where he'd just kissed her. "You're safe, now."

"I know that." She rested her palms against his cheeks, caressed the skin rough with an evening's beard stubble. Tough as he was, he seemed to need comforting as much as she did.

"I won't let anyone hurt you."

"I know that, too." She kissed him on the mouth, a soft, brief touch meant to soothe.

Ray pulled her head against his shoulder, leaned back and relaxed, and held her tight. She melted against him, seeking warmth and solace in his embrace. Sheltered from the world. His arms protected her, his warmth chased away the chill that had grabbed her so completely. She hadn't even realized she was cold until Ray's closeness warmed her. He enveloped her in sweet heat, and slowly but surely the trembling and the fear faded away.

For a while they didn't move at all. It was as if they didn't so much as *breathe,* the stillness was so complete.

This was where she belonged, she knew without doubt. In Ray's arms, her head against his shoulder, his arms folded around her. In the quiet stillness they somehow melded together, completed one another, and the world became a better place.

When Ray did move it was to lift a slow hand to her hair. One by one he removed the pins that had held her once-elegant bun in place. When her hair came down he brushed the strands back and down with his fingers.

Still without saying a word, he kissed the top of her head. Laid his head there for a long moment and sighed deeply. She felt him, finally, relax.

Grace lifted her head and looked at Ray. The sight of his face, handsome and strong, made her heart clench. The lines around his eyes had deepened with worry, his jaw was tense with frustration.

While she studied his face he said nothing. Not a word. After a long moment, he began to feather small kisses on her cheek, her forehead, her neck. He was gentle, achingly tender, but still she saw the distress in his eyes. She felt it in the way his hands held on to her.

She raked her fingers through Ray's hair, through pale

waving strands so soft she didn't want to ever take her hands away. "It's all right," she whispered. "I'm fine, you're fine, nothing else matters."

He didn't look as if he quite believed her, so she laid her lips on his cheek, tasting the saltiness of his skin, raking her mouth over the roughness of his evening stubble as she tried to soothe him. She caressed his neck with comforting fingers, and kissed his other cheek. For a moment she was lost in the scent of him, in the warmth and smell and taste of his skin.

Ray raked his thumbs across her jaw, pushed his fingers through her hair. Repeated her words back to her. "It's all right," he whispered. "Everything's fine, now. Just fine."

The words were not enough. He held her tight, and when she tasted his neck her mouth lingered, sucking gently. The scent of his skin and the sensation of his flesh against her mouth overpowered her. She melted, as if her fear thawed when Ray held her so close.

Ray's hands touched and comforted, easy at first and then moving restlessly over her body. How could hands so large and strong be so tender? As his hands drifted over her body his kisses became harder, quicker, almost frantic, until she could barely catch her breath.

In a rare, motionless moment, she gazed deep into his eyes. "Everything's fine."

When their mouths met this time everything changed, softening, deepening. Slowing down. She felt Ray not only on her skin but all the way to the pit of her soul; she tasted and savored him so completely she knew nothing else. Her body throbbed in time with her heartbeat.

His hands stilled, one in her hair, the other on her bare back. He held her close but soft, as if she might break if he clutched her too tightly.

The kiss went on and on, as if to break it would be the

greatest sin of all. This was all the comfort she needed, all she would ever need. His mouth over hers was tender one moment and demanding the next, his tongue thrusting and then very lightly licking her lower lip as he raked his mouth over hers.

Grace wrapped her arms around Ray and leaned back, placing her head against the armrest, drawing him with her. Their mouths never completely parted, though at times it seemed his lips barely touched hers. Those lips brushed and raked and sucked lightly, teased her relentlessly.

Her body was stretched beneath his, languid and on fire, easing and molding to his body with every passing heart-beat. Ray searched for and found the side zipper of her gown and he slowly lowered it, without ever breaking the kiss.

His hand slipped inside the opening to touch her side gently, possessively, raking over her ribs and stirring her with the easy caress. His palm rested there briefly, and then slid down her side, over her hip, to cup her backside. Gen-tle fingers stroked there, teasing and arousing.

Every breath was an effort, every move calculated to bring some part of her body closer to some part of Ray's. Her body was on fire; she began to shake again. With need, this time, not fear. The quiver went deep. Ray's response was evident in the arousal that pressed against her thigh. Knowing that he wanted her gave her hope. Like it or not, he did still feel something for her. Something stronger than either of them dared to admit.

With a sigh against her mouth, he flicked down one shoulder strap and then another, taking her arms from around her neck, one at a time, to slide the thin straps down and over and then lift her arms back into place. Moving almost lazily, he pushed the gown down to bare her breasts. He languidly teased her nipples with his thumbs while he kissed her.

She felt Ray everywhere, ached for him. The woman in her cried for this; his weight and heat and strength above her, touching her, shielding her. Protecting her completely, making promises with his body that he would never make with his heart and mind.

That didn't matter, not tonight.

She grasped at his shirt and held on, pulling him closer, needing the grip to brace herself against the sensations that washed over her.

When his hand slid up her leg and beneath her gown, she parted her thighs and deepened the kiss. A moan caught in her throat as she held Ray tight and lifted her hips slightly off the couch. He impatiently shoved the fabric of her gown up, past her thigh, freeing her so she was unrestrained and could open herself more fully to him.

Ray touched her where she was already wet for him and she couldn't contain the cry that tried to catch in her throat. A deep quiver twisted and tugged at her body. While he stroked her with insistent fingers he drove his tongue deep inside her mouth and she reveled in it, in the force and the passion he couldn't contain.

Over the sound of their mingled breath and the pounding of her heart, she heard the rasp of a zipper, the soft rustle of clothing.

And then he was inside her, pushing, penetrating and stretching. She lifted her leg over his hip to bring him closer, deeper, swaying against and into him.

Ray broke the kiss with a low growl and Grace let her head fall back. Her flesh tingled from head to toe, her body moved instinctively against Ray's, loving him. Needing him. Needing this. Every stroke took her beyond the last. Every thrust took her higher.

He rocked into her hard and fast, again and again until she gave way to the climax that grabbed hold and shook her to her core. She cried out his name, softly; felt and savored his own completion.

I love you. She couldn't tell him that, couldn't confess her feelings and ruin everything. *I always loved you.* He wasn't going to stay, and she had no right to try to hold him with what they had. He called it sex for the sake of sex, and if that's all he wanted from her she'd give it to him. But in her heart she knew that what had happened between them was much more.

He rested his head on her shoulder and she threaded her fingers through his hair, holding him there. She didn't ever want to let him go.

With the heat of the encounter behind her, she noticed the little things. The couch was not quite long enough or wide enough to accommodate them. Her torn dress was bunched around her waist; Ray was more dressed than undressed; in fact he still wore his holster and gun and most of his rented tux. They should have been uncomfortable, but weren't.

He lifted his head and looked down at her. Ray Madigan, who always smiled, who never took anything seriously, had no laughter in his eyes at the moment. He kissed her, briefly and softly.

He brushed the hair out of her face, looked down at their joined bodies and whispered, "I need you so much, Gracie."

She grabbed the lapels of his white dinner jacket and held him close. Feeling brave, she didn't drop her eyes or her hands, or the leg that wrapped around his and held him inside her. With everything she had, she stared into his blue eyes and told him, with her heart, that she loved him.

"Sleep with me," she whispered. "Hold me all night. Make love to me again."

His answer was another searing kiss.

The dip of the bed woke her from a sound sleep, and at first she thought it was a dream. A familiar dream where Ray came to her in the middle of the night.

But when she felt him slip carefully under the covers, she smiled. This was no dream.

She rolled over and eased her arm over his chest. Oh, he felt so good. "Can't sleep?" she murmured.

"No," he said softly. "I didn't mean to wake you."

His arm encircled her possessively, and she rested her head against his shoulder. "That's okay. I kinda like it." It was real. True. Not a dream at all.

She rubbed her hand against his chest, and her fingers brushed the edge of a scar. In the past week she'd seen the scars, touched them as her hands roamed over Ray's body, but for the most part she'd done her best to ignore them. The scars reminded her of why she'd left him six years ago. Of why he would eventually leave her.

More than anything, she wanted to heal the damage she'd done. She wanted to mend the hurt, try to make him understand. After that…whatever happened was up to him.

"After I moved to Chattanooga, I used to dream about the dip of the bed as you slipped into it. Sometimes the sensation was so real I woke expecting, for a few seconds, to find you there."

He didn't say a word.

"I used to love that feeling," she whispered. "That dip of the bed, the soft rustle of you slithering under the sheet. It meant we were together and safe, and that was all I wanted." It had been too much to want, evidently.

His fingers combed through her hair.

"Sounds silly, I guess."

"Not so silly," he said, but she didn't quite believe him.

Grace sat up and reached over to turn on the light. Ray blinked against the brightness, kept his eyes closed for a long moment before opening them again.

Her unerring gaze landed on the scars on his chest; the one near the center that had almost killed him, the smaller, less threatening one on his left shoulder. She reached out and touched that one, letting her fingers linger on the damaged flesh for a moment.

"Does it ever hurt you?" she whispered.

"Sometimes," he admitted. "But not much and not often."

She covered the scar in the center of his chest with her palm. "It hurts me, too," she admitted.

Her hand skimmed down his chest and to the side, to a newer scar she'd felt more than once. It was long and thin, not a bullet wound at all. "What happened here?"

"Knife," Ray said simply.

Grace's stomach turned, flipped and shuddered. She lifted her head and looked Ray in the eye, silently demanding more.

"There was a bust," he said, his voice low and harsh, his eyes pinned to hers. "This half-crazed kid rushed Luther and the knife came out of nowhere. I guess I could've shot the kid instead of trying to take away the knife, but since he was barely fifteen I just didn't have the heart."

She slid the sheet down, slowly uncovering Ray's hard, muscled, toughened body until she found the scar on his thigh, a small, well-healed reminder of the second time he'd been shot. Without reservation she laid her hand over it. Farther down on the same leg there was a long, rough, almost unnoticeable scar.

"What's this one?"

"Road rash. Guy tried to drive off on me."

"What did you do?" Her stomach revolted again. "Grab on to the car and hold on tight?"

Ray shrugged. "Pretty much."

There were other, smaller scars she didn't ask about. Now that she knew why Ray was compelled to throw himself into the middle of it all, why he had to wage this war, she understood. A little. He had a good heart; he'd been avenging his sister's death all his adult life. She knew that, but it didn't make the pain any easier to take.

She wanted to try again to explain, to make him understand why she'd left…but it would be a waste of time and she didn't want to spoil tonight. But surely there was nothing wrong with telling him to be cautious.

"When you go to Mobile, I hope you'll at least be careful," she said, her eyes on the scar on his thigh. "I hate the thought of you…" her voice almost cracked, so she stopped.

If Ray asked her, right this minute, to go to Mobile with him, she'd say yes. That would be a mistake. A big one. She wasn't sure she could take the uncertainty now any more than she'd been able to take it six years ago. She loved him, she needed him, but she wouldn't try to make this work and then leave him again. Hurt him again. This time he would have to be the one to do the leaving. That was the way it had to be.

Maybe since this time leaving would be his move, his call, it would take away some of the sting of the last parting. He wouldn't be the one deserted, this time.

He took her chin in his hand and pulled her to him for a kiss. They would make love again, she knew, and there would be no more talk of Mobile or scars or the tempting dip of mattresses. This was all they could have, and she'd greedily take it.

* * *

He'd made love to Grace again, slow and easy with the light shining on her face and her body. A short time later she'd fallen asleep with her head on his chest and her hand over the scar on his shoulder. She slept like she didn't have a care in the world; Ray wondered if he'd ever sleep again.

He'd always thought that Grace left because she didn't love him enough, that the nonsense about the job being too harsh was just that. Nonsense. An excuse. He'd told himself that was true again and again, building on the anger he hid so well. The anger that had kept him from literally falling apart without her.

But tonight…he'd seen the pain in her eyes as she'd touched his scars, heard the desperation in her voice as she asked him, so hesitantly, to be careful when he went to Mobile. She didn't ask him not to go, didn't tell him he was crazy for needing to do this. She didn't threaten to hate him if he left or to leave if he didn't change his ways. She just asked him to be careful.

It would have been easier if she'd issued demands, if she'd given him an ultimatum. He knew how to deal with demands and ultimatums. He wasn't sure he knew how to deal with this.

Grace hadn't left him, six long years ago, because she didn't love him anymore. She'd left because she loved him too much. He'd seen the truth in her eyes, as she'd hesitantly laid her hands over his battle scars and asked him to be careful. That realization shouldn't make any difference, not after all this time, but it did. Dammit, it did.

With a gloved hand, Freddie knocked soundly on the door. It was bright and early on Saturday, and he didn't have a moment to waste. He'd promised a half asleep Jenny he'd be right back with breakfast.

When his client answered, the man's eyes widened and he backed up, stumbling over his own feet. "What are you doing here? Shouldn't you be out of town by now?" He looked up and down the deserted street. "Did anyone see you?"

The man looked ridiculous in his silk pajamas. "No one saw me, and I would be far from here by now if everything hadn't gotten so messed up," Freddie said sensibly as he forced his way inside and closed the door behind him. "There's still the witness to take care of. The woman who saw me."

"Then take care of her," the man seethed. "Why are you here? Do you want more money? Forget it. You mucked this up, you handle it on your own."

Freddie looked around the nice, boring house. The furniture was unimpressive, the walls bare. It was a soulless house. No one would miss this man, not really. He was a coward who paid others to do his dirty work. A weasel of a man, in Freddie's estimation. If the cops ever got onto him he'd squeal in a heartbeat.

He had no respect for his client. In truth, he had no respect for any of his clientele, except the occasional woman in need. Like Martha, whose name was tattooed on his bicep, he thought with a fleeting touch of a tender memory. Any self-respecting man took care of his own business.

"I always clean up my own messes," Freddie said softly. "It doesn't pay to leave loose ends."

The man never knew what hit him. Freddie took care of his problem and left the house, taking off his gloves only after he was behind the wheel of Jenny's car.

He had a powerful hankering for a couple of sausage biscuits.

* * *

Grace came awake to an unexpected sound; Ray was singing in the shower. She smiled as she lifted her head from the pillow. This particular song was not familiar, but it was funny and offbeat and *definitely* Lyle Lovett.

Ray had said he didn't sing in the shower anymore, that it was a quirk he'd outgrown. She wondered if that was true, or if, maybe, he only sang for her. The idea warmed her to her soul. He sang just for her, for them, and he probably didn't even know it.

Did she make him happy? Did she free something in his soul?

Grace slipped from the bed and made her way to the bathroom, standing silently in the steamy room and listening. She would remember this moment forever. A man singing off-key shouldn't make her feel so damn good, but it did. She smiled as she listened to the words, then finally laughed out loud as she opened the shower door.

"That's a new one," she said as Ray turned, surprised, to face her. He looked so good, warm and muscled and slick with soap. Water ran down his face, down his hard body. Heavens, she knew every inch of that body, didn't she? Every scar, every sensitive spot.

He tempted her with a smile, with the undeniable passion in his eyes. For today he was hers. Tomorrow could wait a while longer.

"'Skinny Legs' is not a new song," he said with a grin. "You just haven't been keeping up properly."

"Sorry." She didn't think twice before stepping into the shower to join Ray under the fine spray. The stall was large, but she stood so close her body brushed his. A mist of warm water fell over her face and dampened her hair. She gave him a sweet good morning kiss amidst the spray that turned deep and searing. Touching him, just being this close to him, aroused her all over again. After last night she shouldn't have anything else to give, but she did.

So did Ray, apparently.

He wrapped his wet arms around her, rubbed his hands up and down her spine. "Are you here to scrub my back?"

She shook her head and planted a dainty kiss on his wet chest.

"My front?" he asked with a lift of his eyebrows as she rose up on her toes and draped her arms around his neck, pressing her chest to his.

She gave Ray a heartfelt and wicked smile all her own. "Maybe."

Chapter 15

"Maybe we got it all wrong," Grace said dreamily, leaning back on the couch where he'd made love to her last night. She wore one of his T-shirts, shorts that showed off her fine legs, and a pair of white socks to keep her feet warm. And she looked as good right now as she had dancing in her fancy red gown.

"What did we get wrong?" He leaned against the bar, sipping at a cup of terrible coffee and trying to look casual, feeling totally *un*casual. His nerves were too close to the surface, the air crackled with electricity. Something had changed last night. Grace came to him as if the past six years had never happened. As if she still loved him. Skin deep, my ass.

"I don't think Louise is involved at all." Grace tapped her chin thoughtfully with her finger. "She said their marriage had been over for years, and yet neither of them made any move to get a divorce. Why? I mean, if Louise wanted out she wouldn't have hesitated. Maybe she isn't as tough as I originally thought she was, but she is a strong woman. I can't see her taking a lot of grief from Carter without doing something about it.'' She stretched her arms over her head.

Watching her, Ray smiled. Skin deep or not, Grace touched him in ways no other woman ever had. Or ever would. ''Maybe they didn't divorce because they liked things the way they were.''

''Exactly,'' she sat up straight and looked squarely at him. ''Let's face it, there was plenty of money to go around.''

''Some people never get enough,'' he said with a shake of his head. ''They can't stand to part with a dime…''

''But a divorce would've left Louise and Carter both fairly well off, and if they were truly miserable…'' She narrowed her eyes. ''Maybe they weren't completely miserable. Maybe they were…*comfortable.*''

Ray shrugged his shoulders and set the bad coffee aside. ''Carter had his affairs and Louise had hers. They were fairly discreet, so they fooled around when the mood struck them but still had the prestige and the money and the big house and the society crap that comes with it all.''

Grace nodded. ''And if a paramour got too close, maybe thinking about getting their hands on some of that money, the marriage was a quick way to put an end to things. Sorry, honey, you're fun in bed but I have this wife at home…''

''Or this husband,'' he interjected.

''Or this husband.''

Ray began to pace. Maybe she had a point. ''So everything was hunky-dory until Heather came along. She threatened to throw a monkey wrench into the works. The affair got too serious. Carter was going to leave Louise for her.''

Pacing still, he laid his eyes on a contemplating Grace. Talking with her about someone else's marriage and divorce made his mind turn, unwillingly, to their own. Maybe their marriage hadn't worked, maybe they'd screwed everything up royally. But he never would've cheated on her, and he knew without a doubt that she never would've cheated on him. If they were right about the Lanfords' situation…hell, that wasn't a marriage at all.

"Was he really going to leave Louise?" Grace asked softly, thinking aloud. "All we have is Heather's word on that. No one else has mentioned anything about a possible divorce."

"True," Ray agreed. "Besides, if the object of the hit was to put an end to a relationship that got too serious, Heather is the obvious target. Her death, if arranged properly, raises much less fuss than Lanford's and ends the threat just as permanently."

"So it wasn't Louise," Grace said with finality. She looked almost relieved.

Ray wandered about the room until he ended up before the couch where Grace lounged. He stopped pacing and stared down at her. "What about Reed?"

She shook her head. "I don't think so. His affair with Louise was over long ago. Heather said they were on again off again, but I think they were definitely off for good. Reed might've felt a little put out about the way the relationship ended, but murder? It doesn't make sense. Even if he did away with Carter, that didn't mean Louise would come back to him. What did it really accomplish for him?"

Reaching out casually, she laid a soft hand against the side of his leg. The touch wasn't sexual or demanding, it was just an unconscious search for attachment. A casual, intimate contact. He liked it. He liked it too much.

"Besides," she said, "assistant D.A.s don't make that

much money. The family wealth is there, but I have a feeling Elliott has to explain away every dime he gets from his mother. Do hit men give receipts?''

Ray grinned. She was getting into this. "Okay, Sherlock. What about McCann?''

She shook her head and trailed her hand down his thigh to his knee. "I can definitely see Ben killing for love. He has that kind of fiery passion in his eyes.''

"Fiery passion?'' Ray repeated. He didn't much like the fact that Grace so obviously liked McCann.

She ignored him. "But he's not the type to hire it out. If he wanted Carter dead, he would've done it himself.''

"That leaves Heather,'' Ray said. "Maybe things went south with her and Carter and no one knew about it but the two of them. A woman scorned, and all that.''

Grace shook her head again. "Nope. I don't think so. But even if it is, she loses too much by getting rid of Carter. She would've been better off blackmailing him. Louise probably knew all along what was going on, but if Heather went public with the affair it would be damaging to them both.''

She made sense, and he trusted her instincts. She knew people. Always had. She'd seen right through him, hadn't she? "So who?'' He sat beside her and draped his arm over her shoulder.

Snuggling against him, she continued her line of reasoning. "Unless there's some other ingredient here we don't have, like a mob connection or a dirty business deal…''

Grace closed her eyes and made herself more comfortable, wriggling against his side so warm and soft he was ready to forget Carter Lanford completely. He was ready and willing to forget everything. Damnation.

"I think Heather is the key,'' Grace said. "She didn't

do it herself, but maybe someone who cares about her, someone who loves her and hated to see her used, would despise Carter enough to do away with him.''

Ray leaned back and decided to simply enjoy the way Grace felt right this minute. Her softness. Her presence. And still his mind worked.

''And then this person would be there to comfort Heather when her sugar daddy's gone,'' he said.

''Maybe.''

Ray knew without doubt that he would kill for Grace, if he had to. She was his in too many ways to count, and he would do anything to protect her. Like it or not. So, who loved Heather that way?

Only one name came to mind. ''Hatch,'' he said softly. ''Christopher Hatcher. He follows Heather around like a puppy dog, her moony-eyed, adoring slave. At the office, last night at the ball...'' Unfortunately the scenario didn't quite work. ''But he wouldn't have the money to hire a pro like Potts.''

''Are you sure?''

There were too many unknowns here. Heather might have a dozen secret admirers, an old boyfriend with a screw loose, a skeleton in her closet. ''I can mention the possibility to Luther and have him check it out. I just don't see the money trail. Hatch's job at Lanford Systems is definitely low level. He's a techie, not a corporate guy. The money didn't come from there.''

Grace sighed, a long despairing sigh that came awfully close to a moan. ''Luther will take forever, if he bothers to check at all.'' After a moment a smile bloomed on her beautiful face.

Ray placed his face close to hers. Nose to nose. Not quite mouth to mouth. ''What are you thinking?''

''Do you have your laptop with you?''

She started with a search on Hatcher's name, and a quick e-mail to a couple of talented cyberfriends. She'd never met Badger or Crash, didn't know their real names and never would, but when it came time to do the impossible with a computer, they were good friends to have. They had taught her that with the right software and enough talent and patience, you could find out just about anything with a laptop and a phone line.

What came next was a little more complicated than browsing through old newspaper articles, and it took a while longer. She couldn't ask Badger or Crash to do this particular chore for her.

She had to get in and get out as quickly as possible, before someone on the other end tried to trace her. Going through Christopher Hatcher's computer system at work, she was able to access the personal information he had stored there. For a computer geek, he was incredibly lax. Then again, maybe he didn't think anyone was as smart as he was, and wouldn't know how to hack into his system.

The longer she was connected the more likely she was to get caught. As it was, she was leaving a trail a mile wide. Just as she was about to sign off and tell Ray what she'd found, she got an e-mail from Badger that confirmed what she'd found.

She'd been sitting here with the computer in her lap for more than an hour, probably closer to two, and Ray had hardly moved. He stood nearby, he paced restlessly, but he didn't let her out of his sight.

"Okay," she said, glancing up at Ray. "Hatch's father died last year and he got a big inheritance and a pretty decent insurance check." She leaned toward the computer screen. "It all went in the bank, where it sat untouched until…two months ago. He made a large withdrawal, and last week he made an identical withdrawal."

"What kind of money are we talking about?" Ray asked.

"He definitely didn't have to stay on as Lanford's number one techie, that's for sure," Grace said as she logged off.

"Unless he wanted to stay close to Heather," Ray added.

"Which would be kinda sweet if he hadn't hired Freddie Potts to kill off the competition," Grace said as she closed the laptop and set it aside.

"How did you get all this?"

Grace smiled, glad she could impress him. "Lanford Systems has a T1."

He raised his eyebrows in silent question.

"Which means they have a set IP and are basically on and vulnerable all the time. I got into Hatch's system at work, where he foolishly kept a lot of personal information." She shrugged her shoulders. "My online friend Badger got some of the info on the insurance and the bank balance."

"Badger," Ray deadpanned. He crossed his arms and stared down at her, temptingly impressive as always. "I could've used you a thousand times in the past year. If you ever want a job as a P.I., give me a call."

Her heart hitched a little. Had she ever really thought that she didn't love him anymore? That she could look at him and convince herself that what they had was over and done? She looked at him and saw the man who protected her; who loved her, whether he liked it or not.

Working with Ray sounded great, like a dream come true, but he was going to Mobile as soon as this threat was over. Wasn't he?

"What do we do now?" she asked, ignoring his suggestion.

"Call Luther."

This time her heart leapt unpleasantly. "You can't tell Luther that I hacked into Hatcher's computer," she said, horrified. "He'd *love* to arrest me and hand me over to the FBI. And you absolutely can't tell him about Badger."

Ray looked supremely unconcerned. "I'll tell him I have a hunch and let him follow it from here and see where it lands."

"He won't follow through, you know he won't. Luther never believed in anyone's hunches but his own," she argued. Besides, she didn't want to bring the cops and the FBI in now. There were too many other explanations for the information she'd found.

"He will," Ray said, not sounding very convinced. "Eventually."

Grace stood and looped her arms around Ray's neck. Rested her body against his and breathed deep. "I have a better idea."

Hatch's house wasn't nearly as upscale as Heather's. It was an ordinary little frame house on an ordinary little street. The lawn had been mowed, but no attempt had been made to pretty the place up with flowers or neatly arranged bushes.

Ray glanced at Grace, caught her studying the house as if she could see through the drawn curtains.

"You're becoming quite the little investigator," he said as he shut off the engine at the curb.

She turned her head to look at him. "I just want to get Potts caught and put behind bars. Don't you?"

"Sure." He threw open his door and stepped onto the street. Grace waited in the passenger seat while he rounded the car to open her door for her.

Once this was over and Grace was no longer in jeopardy, what would happen? When the pursuit of Potts and the threat to her life was done, she wouldn't need him anymore. He could head to Mobile and report to Stan's undercover unit, and Grace could go back to her quiet, uneventful life. A life without worry or danger or passion. And without him. Was that what she really wanted?

Their conclusion that Hatcher might've been the one who'd hired Potts was reaching, at best. And Grace's suggestion that they call on Hatcher themselves instead of calling Luther was unlike her. Maybe he was bringing out a long hidden adventurous spirit. Then again, maybe Grace had simply wanted to get out of the suite for a while. Maybe the walls were already closing in on her.

He rang the bell, then knocked loudly. Nothing.

"Maybe he's not home," Grace said, her voice low and soft. This had been her idea, but she was obviously having second thoughts.

Ray grinned. "You don't have to whisper."

She looked annoyed and properly chastised as he banged on the door again.

Nothing.

Ray cocked his ear toward the door. "Did you hear that?"

Grace held her breath. "What?" She still kept her voice at a whisper.

"I could've sworn I heard someone say *come in*. Didn't you hear it?"

She shook her head.

"There it is again," Ray said, lowering his own voice. "Didn't you hear it that time?"

Grace shook her head. "I didn't hear anything."

"Yes, you did," he insisted, looking deep into her warm, dark eyes.

She started to shake her head again, and then stopped. The shake turned into a nod. "Oh."

He reached for the doorknob. Grace's hand shot out and covered his.

"This is breaking and entering," she whispered.

"What's a little B and E to a hacker?"

She blushed.

"Besides," he said as together their hands turned easily. "The door's unlocked. I don't think *entering* alone is much of a crime."

She cowered behind him as he stepped into the small foyer and called out. "Hello?"

"I don't think he's here," Grace said. Her whisper was now no more than a soft wisp of air. She grabbed onto the tail end of his shirt and held on tight.

"Let's have a look around." He glanced over his shoulder as he stepped into the living room. Grace's face was pale, her eyes wide and afraid. His Gracie? Adventurous? Never. "Don't touch any…"

Her focus changed, her grip on his shirt tightened, and she clapped a hand to her mouth. Ray snapped his head around to see what caused her reaction.

Christopher Hatcher, dead, was slumped in a heap of flesh and bones and wrinkled green silk pajamas on the floor of his living room. There was no blood, but his head was twisted in an unnatural position and his open eyes stared sightlessly to the ceiling.

Ray grabbed his Colt and spun around slowly. Nothing in the room breathed or moved, but for him and Grace. Hatch was long dead; Potts was long gone. Grace hid her face against his back and cursed low and soft, her words lost in a sob. He steered her into the foyer, where Hatcher's body would be out of her sight.

While he held her he studied the area around the knob

on the front door, checked out the condition of the frame. There was no sign of forced entry, not at this entrance, anyway.

"What do we do now?" Grace whispered when she'd regained her composure.

"Call Luther."

"He'll arrest us," she said. "We can't claim that Hatcher said *come in,* now can we?"

"We have no choice."

They went into the kitchen and, using a kitchen towel to protect possible fingerprints on the phone, Ray called Luther at home.

Again, he woke the homicide detective up.

"I didn't get to bed until six," Luther grumbled when he was awake enough to realize who was on the other end of the line.

"You get back to sleep, then," Ray said tersely. "I'll call the Feds and let them handle Potts's latest victim. You know, the one most likely who hired him to kill Carter Lanford."

Luther's voice changed, was immediately alert. "Where the hell are you?"

She'd seen enough death to last her a lifetime.

By the time she and Ray got back to the suite and closed the door behind them, Grace was ready to collapse. Luther had been unrelenting in his interrogation, and had made it clear that they were both very lucky not to be spending the night in jail.

All she wanted to do was hold Ray and cry. She didn't know exactly why she wanted to cry. Not for Christopher Hatcher, who had almost certainly hired Freddie Potts to kill Carter Lanford. Not even for Heather Farmer, who had lost both her lover and her friend in a little more than a week.

Ray, knowing she was upset, gathered her against his chest as soon as the door was closed and locked behind them. And she knew, as he held her close, that what she wanted to cry for was *them*. For Ray and for her. For everything they'd missed and would miss in the years ahead. Tears stung her eyes. Luther was right. If she and Ray couldn't make it, how did anyone in the world have a chance at lasting happiness?

He lived with death and danger. She needed to be safe. He lived on the edge. She needed *him* to be safe. All they had was their love for each other, and dammit it wasn't enough.

No matter how shaken she was, she remained determined to stay as long as Ray would have her. He'd made the choice to go to Mobile, and she would not walk away from him again, no matter what. She would not offer ultimatums or demand that he choose her over his life's work. But she wouldn't follow him, either.

All they had was this moment, and she was determined to savor it the way she continued to savor her memories of the time they'd had before their marriage had started to fall apart.

He stroked her hair. "You have to put it out of your mind. Dismiss it. Forget what you saw."

He made it sound so easy…

"Come on. Change your clothes, brush your hair, and I'll take you somewhere nice for dinner." His hands stroked her back comfortingly, with an easy, tender strength. "Steak. Chinese. Seafood. You pick. Anything you want, Gracie."

She lifted her head to look at Ray. The tears in her eyes were already dried, leaving only a hint of a sting behind.

She studied him carefully, lovingly, memorizing the cut of his jaw, the softness of his mouth, the depth and passion in his startling blue eyes. The strength and gentleness that made him who he was. As she looked, she traced his jaw with a lazy finger. She was tempted to tell him she loved him, still. That she had never fallen out of love, no matter how hard she'd tried.

But all he wanted was this, their physical connection, a temporary affair before he moved on. He was no doubt working her out of his system the same way she'd so foolishly planned to work him out of hers.

Once he went to Mobile he would replace her. The way he'd replaced her before.

But she didn't care about that. Not now. All she cared about was this moment. Tonight.

"I have a better idea," she whispered, rising up on her toes to softly kiss Ray. "How about you order us a pizza."

Chapter 16

They ordered pizza, ate it hot *and* cold, and then settled on the couch in front of the television. Ray in a pair of boxers, Grace in a T-shirt. She leaned against his side, and Ray wrapped his arm possessively around her. Exhausted, sated, snuggled against his warm, male skin, she was perfectly contented.

Where did he get his courage? she wondered. Had he been born with it? Or had his bravery been built, one iota, one crisis, at a time. She could use a little courage herself, right now. Courage to stay. Courage to speak the uncensored truth.

It was nearly ten o'clock when someone banged on the hotel room door. Ray reached for the pistol on the table by the couch and shooed Grace toward the bedroom. She hadn't taken two steps before Luther called out, letting them know it was he at the door.

Grace went to the bedroom and pulled on a thick terry-cloth robe, and Ray grabbed his jeans from the chair near the blue couch, where he'd tossed them a while ago. She reentered the main room as Ray opened the door and Luther breezed in. She wasn't hiding from this. Whatever he had to say, she wanted to hear it all.

"You all right?" Luther asked Grace, gruff and semi-concerned.

"I'm fine," she answered softly, remembering their conversation from last night. Luther thought she was bad for Ray, would hurt him again. Not for the world...

She would like to think that this was a purely social call, but after the day's grisly discovery she assumed Luther had more questions about Christopher Hatcher's murder. Besides, with his rumpled suit and piercing eyes and clenched jaw, he looked to be all business.

"Do you know her?" Luther thrust his hand out, showing Grace a simply framed 5 X 7 photograph of a fair-haired woman.

"She looks familiar," Grace said, racking her brain.

"She lived one street over and a block down from you."

Knowing that, the vague memories came together easily. "I used to see her out running. We'd wave, but I didn't know her."

"Gillian Bickmore."

"You said *lived*," Ray said tersely. "Past tense."

"Her body was found this morning, by a neighbor wondering why she hadn't collected her papers for the past couple of days." Luther reached into his pocket for a hard candy, but didn't open it. He played with it, rolling it in his nervous fingers. "He snooped around, peeking through windows until he saw her. It appears that she was poisoned, though I won't have the results of the autopsy for a few days."

He told them about Gillian's missed days at work and

the new boyfriend, Jimmy, she'd told her co-workers about. And that she'd been dead a couple of days.

"Since we ID'd Potts," Ray said.

Luther nodded. "Yeah. This one was weird, too. Gave me the creeps. The woman was laid out on her bed dressed in a sexy nightgown. Her hair was combed, she was wearing makeup, it looked like someone had straightened the sheets and covers around her so she'd look nice and neat once she was dead. Whatever poison or drugs he used, it wasn't something that caused pain. The expression on her face was almost peaceful." He shuddered and slipped the cellophane off his candy. "The pillows were fluffed up, a dim bedside light was left burning. It was almost as if the man who killed Bickmore...*liked* her." He shuddered as he popped the candy into his mouth.

"Any hard evidence?" Ray asked, his voice soft.

Luther shook his head. "Not yet. Crime scene techs are still there, but so far they haven't found a single fingerprint in the whole house." He cursed under his breath and bit down on his candy with a loud crunch. "If Potts is staying with a woman, or moving from one to another, unless someone recognizes him there's no way we can track him. He's apparently changing his look regularly, since Gillian's co-workers said she described him as a brown-eyed blond hunk," he rolled his eyes in apparent disgust, "and Grace said when she saw him kill Lanford he had brown hair and pale blue or green eyes..."

"He did," she said softly.

"And you said he had dark hair when you saw him last night."

She nodded her confirmation.

"Maybe we're talking about two different men," Ray suggested. "We don't know that Gillian Bickmore's

Jimmy is Freddie Potts. Method of death is different, and the physical descriptions don't match.''

"Only hair and eye color are different," Luther snapped. "They can be easily changed. He's a big guy, and he was in Grace's neighborhood. This *Jimmy* picked Gillian up while they were both jogging."

Ray muttered something foul, and Grace winced. It was Potts, she knew it. He'd watched and waited and hooked up with a poor woman who had simply been in the wrong place at the wrong time. The hit man had been close, all this time.

"One way or another we have to find this guy. I don't need any more dead people in my town, you hear me?" Luther ran a distracted hand through his hair. "Unfortunately we have no way to go to Potts," he said softly. "We're going to have to wait and hope he comes to you."

"No," Ray said without hesitation, pointing an accusing finger at his ex-partner. "Grace is not going to be your bait. I'm not going to troll her around town and wait for this guy to bite."

The tired homicide detective grabbed another hard candy from his jacket pocket, glanced at the peppermint and then dropped it back. He looked plumb worn-out. "Do you really think we'll have to do that?"

Grace looked up at Ray. Luther was right. They might be able to hide for a while, but Potts was still out there and he was coming for her.

Luther had delivered nothing but bad news, and he wasn't finished. "Ray," he said. "Can I have a word with you?" He jerked his head toward the door that led to the hallway.

"I'll go…" Grace began.

"No," Ray said, grabbing her arm and pulling her to him, forcing her to remain at his side. "Whatever Luther's got to say, you can hear it.'' He laid sharp eyes on Luther and silently dared him to argue.

Luther just sighed. ''It's Morgan,'' he said, jerking his head to the hallway again as if he expected that bit of information to change Ray's mind.

Ray groaned softly, low in his throat. It was a growl of pure frustration. ''She knows. What about him?''

''Daniels opened his big mouth and blabbed.'' Luther scowled. ''He denied it, but Morgan and his cameraman were at the Hatcher house less than an hour after you left, and he was asking a lot of *very* informed questions. He already knows too much.'' Luther laid his almost-apologetic eyes on Grace. ''He knows about you.''

Ray cursed, low and long, and pulled her tighter against his side. ''I swear, if Morgan uses Grace's name or picture on the air, I'll do a hell of a lot more than break his damned nose again.''

''Doesn't he have a restraining order against you?'' Luther asked.

''Yeah.'' Ray raked a distracted hand up and down Grace's arm. ''And if he's smart, he'll stay far enough away to keep me from violating that court order.''

Knowing Potts was still around, and that he had most likely killed again, made Ray edgy. He wasn't any calmer than he'd been last night when Luther had delivered the news.

He didn't want her to leave the suite at all; every time someone passed in the hallway he tensed. And he couldn't stand still. He fidgeted and mumbled and paced.

Grace tried to convince herself that the last two nights had been a mistake. She couldn't do it. Nothing that felt so good and right could be a *mistake*. She loved Ray, she adored him, and together they had something special. Until he stirred things up by getting himself hurt. Until she ruined everything by bolting like a frightened rabbit.

She couldn't stand to sit here and watch Ray pace, so she left the couch on silent sock-covered feet and crept up behind him, wrapping her arms around his waist and resting her head against his back. This was such a wonderful place to be, safe and sheltered. Together after so long. All those years ago, when she'd known she couldn't live without Ray, she'd been right. For the past six years she had not been living. She'd been existing. Making it from one indifferent day to the next waiting for the numbness to go away, waiting for this moment.

He covered her hands with one of his, threaded his fingers through hers.

"Looking to kill a few minutes in the sack?" he asked, his voice not quite as casual as he tried to make it.

"No," she whispered.

"Well then, don't go pawing all over me, baby," he said gruffly. "I have a hair trigger where you're concerned."

She didn't back away, but rested her cheek against his back and held on tight, closing her eyes and breathing deep.

She'd been a coward for so long, and in so many ways. If only she had a touch of Ray's strength, just a little of his daring…

"I love you," she whispered.

He didn't say a word, but tensed in her arms. The muscles in his back and his stomach went rigid. As far as she could tell he didn't breathe.

"Don't go ruining a good thing," he finally said softly. "Just because we're good in the sack and I'm keeping watch and you're scared…"

"That has nothing to do with it." She rotated her head

and rested her chin against his back. It was easier this way, not looking at his face, not staring into those intense blue eyes. Maybe she'd found a little courage, but she was still far from brave. "I've always loved you, Ray."

He turned around, took her chin in his hands and forced her to look at him. He had always made her face her worst fears, hadn't he? He'd always asked for just a little too much.

"Then why did you leave?" he asked softly. "Give me a reason I can understand."

She couldn't think of another way to tell him, she couldn't explain anymore. "I love you."

The pager he had clipped to his belt beeped; a discordant noise at the most wrong of times. He reached down and touched it blindly and the beeping stopped.

"You love me when everything's going your way," he said darkly, frustrated. "When all the pieces of the puzzle fit to suit you." He placed his face close to hers. "What if I ask you to go to Mobile with me? Would you? Could you take it? Or would you run again? Would you try to make it work and then leave a year from now? A month? I couldn't take that, Grace, wondering if you'd be there or not when I got home." He stroked her arm once. "So tell me," he asked again, his tense voice telling her he thought he knew what her answer would be. "What would you say?"

"I don't know," she whispered, trying to be honest, trying not to hide her fears this time. "It's not...it's not that easy."

"Yes, it is." He lowered his head as if to kiss her then stopped suddenly, as if he'd changed his mind.

The pager went off again, and this time he cursed as he snapped it up to look at the display.

"Who is it?"

"Trish," he muttered, returning the pager to its place and making no move toward the phone.

Of course, Trish. Grace had to make herself remember that while she hadn't been able to move on, Ray certainly had. He'd married two more times after she'd left. Who knows how many other women there had been in his life? He hadn't moped around for the past six years, he hadn't stopped living or loving.

"I'm sorry," she said, backing away one step. "I just got carried away, I guess. The two of us being back together, all this excitement..." her voice cracked. "The past couple of nights."

"Are you taking it back?"

It would be easiest to say yes, wouldn't it? To blame her declaration on sentimentality and laugh it off.

"No," she said, her voice low but very clear.

The pager went off again.

"Dammit," Ray muttered, lifting the pager again and glancing down at it. "What the hell does she want?"

"Call her," Grace said, turning her back to Ray. "It must be important for her to page you three times."

"I might as well," he said as he walked to the telephone on the table by the end of the couch. "She'll just keep paging me until I do."

Grace busied herself, frantically straightening the Sunday paper until it was needlessly neat.

She tried not to listen to Ray's conversation with his second wife, but his urgent tone stopped her cold.

"What? No...no...I'm on my way."

He slammed the phone down. "Trish has had an accident."

"Is she okay?"

Ray nodded. "Her car's totaled and she's a basket case.

Her fiancé is with her, but she says he's as upset as she is and isn't much help at the moment. I gotta go.''

Of course he wouldn't turn his back on Trish, any more than he would have turned his back on her when she needed him. It was in his character to be there, to watch over those who couldn't take care of themselves. Was that all they had?

"I'll stay here."

"No, you won't." He took her arm and steered her toward the door. "I'm not leaving you alone and it would take forever to get Luther over here."

Unwilling to argue with him, Grace stepped into her shoes. "Any more ex-wives and you won't have time for any career at all, much less undercover work," she snapped, annoyed that their conversation had not taken the turn she would've liked.

"Tell me about it," Ray muttered as he checked the deserted hallway before he pulled her into the hall and closed the door behind them.

Freddie sat on the hill above Trish Madigan's apartment complex, his back against a leafy tree, the gun in his lap hidden from view by a magazine he'd picked up at a convenience store, along with his soda and cigarettes. He wished he'd picked a more interesting magazine. He needed something to cover the gun, in case anyone happened to walk by. Not likely up on this tree-covered hill, but he had to be prepared for anything.

He grumbled. His accountant handled all his financial matters. Why had he picked up this magazine that was about nothing else?

Tracking Trish Madigan down had been a breeze; running her off the road had actually been fun. Like the old days, when he'd been just starting out. The boyfriend had driven the blonde home a half hour ago, and if he knew this broad at all the first thing she'd done was call her ex. And if he knew Madigan at all, the man was on his way.

Madigan would either have the witness with him, the simplest scenario from Freddie's viewpoint, or else he'd come alone. If that was the case, when he left Freddie would follow to wherever he had the witness stashed.

Once the witness was disposed of, he'd be out of Alabama in a flash. Florida, he thought with a smile. Maybe the Keys. He wished he could ask Jenny to go with him, but that was a complication he'd have to do without. When he'd left her this morning he hadn't even told her he wouldn't be calling her or coming back, he'd just walked out. Made him feel sorta like a heel.

A gray car pulling into the parking lot made Freddie forget all his regrets. He saw Madigan in the driver's seat and, as he pulled into a parking space, a dark-haired passenger at his side.

Show time.

"I'll wait in the car," Grace said calmly as Ray turned off the engine.

"You will not," he responded without so much as glancing at her.

How could she tell Ray that she had no desire to stand back and watch while he comforted his second wife? She'd already made a fool of herself and confessed that she still loved him, for all the good it did. He'd been right all along. All they had was a physical connection, a sexual affinity for one another. When this was over he'd head to Mobile and find wife number four, a Lyle Lovett fan who wouldn't mind so much when he didn't come home for days at a time, when he threw himself in front of a bullet.

"Trish asked for you, not me," she said, looking out

the window. "I'm not as good with hysterical women as you are."

"Yeah, well, it's a gift," he muttered, throwing open his door and stepping out.

For a moment, Grace thought he was going to allow her to sit in the passenger seat and mope to her heart's content, but he crossed behind the car and threw open her door. Offered his hand insistently even as he suspiciously searched the parking lot. He watched a man at the other end of the apartment building gallop down the stairs, car keys in hand.

"I can't leave you sitting out here unprotected. Come on, Grace. Don't be unreasonable." He was impatient, at the end of his rope.

She placed her hand in his and swiveled, placing her feet on the ground. "Heaven forbid that I should be *unreasonable*," she said as she stood.

He stared at her, hard and unflinching, unforgiving and unrelenting.

A split second before she heard the shot, Ray threw her to the ground. She hit the asphalt, Ray on top of her, as a bullet smacked into the building behind them.

Ray muttered profanely, drawing his own gun and looking toward the hill behind the car. He shielded her with his body, pressing her against the car as he turned his head and searched.

"How did you know..." she began, breathless.

"I saw a glint up there," he said, nodding to the tree-covered hill. "Out of the corner of my eye."

Trish's front door opened. She took one look at the scene before her, screamed, and slammed the door shut. The man who'd been climbing into his pickup truck at the end of the parking lot turned and ran up the stairs.

"Get under the car," Ray ordered.

Grace did as he asked, laid flat on her stomach on the asphalt and scooted under the car. She moved almost to the middle of the sheltered space, leaving room for Ray, but he didn't follow her. When he started to move, she reached out and snagged his pant leg.

"Stay," she whispered.

He lowered his head just enough to look at her. "I can't. You stay here until I get back."

And he was gone, sprinting away.

Trish and the man at the end of the parking lot had probably both called the police. They were on the way, she assured herself. Help was on the way. Would they be in time to help Ray?

Grace looked at oil-stained asphalt close to her face and tried to slow her heartbeat and find her breath. Ray was good, he was very good at what he did. He hadn't survived all these years by being careless. But Potts was good, too. Why couldn't Ray have just stayed here with her? Safe and sound. Protected.

A shot rang out and she flinched. Who had fired? Ray or Potts? From her sheltered spot under the car she had no way of knowing, no way to see what was going on out there.

The seconds ticked past. Or were they minutes? Surely it wasn't long before she heard another shot. Then all was quiet.

She couldn't stand it. What if Ray was out there, bleeding in the parking lot? What if he needed her?

"Ray?" she called softly, peering out from beneath the car, seeing no sign of life nearby. She called again, a little louder, and got no response.

Moving very cautiously, she scooted to the side and peered around the tire. Still no sign of Ray. She scooted a little farther, and saw him walking down the hill. She rolled from beneath the car and slowly up onto her knees. When he saw her, he started to run.

"I haven't found him," he shouted. "Get back…"

She felt the impact of the bullet before she heard the shot. Her shoulder burned, her head swam as she listed back so that her spine rested against the car. Her vision blurred and narrowed. And over Ray's shoulder she saw him. Potts, emerging from the trees like every little girl's bogeyman. His gun was raised. Aimed at Ray.

She tried to scream, to warn Ray, but her voice was much too weak. His name came out as a whisper.

Her image of Ray started to fade away, but before it did his eyes caught hers and he spun around, dropped to the ground, and raised his weapon. He fired, once. Twice. Again. Potts fired in return.

It all happened so fast… On her knees by Ray's car she listened and watched, but she finally lost count of the gunshots and closed her eyes. Unable to remain on her knees, she rolled to the side and rested her cheek against the gritty parking lot.

In the distance she heard sirens.

"Grace?"

She opened her eyes and saw Ray bending over her. He took off his shirt, the plaid one he wore over his T-shirt, and quickly folded it in his hands.

"He shot me," she said weakly. "Are you okay?" she asked, trying to check him out for wounds, blood, a tear in his clothes. He looked to be unhurt.

"I'm fine," he said, pulling her up and toward him to place the folded shirt over her shoulder, supporting her in his lap while he applied pressure to her shoulder front and back. "Potts is dead," he said, his voice shaking.

Trish ran out of her apartment, crying and squealing.

Ray told her to settle down, call 911 and fetch a blanket. She backed off to do as he asked, crying still.

"I should've stayed under the car," she said weakly. "But I couldn't see you, Ray. I heard the shots and I thought that maybe…maybe…" That you'd been shot again. That this time, this time I would have to watch you die.

Trish scurried out of her apartment, bearing a hand-knitted blanket in many pastel colors. She handed it to Ray and peered down at Grace, then turned her eyes out to the parking lot, where Potts lay dead.

"Was that the same guy who ran me off the road?" she asked, her voice faint and slightly squeaky.

"Someone *ran* you off the road?" Ray snapped as he wrapped the blanket around Grace, making sure her legs and arms were covered. "Why the hell didn't you tell me that when you called?"

"I was upset," Trish whispered. "I was going to tell you all about it as soon as you got here."

Ray glanced sharply up at Trish and the slender man who joined her, and they both backed away. Far away.

"Are you sure you're okay?" Grace asked, her voice weak.

"Don't talk," Ray ordered softly, pulling her gently into his arms, keeping the pressure on her shoulder. "This is nothing," he said, his voice oddly unsteady. "The police are coming, an ambulance is on its way, they'll have you fixed up in no time."

She wasn't so sure. Should she be so cold? She started to shake, and Ray held her tighter.

Grace laid her head against his shoulder and closed her eyes. A little nap would be nice, right about now. But not just yet.

"I meant what I said," she whispered. "I do love you."

"Stop this," he ordered. "You're going to be okay. You don't have to make any…any…"

Deathbed confessions. He couldn't say it and neither could she.

Ray tried to hold her close, and keep pressure on her wound, and for a few minutes he whispered calming words she knew he didn't believe. She heard the fear in his voice. Ray Madigan, who was never afraid of anything, was terrified.

Thinking wasn't as easy as it should be. Staying awake was an effort. She made the effort.

"Why didn't you come after me?" she asked. "I never could've looked you in the eye and pretended not to love you anymore. I was just so mad at you for putting yourself in danger all the time. It hurt Ray, it was killing me. I had to do something."

"Don't talk," he said. "Save your strength."

As always, Ray didn't want to talk about it. He didn't want to go back in time and suffer through their divorce all over again. Maybe he was right. Maybe rehashing the past wasn't going to fix things. It certainly wouldn't change what had happened. Grace closed her eyes and rested against his chest. He held her close. So close.

"I left," she said lowly, her breath steady against Ray's shirt, her body shivering. "But you *let* me leave. You weren't supposed to let me leave. Why didn't you come after me?"

He held her tight and rocked gently, the movement slow and steady.

"I did," he whispered. "Dammit, Grace, I went to Chattanooga twice. You weren't hard to track down."

"I wasn't supposed to be," she murmured.

"But when I got there I couldn't face you. I sat in the parking lot and watched the door to your apartment…and

I couldn't make myself go up and ring the bell. I could face bad guys and whatever weapons they threw at me seven days a week, but I knew I couldn't survive you looking me in the eye and telling me you didn't love me anymore.''

"I couldn't have done it."

Ray held her tighter, warmer. Good, she needed that warmth.

"What an idiot I was," he whispered in her ear. "I couldn't face you, so I came back here and tried to pretend that everything was all right when *nothing* was all right. I worked myself up, I made myself angry. If you and I had a good marriage, I could by God have a good marriage without you.''

"Trish and Patty," she whispered.

"Yeah.''

She snuggled closer. The truth came easier at a time like this. Games seemed senseless. All they had was the truth. All they had was each other.

"Have I ever told you how much I hate those two?'' she confessed. A wave of cold shot through her body and she shuddered. It would be so easy to go to sleep, to lie here in Ray's arms and drift away. "I just can't help it. I really, really *hate* them."

Was that a laugh she heard? Maybe…maybe not. It was either a laugh or a sob, and Ray never cried. If she had the strength she'd lift her head to see if it was laughter or sorrow on his face. She didn't though. Couldn't.

The ambulances were near, Trish and her fiancé hovered somewhere close but not too close. All around there was the shuffle of feet and lowered voices as the residents of the apartment came out to see what the excitement was about. And still, she felt like she and Ray were all alone.

"I love you, Gracie," he whispered.

I'm going to die, Grace thought dreamily. Ray would never say such a thing if he thought I was going to make it.

The sirens were closer now, so close the blaring noise hurt her ears. Ray placed his mouth close to her ear. "You're going to be all right," he whispered, sounding almost like he believed it.

It was just a shoulder wound, he told himself again and again. Nothing vital had been hit, the bullet had gone straight through.

But she was so cold, and he had a feeling that if he let her drift away she'd never come back. She had lost too much blood. No matter how much pressure he put on her wound, she continued to bleed.

"Grace," he said as he felt her slipping into unconsciousness.

She didn't answer.

The paramedics forced him to release her, to move out of their way. Something deep inside shouted insistently that if he let her go she'd die. They couldn't take proper care of her. Only he could do that.

His brain knew better, and he reluctantly backed away to let the paramedics do their work.

Everything inside him wanted to kneel back down beside her and order her to open her eyes. Her face was too white, her lips too bloodless, the blood staining her clothes and the blanket a paramedic tossed aside too red.

Luther appeared beside him. Hell, he hadn't even seen the car pull into the parking lot.

"Son of a bitch shot Grace." He never took his eyes from her face. "It's just a shoulder wound," he said, for his own benefit as well as Luther's. "She's going to be all right."

"That's good."

"I told her to stay under the car. Dammit, why didn't she stay under the car?"

The paramedics worked quickly and efficiently, checking Grace's vital signs, restricting the flow of blood.

"You got Potts good," Luther said, glancing over his shoulder to where the hit man's body lay in the parking lot, just beyond the trees he had emerged from firing his weapon. "That is one seriously dead hit man, I tell you." He grabbed a peppermint from his jacket pocket, slipped off the cellophane, and popped the mint into his mouth.

A new commotion started behind them, and Ray groaned as Sam Morgan and his cameraman leapt from the car that had stopped in the middle of the parking lot. Almost immediately, Morgan's eyes landed on Ray.

"What the hell is he doing here?" Ray muttered.

"Someone probably called him," Luther said.

At the moment Ray couldn't care less what Morgan said or did. The man was a pest, an annoyance, a flea. He turned around and watched the paramedics prepare to transport Grace to the hospital. They took good care of her, he knew. The best. That knowledge calmed him, a little.

He'd ride with her in the ambulance. He'd hold her hand and give her his strength, and everything would be fine. Just fine.

They strapped Grace to a board and lifted her, two paramedics carrying, another leaning over her and continuing treatment.

"Heartbeat's thready, she's not warming up like she should. She's going into shock," that paramedic barked as they hurried her toward the ambulance.

Ray took off running, determined to stay with Grace. No matter what. *No matter what.*

But he was stopped cold at the ambulance doors. There was no room, they told him as they shut the doors in his face. And they had no time to waste. They were working on Grace as they pulled away.

Ray stood there feeling, for the first time in his life, completely helpless. He'd been fine until they'd ripped her away, and now he shook as badly as she had, his heart beat just as thready and uncertain. Shock could kill her, her body could simply…shut down. He had to get to the hospital. Now.

"Come on," Luther said, taking Ray's arm and leading him to his car. "I'll drive you."

"I can drive myself," Ray said angrily.

"Like hell you can. You don't look any better than Grace did."

Sam Morgan had apparently gathered enough information to know that Ray was directly involved in the afternoon's excitement. He approached with the microphone held high and his cameraman directly behind him, the lens focusing on Ray's face.

"Mr. Madigan," Morgan called, a touch of false concern and sick excitement in his voice. "Can you tell us what happened here today?"

"Back off, Morgan, before I decide to break your nose all over again," Ray said as he approached Luther's car.

"Someone tells me the woman who was shot was a friend of yours, that you two arrived here together this afternoon." A sick light of excitement lit Morgan's eyes. "Was the bullet she took meant for you, Mr. Madigan? How do you feel about that?"

Ray took a split second to flick the microphone from Morgan's grasp and toss it to the ground, and to grab the front of Morgan's shirt and pull the man close so he was nose to nose with the detested reporter. "You say one more word to me and I'll rip out your liver. Here and now, in front of all these people.''

Morgan trembled and cut a panicked gaze to Luther. "He threatened me, Detective. You heard it, he threatened to *kill* me.''

"I didn't hear anything,'' Luther grumbled.

Ray released Morgan and sent the man stumbling backwards. "All I did was tell the man how I *felt*. Hell, he asked.''

There was no time for this, not a single moment to waste. Ray jumped into Luther's car. Luther was right behind him. He threw a red-domed emergency light onto his dash and turned it on, and took off at top speed. Traffic parted and pulled to the side. The ambulance was already out of sight. Ray clenched his fists and forgot about Morgan and Potts and everything but Grace.

Shock. It could kill her. She could be dead or dying right now, and there was nothing he could do. He'd never felt so helpless.

"What am I going to do if she dies?'' he whispered. "I screwed everything up, Luther. Everything.''

"You did the best you could,'' he said, his eyes and attention on the road.

"It wasn't good enough,'' Ray muttered. "How am I going to survive without her?''

Luther shook his head. He tsked and grumbled and cursed. "Well, this sounds awfully familiar,'' he finally said coherently.

Ray took his eyes off the road to look at his friend. "How?''

Luther kept his eyes on the road, hesitated thoughtfully.

"How?'' Ray demanded.

"Every time I drove Grace to the hospital, when you were shot, she'd sit in the passenger seat and mumble the exact same thing. *What if he dies? How will I make it without him?* She'd sit there and shake and cry and talk to herself, even when I told her your injuries weren't serious.''

A chill shimmied down Ray's spine. She'd tried to tell him, hadn't she? He'd realized for a while, that she hadn't left because she didn't love him, but because she loved him too much. Finally, he understood.

''I did this to her,'' he said, his eyes intent on the traffic ahead. ''Three times, I did this to her. She tried to tell me, she asked me to quit...and I just patted her on the back and told her not to worry.''

He shook his head. ''No wonder she left me. I put her through this again and again and when she asked me to quit and I didn't take her seriously...she had every right to walk out. Every right in the world.''

How could he blame her? The pain he felt at this moment was hideous, it was by far the worst pain he'd ever experienced. He'd rather be shot a hundred times than go through this again.

Chapter 17

Grace opened her eyes to see Ray pacing by her bedside. It was dark outside, and the room was lit by a low-watt lamp directly above her hospital bed. The only sounds she heard were Ray breathing and muttering low to himself and the occasional squeak and swish of a nurse passing in the hallway.

The events of the day came back to her in a flash. Telling Ray she loved him. Getting shot. Hearing him tell her, at last, that he loved her.

Ray spun around and his eyes lit on her face; he seemed surprised to find her awake. He pulled a chair to the side of the bed, sat in it and took her hand in his. He looked haggard, plumb worn-out. The lines around his face deep, his eyes red.

"How do you feel?"

"A little dopey," she said with a smile.

"It's the pain medication," he explained.

She closed her eyes and took a deep breath. Her shoulder ached and her head was spinning, a little, but she felt better than before. Stronger. She shuddered, remembering the way Potts had fired his gun at her and at Ray.

"That man…Potts…"

"He's dead," Ray whispered.

"You killed him."

He nodded once.

It was finally over. Potts was dead, she was still alive, and Ray was with her. For how long?

She wondered if he thought she'd forgotten that he'd told her he loved her, when he'd thought she might die. She wondered if he hoped she'd forgotten. He'd confessed a lot to her as he'd held her. More than he was comfortable with, surely.

A thin nurse who probably didn't stand a full five feet tall opened the door and stepped in with an air of unmistakable authority. "You're still here," she said, narrowing her eyes at Ray. "I told you the last time, visiting hours are over."

"But this is my wife," he argued, snapping at the nurse. "You can't expect me to just leave her here."

Ray narrowed his eyes and glanced down at her, perhaps waiting for her to contradict him as she usually did with an insistent or muttered "*Ex*-wife." She didn't say a word.

"That's exactly what I expect," the nurse cracked back.

Ray ignored the nurse and smiled at Grace. The smile was tired, and weak, but it was a Ray Madigan grin just the same. The new, easier expression on his face wiped away some of the tiredness there.

"It's going to take someone a lot bigger than you to drag me out of here," he said softly. "Several someones."

The nurse snorted, checked Grace's pulse and rolled her eyes. "All right, stay. But if you give me any trouble I will haul you out of here myself. I'm stronger than I look."

When the nurse was gone, Grace squeezed Ray's hand and gathered her own strength. Now or never. "Ray, you asked me this morning what I would say if you asked me to go to Mobile with you."

"Gracie, don't…"

"I'd say yes," she said quickly, before he could stop her, before he could take back his offer. "I won't lie to you. Watching you put yourself in danger won't be easy, I won't enjoy going through that again. You may have to comfort me now and then, and you may have to remind me why you do what you do…but living with the uncertainty of what each day will bring is better than living without you. I found that out the hard way."

He shook his head. "I can't ask you to do that."

Her heart sank, and the unpleasant chills that worked through her body had nothing to do with being shot. Ray didn't want her with him. He'd rather go on alone. She shouldn't be surprised.

The least she could do was to let him go without tears and recriminations. He had been completely honest with her, telling her again and again that all they had was a physical connection. Hadn't this been a part of her plan? To let him be the one to do the walking away, this time.

"I understand," she whispered, determined to make this as easy for him as she could. After all, he had never promised anything beyond today.

Ray threaded his fingers through hers, and she took a good hard look at his face. Even though his short-lived smile had eased the weariness there, he still looked drained and years older. In truth, he could probably use a hospital bed of his own.

The hand that held hers tightened. "I was thinking maybe I'd stay here," he said lowly. "And I was thinking maybe you'd like to quit working for Dr. Doolittle altogether and come to work for me.''

She smiled softly, afraid to hope, afraid not to. "Really?"

"My own hacker," he said with a forced grin. "What more could I possibly ask for?"

The offer sounded good, truly wonderful, but she wondered if Ray could really let his crusade go, if he could forget about his sister's death—the death that had driven him all these years.

"Can you be satisfied with that?" she whispered. "Can you live with the knowledge that there are bad guys out there someone else is bringing down?"

He hesitated, but nodded once and then leaned over the bed rail to kiss her, gently, lovingly. "I think from now on I'll save all my adrenaline for you."

"I'd like that."

He brushed her hair away from her face and laid his palms on her cheeks. "Marry me again?"

"Ask away."

"I just did."

"No, the Lyle Lovett trivia test," she whispered. "I've been studying up."

"When?"

She laid one hand over his, rested it there. "This morning, on the Internet, while you were asleep. I probably know more about Lyle than you do."

He grinned crookedly. "I doubt that."

"I'll need a little time to learn a song in its entirety, though," she said. "I think I know most of the words to 'She's No Lady,' but I wouldn't want to make a mistake."

"I'll be happy to tutor you," he moved in for another soft kiss, touching her as if he was afraid she would break if he kissed her too hard.

"You knew I would ask," he said as he pulled away, sounding content and a little puzzled. "Why else would you study for that silly test?"

"I didn't know," she said, lifting her hand to touch his rough cheek. "I hoped. I really, really hoped."

The nurse breezed back in, a paper cup in her hand. She cast a sharp glance at Ray as he reluctantly returned to his seat. "Time for your sleeping pills," she said enthusiastically.

"I don't want any sleeping pills," Grace said strongly. "I think I have more than enough drugs in my system at the moment."

"If this man is going to keep you awake…" the nurse began to reprimand.

"*This man* is my husband," Grace snapped. "If he goes, I go."

The nurse harrumphed and left the room, sleeping pills in hand.

Ray gazed at her with a sinfully satisfied expression on his tired face.

"I love you, Gracie."

"I love you, too," she whispered.

He took her hand again, made himself comfortable at her side, and by the time the nurse came around again they were both sound asleep.

She should've known that Ray would not be able to completely let go of his crusade. They'd been married two months, and already he was doing his thing.

Ray had somehow convinced Beatrice Reed to start a drug rehab program at the Children's Hospital. As a former narcotics officer, he would be instrumental in the fund-raising activities that were scheduled for the next year. He had lots of ideas about the way the program should be run, who should be involved, how they could get the kids who really needed help into the program.

At the end of a long day at the office, they lay together in their bed. They lived in a new house in the same neighborhood they both loved, and the place was a marriage of her snow globes and soft colors and Ray's sound system and Lyle Lovett collection. It was perfect.

"I found Timothy Reynolds," Grace said softly. "He's working in Houston. Making good money, dating the boss's daughter, just bought a new car. Will Mrs. Reynolds be pleased?"

Ray pulled her close, and she rested her head on his shoulder. There in just the right spot, where she fit so well.

"Yeah," he said softly. "She just wants to find him and make amends. Five years is too long for a mother to go without seeing her son."

She agreed with a contented murmur. Working with Ray was a never-ending adventure. Business was going so well, he was already talking about hiring another investigator. Doris thought she needed her own secretary.

"Is Luther coming for dinner tomorrow night?"

"He said he would. He also said that if you tried to fix him up with another bimbo he would never forgive you."

Grace smiled. "Tara is not a bimbo."

Ray groaned, then laughed lightly.

They snuggled in the dark, fitting together as easily side by side as they did sexually. Ray was her place in the world, and she was his.

"You never did ask me to sing that song for you," she whispered, laying her hand on his chest and rocking her fingers there.

"I tutor you on a regular basis."

"Just about every morning," she said with a smile.

He rolled on his side to face her, propped himself up on his elbow, and grinned. "I take it you're ready?"

She nodded. This was not a song Ray normally sang in the shower, but she'd heard it on the CD several times. Enough to get the first part right, which was all she'd need.

Grace placed her face close to his, almost nose to nose, and broke into a soft, hesitant, slightly off-key version of "Fat Babies."

She hadn't gotten far into the song before Ray laughed and rolled her onto her back, laying his hand over her still flat stomach. Of course he knew exactly what she was trying to tell him.

"Are you sure?"

"Positive."

"Happy?"

"Deliriously."

Ray placed his face against her stomach. "Me, too," he said softly.

She cupped his head while he kissed her belly gently, just once.

"God, Gracie. A baby," he whispered reverently as the news sank in. "A *baby*."

He rose up, hovered above her and looked down. "I love you."

She touched his jaw with tender fingers. "I love you, too. I always have." When he smiled at her she took his face in her hands. "Being the first Mrs. Madigan was pretty darn good most of the time," she confessed. "But, Ray...I dearly love being the *last* Mrs. Madigan."

Ray kissed her briefly then returned to his original position with his mouth against her belly and his hands on her hips. He started off talking to the baby, cooing sweet words against Grace's skin. Holding her close as he kissed her stomach, stroked her there with the palm of his hand, then rose up slowly to take her mouth with his, deep and gentle and all consuming.

He made love to her, a slow, sweet, delicious joining of hearts and bodies.

As always, he was a *very* nice guy.

* * * * *

Remember Shea Sinclair, the weather girl?

Well, she's about to get the story—and love—of her life this summer.

Only from Linda Winstead Jones and Silhouette Intimate Moments!

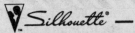

*Two powerhouse writers
tell compelling tales of
love lost—and won.*

What happens when you wake up—
and don't know who you are?

These two women
are about to find out in

FORGET ME NOT

Featuring

THE ACCIDENTAL BODYGUARD
by Ann Major

&

MEMORIES OF LAURA
by Marilyn Pappano

Be sure to pick up your copy—
On sale March 2001
in retail stores everywhere!

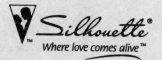

Silhouette®

Where love comes alive™

BR2FMN

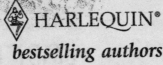

HARLEQUIN®

bestselling authors

Merline Lovelace
Deborah Simmons
Julia Justiss

*cordially invite you to enjoy three
brand-new stories of unexpected love*

The
Officer's
Bride

Available April 2001

HARLEQUIN®

Makes any time special ®